Fasci

Fascinated
Miles Gibson

SINCLAIR-STEVENSON

First published in Great Britain in 1993
by Sinclair-Stevenson
an imprint of Reed Consumer Books Ltd
Michelin House, 81 Fulham Road, London SW3 6RB
and Auckland, Melbourne, Singapore and Toronto

This paperback edition published
by Sinclair-Stevenson in 1994

A CIP catalogue record for this book
is available at the British Library
ISBN 1 85619 508 2

Typeset by Hewer Text Composition Services, Edinburgh
Printed and bound in Great Britain
by Cox & Wyman Ltd, Reading, Berkshire

For Susan

'Scum always floats to the top'

Conrad Staggers

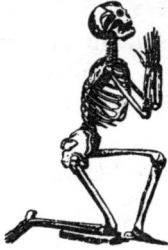

One day Frank Fisher leaves his house, walks to the post box on the corner of the street and disappears.

He turns the corner and is suddenly gone, as if the street has swallowed him. The neighbours see nothing. His wife, Jessica, slumped in the sofa, watching TV, makes a nest from a pile of embroidered cushions, yawns and falls asleep. No one sees Frank vanish.

It is a little past three o'clock but on this dismal winter afternoon the city is already steeped in darkness. Lights shine from parlour windows along the terrace of narrow houses. The sky is a swirling, sulphurous gravy. The pavements are greasy with rain.

Frank turns the corner and is about to step from the kerb when he sees a Mercedes swerving towards him and a man somersaulting into the gutter. The man has been thrown from the back of the car. He's a large old man in a black overcoat that fans from his shoulders like wings. He hits the pavement, rolls forward, grunts and turns his face to the sky. The face is bruised and flecked with blood.

Frank shouts and shrinks back on tiptoe. He thinks the old man is dead. And as he stands there, shivering and confused, two men climb from the car and saunter towards him through the gloom. They are tall men, as lean

1

as shadows, dressed in expensive charcoal suits and highly polished shoes. They are silent and staring. They move with the easy grace of panthers.

'Did we kill him?' asks the first of them as they approach Frank. His name is Harry Cocker but everyone calls him the Beast. He bends his head and grins. His green eyes shine with satisfaction.

The corpse groans and blows a glistening bubble of blood.

'No,' says Frank. 'Thank God, he's still moving!' He glances up at the two men. His breath is a soft explosion of steam.

'Stubborn bastard!' says the second stranger. His name is Lloyd and he's proud to be Harry's half-mad brother. He pushes Frank aside and begins stamping on the old man, snorting and clapping his hands like a murderous flamenco dancer.

'Leave him alone!' shouts Frank. He is so astonished that he runs forward to knock Lloyd Cocker from the old man's chest, catching him with his shoulder and pushing him away. He's forty years old next birthday and that's too old to brawl in the street. But he won't stand and watch an old man beaten to death.

'I'm trying to kick-start his heart,' grins Lloyd, stepping aside and watching Frank spill onto the pavement.

Frank scrambles to his feet and nurses his elbows in his hands. He's twisted a leg and his knuckles are bleeding. He hobbles in circles, trying to shake out the fire in his bones. The Cocker brothers ignore him.

'Help me get the bastard into the car,' says the Beast as Lloyd returns to the trampled corpse.

Frank watches them haul their victim from the gutter and drag him across the street. They drag him by his ankles with his arms trailing loose and his head wrapped up in his coat.

'That man needs a doctor!' shouts Frank. 'You've got to get him to a hospital. He could have internal injuries.'

2

His voice sounds small and remote, like a cry for help from a locked room. He can't believe this is happening.

'It's a waste of time,' says the Beast mildly. 'But don't worry, Skipper, we'll give him a decent burial.' They cram the old man into the back of the car and try to cover him with a blanket to prevent him leaking into the pigskin upholstery.

'I'm calling the police!' warns Frank. He glances up and down the empty street. He doesn't know where to turn. Why doesn't someone run out to help him? He wants to see large and angry women, dressed in pinafores and slippers, emerge through the rain like a battle fleet, armed with rolling pins and pokers. He wants to see big-bellied men in shirtsleeves, horse brasses on belts, marching shoulder to shoulder towards him. He wants the world to be different. He doesn't want to be Gary Cooper. He begins to limp towards the nearest house with a lighted window but, as he approaches the privet hedge, the light flicks out before him.

The Beast shakes his head and turns away from the car. He is holding a baseball bat in his fist. As he moves towards Frank he raises the bat against his chest. He advances with a queer little dancing stride and the rain seems to spark on his black leather shoes.

The first strike catches Frank against his neck, nearly knocking his head from his shoulders. His mouth springs open and blood sprays from his nose. He twists and staggers and falls to his knees.

The second strike catches him across the spine, knocking him forward and cracking his face against the kerbstone.

The Beast raises the bat for a third and final strike but Frank has already gone.

When he opens his eyes he is slumped in the back of the car and sharing the blanket with the corpse. His head feels crushed and his shirt is clammy with blood. He tries to search for his face and probe the pain in his neck and throat but, when he makes an effort to raise a hand, his arm refuses to obey his command and he finds he can't work his fingers.

He manages to tilt his head and squint through the window but sees nothing beyond the darkness and rain.

He thinks, in a few minutes I'm going to die. They'll stop the car and drag me into a ploughed field, set me loose to flop around until I suffocate in the mud. They'll shoot me in the back of the head and roll me into a ditch where the dogs and the crows will pick at my bones. He thinks of Jessica, watching TV, waiting for him to walk through the door. How long has he been away? How long will it take her to miss him? He's going to die and she'll never find him. He's going to die without warning or reason.

The Mercedes swings from the road, lurches down a flooded gravel track and shudders to a halt. For a few moments there is nothing but the hammering rain and the click of the windscreen wipers. The brothers sit, as silent as lovers, staring out at the night.

With a great effort Frank manages to pull himself up against the edge of the door. Through the beams of the headlights he can see a landscape of twisted peaks and toppling spires. A nightmare of rusting carcasses, ashes, rags and bones. Ribbons of tattered polythene slap like prayer flags from the spires. Glass glitters in the floodlit peaks. Below, in the gulleys and ditches, melting into a poisonous broth, lie the bloated bellies of mattresses and the skeletons of small machines. They are perched on the edge of a rubbish dump that seems to stretch to the end of the world.

As Frank struggles to make sense of these surroundings, the Cocker brothers clamber from the car and retrieve the old man. The body topples from the seat and slithers softly to the ground. The brothers roll it to the edge of a crumbling precipice and pitch it into the darkness. Lloyd grins and peers after it. The Beast finds a handkerchief and carefully wipes his hands.

4

Frank closes his eyes and tries to hide beneath the blanket. These are his executioners. Here is the killing ground. He wants to shake himself awake. He wants to find himself, thrashing and shouting, in the safety of his own bed with Jessica complaining beside him and the radio playing the early news and the dream dissolving in morning sunlight. He wants to gather her into his arms and tell her how much he loves her and run his hand beneath her pyjamas until she pushes him away, protesting and laughing, and struggles downstairs to make coffee.

Lloyd seizes him, yanks him out and throws him into the mire. Frank shouts in pain and starts to crawl away on his hands and knees. His arms collapse and send him sprawling. He reaches out, choking in mud, groping for a hiding place under the car, but the Beast drags him back and Lloyd kicks him over the precipice, down the slippery slope to hell.

Jessica wakes up and knocks a cushion to the floor. She swings her legs from the sofa, reaches out and switches off the TV. It is dark. She stretches and yawns and wanders into the kitchen. She calls out to Frank but the house remains silent. It is four fifteen by the clock on the wall. A little after six thirty by the electric clock on the oven. She turns, walks into the hall and calls again.

'Frank?'

The hall is empty. The light from the street is a soft, phosphorescent bruise in the frosted fanlight above the front door. She walks quickly to the back parlour but the room is deserted. She returns to the hall and creeps up the stairs, waiting for him to pounce from the darkness, shrieking and laughing and rolling his eyes. She hates it when he plays this game! Ten years of marriage and still he behaves like a schoolboy.

'Frank!'

She stand motionless, a pale ghost on the empty stairs, listening for the slightest movement in the rooms above, refusing to be drawn any closer into his trap. She imagines him wedged behind the bathroom door, pressed on tiptoe against the wall, trembling and tense, an immense grin on his shining face. She throws open the door, banging it hard against the wall, and glares indignantly at the empty bath, the gleam of the washbasin, the clutter of bottles and tubes on the shelf. The cap is missing from the Colgate pump. The Listerine bottle is empty. The basket of fruit-flavoured novelty soaps still gathers dust in its corner.

'Frank?'

He has to be somewhere in the house. How long does it take him to post a letter? She creeps into the bedroom. The furniture is steeped in darkness. Rain rattles against the window. The bed with its winter eiderdown remains undisturbed, a slumbering elephant. She snaps on the light, hurries barefoot across the carpet and closes the curtains, turning quickly to catch any demons that might have followed in her footsteps.

'Frank?'

She whispers his name to the wardrobe, the bed and the chest of drawers. It is nineteen thirty by the clock on the bedside table. A little past five o'clock by the watch on her wrist. She shivers and tries to wipe away the gooseflesh on her arms. It's stupid to feel so frightened. How long does it take him to post a letter? She stares at herself in the wardrobe mirrors. She is wearing one of his old shirts, the collar frayed, a button missing, the big sleeves rolled to her elbows. She makes an attempt to push the shirt-tails into her skirt. She needs a drink. She must try to pull herself together. Her face is still creased from the crush of the cushions and her cropped hair is standing in spikes.

'Frank?'

The reflection makes no answer but stands staring hopelessly into her face. She swears softly, raking her scalp with her fingers, and turns in a circle, spooked by the swirl of her own leaping shadow.

She runs downstairs, switching on lights in every room, shouting his name and banging doors to drive away hordes of scuttling goblins. She pulls on her shoes, throws a coat round her narrow shoulders and runs from the house, into the bitter winter night, towards the corner of the street.

7

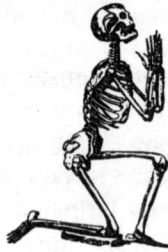

It stops raining. The sky clears and the moon sails over the peaks and spires, turning mud into molten bronze and broken glass into diamonds.

Frank lies sprawled in a bed of shattered chicken bones. For several minutes he's been watching the corpse struggle to rise from its shallow grave. The battered body keeps clambering to its feet and then falling backwards into a pool of luminous water. When it finally manages to balance itself, it stands pulling coathangers from its limbs. Now it turns, totters forward in its squelching shoes and looms over him, its big face varnished with mud and its fingers dripping moonlight.

'I thought you were dead,' whispers Frank. His tongue feels torn and his throat is filled with gravel.

'I thought *you* were dead!' grins the corpse. He stretches out an arm and shakes Frank warmly by the hand.

'Frank Fisher,' croaks Frank.

'Webster Boston,' beams the old man. He tightens his grip and tries to haul Frank to his feet but Frank shouts in pain and falls back into the chicken bones.

'Where does it hurt?'

'Everywhere!' gasps Frank. He counts his fingers with his thumbs and moves his head in a crunching circle. The

8

pain is trapped in his ribcage, kicking against his heart and lungs.

'Stay there.'

'Where are you going?'

'I'm going for help,' says Webster Boston. He plunges his hands in his waterlogged pockets and strolls away, picking a path through the petrified forest.

Frank settles back in the chicken bones and turns his face to the moon. He must be patient. He must keep his courage a little longer. He is waiting for a rescue team to appear above him on the ridge, men shouting down to him, rope ladders, flashlights and dogs. They'll haul him from hell in a cradle and bundle him into an ambulance. He can call Jessica from the hospital, explain what happened and ask her to collect him. Will they try to hold him overnight, marooned in a pair of borrowed pyjamas, left to sleep on a rubber sheet in a ward full of shrunken old men? He hates hospitals. He's afraid of them. The smell of death and disinfectant. He won't do it. He'll walk home barefoot if they take his clothes. He wants a hot bath, something to drink and the sweet oblivion of his bed.

He might be interviewed by the police and asked to describe the attack. Vicious. Nasty. Unprovoked. The assailants. A brief description of the assailants. Unpredictable. Dangerous. Violent. Sympathetic noises from the assembly. Helping the police with their enquiries. And he is prepared to pick them out at a formal identity parade? He doesn't know. It was dark. It happened so fast. He realises, with dismay, that the faces have already turned into phantasmagorical masks, with scarlet sequins for eyes and the grinning jaws of wolves.

The moon drifts higher and the wind begins to sweep through the crumbling parapets and towers, ploughing puddles and whipping at a thousand polythene banners. It must be late. How long does it take him to post a letter? He manages to raise an arm against his chest and tries to search for his watch, but the wrist is thickly bandaged in

9

mud. It's so cold that he can't feel his legs. He won't last long if they fail to find him. He'll die in the ditch and his pickled body will turn to leather. The peat-bog man. Recovered in a thousand years. His head on a plate in the British Museum.

He must find shelter. The carcass of an old armchair lies, trapped in mud, a few yards away on the other side of the pit. If he can crawl into its sagging arms he'll be saved from the freezing wind.

He levers himself against one shoulder, paddles his feet and manages to roll himself onto his stomach. His ribcage seems to bend out of shape beneath his weight and he screws up his eyes, concentrating, waiting for the pain to loosen its grip. He slithers forward, folding and kicking his legs, a swimmer in a dark, gelatinous sea.

When Webster Boston returns, Frank has managed to drag himself to the armchair and lies exhausted before it, with his head half-buried in its rusted springs.

'Frank?'

Frank groans and tries to pull out his face but he knows that he hasn't the strength to do any more than work his lungs and keep his heart beating.

'I found a telephone at the top of the road – we'll soon have you out of here.'

'Webster?'

'What is it, Frank?'

'Can you help me into this chair?'

Webster bends down and gently hoists Frank into the mess of stuffing and springs. He straightens Frank's shoulders and tries to scrape the mud from his face.

'What's your line of work, Frank?'

'I'm a marketing man. You've probably heard of the Fancy Wholesale Tropical Fruits Corporation?'

'No.'

'They trade in fancy tropical fruits.'

'Is that right?' Webster looks baffled. He casts around

10

in the mud, finds a twisted metal crate and sits down beside his companion.

'Kumquats and pawpaws,' whispers Frank, trying to explain, wanting to talk away the pain that is burning under his skin. 'Pomegranates and limes.' Twenty years in command of a desk. He'd been planning to die from atrophy. Laid to rest on the boardroom table, mourned by the senior secretaries, his long-service medal around his neck. He hadn't expected a stranger to beat out his brains with a baseball bat.

'Remember Spangles?' says Webster, staring at his hands.

'What?'

'Life's always sweeter with Spangles.'

'I don't remember.'

'Spangles. Five-fruit Spangles. They used to cost thruppence a packet. You never see them any more. It's like White Heather Assortment and Blue Bird Liquorice Rolls. You get used to them. You get a taste for them. And then, overnight, they've vanished.' He sighs and pokes an ear, grieving for the fate of Five Boys Chocolate and long-lost rolls of Army Mints.

'What's your line of work?' prompts Frank, fighting the silence, trying to get him talking again.

Webster blinks and pulls the finger from his ear. 'I'm a soldier of fortune.' He begins to fish in his pockets. His overcoat has been torn to rags and the rags hang from his arms like strands of melted tar. After a long search he pulls out a shrivelled bag, which he peels apart to reveal a handful of amber buttons. He picks at one between finger and thumb and offers it to Frank.

'What is it?' Frank looks suspicious and pulls back his head as the button is waved beneath his nose.

'Fowler's Old-Fashioned Acid Drops,' says Webster, pushing the button into his mouth and rolling it against his teeth. He breathes a deep and satisfied sigh. 'Do you want one?'

11

Frank accepts an acid drop and sucks at it slowly, feeling the sweetness dissolve on his tongue and trickle against his throat.

'Who were those men?'

'The Cocker brothers.'

'Why did they push you from the car?'

'I wasn't pushed,' said Webster indignantly. 'I jumped!'

'Why?'

'They were trying to kill me,' he says softly. He glances up at the moon and smiles as a large green Bentley glides silently to the edge of the ditch.

'Look. Here's Valentine.'

She stands at the foot of the bed and stares down at him.
She is tall and lean with waxed black hair and a brightly
painted face. She is wearing a charcoal chiffon dress and
a pair of long satin evening gloves. Her perfume fills the
room with a sweet incense of roses, jasmine and cloves.
Whenever she moves the perfume wafts from her limbs,
makes the air shimmer around her head like heat haze
on a desert road.

Frank groans and tries to unglue his mouth. He doesn't
know how he reached this place. He doesn't recognise
the bed, the candy-striped pattern on his pyjamas or the
woman who is standing there watching him.

'What happened?'

'I brought you home.' The woman smiles. A flickering
curve on her crimson mouth. Her eyes glitter in their
scoops of darkness.

Frank drifts back to the land of the living. He remembers being hauled from the mud, wrapped in blankets and
carried away in the back of the Bentley. The bed and
pyjamas remain a mystery. The pyjamas are huge. He
pulls an arm from beneath the covers and peers up the
sleeve at his missing fingers.

'We had to scrub you down. You were filthy.' She raises

a hand against her breasts as if protecting herself from the spectre of his nakedness. The long satin fingers are covered in rings. Emeralds and amethysts. Rubies dark as blood clots.

'Where's Webster?'

'He's with the doctor.'

'Is he badly hurt?'

'The doctor's for you.'

'What's the time?'

'Around midnight.'

'I have to phone home!' He tries to shake off the sheet and clamber from the bed but the pain in his chest stakes him securely against the mattress.

'You want to phone Jessica?'

He flinches, shocked by the sound of his wife's name. 'How do you know?'

'You were calling her name when we brought you here.' She shrugs, charging the air with more of that sweet, narcotic perfume. 'Are you married?'

'Yes.' He yawns. His eyes feel heavy and he can't raise his head from the pillow.

'She'll be worried.'

'Yes.' His voice is no more than a whisper.

'Wait for the doctor.'

She turns quickly and walks from the room, making the chiffon swirl around her as if she were wearing nothing but shadows.

When Frank opens his eyes again he is staring into the face of a man with a dainty pencil moustache and a pair of soft blue eyes. One of the eyes is small and rheumy, the other is a monstrous fish swimming in the bowl of a monocle. He is dressed in a plain dark suit and a fancy white silk shirt. He smells of whisky. He is wearing a stethoscope as a necklace.

'Are you the doctor?'

'Do I look like a doctor?'

'No,' whispers Frank. He grins, unbuttons his pyjama

jacket and lets the stranger prod his chest. He is waiting to be asked questions about the cause of his injuries. He is waiting to explain the circumstances of the fight and give a description of his assailants. But the doctor examines him in silence.

'What's the damage?' he demands, when every part of him has been thumbed, turned, twisted and tweaked.

'Minor abrasions to the legs, upper arms, neck and chest. Some extensive bruising to the ribs, throat and shoulders. Nothing serious.'

Frank sighs. He was lucky. Nothing torn or broken. He pulls the big pyjamas closed and wraps himself in the sheets. 'My throat is sore,' he complains, pressing his fingers against his neck.

'Are you thirsty? Here. Drink.' The doctor produces a waxed paper cup filled with a measure of bitter milk.

'What is it?' gasps Frank, draining the cup and scraping his teeth against his tongue. His mouth is suddenly sprouting hairs.

'Something to make you sleep. Something to help the aches and pains.' The doctor smiles, plucks the stethoscope from his neck and throws it into his leather bag.

'No . . .' Frank yawns and finds that he cannot untangle his arms.

'You should rest,' says the doctor gently. He steps away from the bed. His monocle glints like a silver medal.

'I must get home . . .'

'It's too late.'

'I have to call my wife . . .'

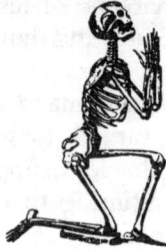

At midnight Jessica calls the police.

A woman answers the phone, surprising her, demanding to know her business, finally takes her name and number, transfers her to the duty sergeant.

'Can you describe him?' asks the duty sergeant, when Jessica has been made to repeat her story. His voice isn't old or mature enough to inspire a sense of confidence. He sounds like a rather bored shop assistant. She feels cheated. She wanted a voice in uniform.

'Average height . . . average build . . .'

It sounds so stupid. It sounds like the sketch of a stranger. Why can't she describe her own husband? He is tall and lean with a slow smile and a touch of early frost in his hair. She is proud of him when they walk in the street. He bears no likeness to the wheezing, wheedling, swag-bellied husbands of the other women she knows. These men, softened to fat, losing their hair with the rest of their teeth, have thickened into monstrous babies.

'Is there anything in particular?' prompts the duty sergeant. 'Does he have any distinguishing marks?'

'What kinds of marks?'

'Birthmarks. Tattoos.'

'No.'

His body is printed with several fine scars, an intimate history of boyhood battles. She knows the coarse white thread that copies the curve of his shoulder blade, the raised red crescent beneath an elbow, the small silver moons punched into his knees.

'Is he an epileptic or diabetic? Does he take any form of medication?'

'No.'

'When was the last time you saw him?'

'This afternoon. He went out to post a letter at the top of the street. I waited. He hasn't come home . . .'

'Did you have a disagreement?'

'I was alseep. No. There was nothing.'

'Had he been drinking?'

'What?'

'You said you were asleep. Had your husband been drinking?' There's an edge of impatience on his voice to let her know that she's wasting his time.

'No.'

She has never seen him drunk. When *she* breaks into a bottle of wine she becomes a shrieking, rubber-faced harpy, the kind of drunk you try to avoid. She shouts and sings and dances on tables, opens her dress and flaunts her tits, falls down and vomits on carpets. He stands impressive, superior, bored. She does not admire his moderation.

'Perhaps he went to visit someone . . .'

'I've phoned everywhere. I've tried everything.' She rakes at her hair with her fingernails. Why doesn't he want to help? What's wrong with the fucking system! People can't disappear! When she'd phoned the local hospitals they'd treated her with the same suspicion, refused to check their casualty lists, left her hanging on an empty line.

'Are you sure he didn't meet a friend?'

'People don't vanish into the rain! The ground doesn't open and swallow them!' She is suddenly shouting, blinking back tears, frightened by all these senseless questions.

The duty sergeant falls silent for several moments, leaving her time to regret the outburst and giving him an opportunity to take a sip from a cup of instant coffee beside him. The coffee is cold and contains too much sugar. He swallows and sucks at his teeth. 'If he met a friend,' he begins again, 'there's a chance he'll be home in the morning.'

Jessica winces and tightens her grip on the telephone. What's that supposed to mean? Does Frank have some little tart waiting for him in a rented room? Is that it? A popsy in leg-spreader underwear? Is she supposed to remember the smell of cheap perfume on his shirts, his strange moods, the late nights he spends at the office, the whispered weekend telephone calls? It's crazy! She can't believe it. Other women find him attractive because he seems not to notice them. At parties they surround him, flashing their eyes and their naked shoulders, while he stands patiently, smiling but distant, waiting for her to rescue him.

'What happens if he *doesn't* come back in the morning?' she snaps back at him. What happens if he's been involved in an accident and he's hooked to a life-support machine? What happens if he's gone crazy and tries to walk into the sea? What happens if his life depends on their finding him tonight?

'If he's not there in the morning we'll ask you to come down and make an official report.'

'Is that it?'

'That's it.'

'Nothing else?'

'It's not a crime to leave home.'

'Thanks for nothing!'

Jessica bangs down the phone and sits alone in the empty house, praying for Frank to step from the darkness. It's two forty-seven by the clock on the bedside table.

18

Something past midnight by the watch on her wrist. At daybreak she'll walk down to the police station, confront the duty sergeant and enter Frank's name in the Book of the Disappeared.

Frank wakes up to find Valentine sitting on the edge of the bed with a breakfast tray in her hands. The room is large and filled with sunlight from a long window. The window is dressed in gold braid and fat swags of purple velvet. The surrounding walls are bare. The floor has been stripped to polished planks, on which a threadbare Persian rug seems to float like an empty raft.

'How do you feel this morning?' she asks as she places the breakfast tray in his hands and helps to prop his shoulders with pillows.

'Fine. I feel fine,' he says, wiping the sleep from his eyes and checking his pyjama buttons.

'You look like shit,' Valentine says cheerfully, pouring coffee from a silver pot.

She is wearing a long silk dressing gown tied with a richly embroidered sash. Crimson flowers on a dark green band. Her black hair, still damp from the shower, has been pulled from her neck and tied in a knot.

'I always look like shit in the morning,' says Frank. He grins and studies the breakfast tray. A rack of toast, curls of butter in a silver dish, boiled eggs, madeleines the colour of honey, hot milk and soft, brown sugar.

'What's the time?'

'Eight o'clock.'

'I've got to leave! I'll be late for work!' He looks around the room in dismay and grasps the sides of the breakfast tray. He doesn't know where they've hidden his clothes but his wristwatch and keys have been placed within reach on the bedside table.

Valentine looks startled, catches him by his pyjama sleeve and gently squeezes his wrist. 'Take it easy. Drink your coffee. My father wants to meet you.'

Frank sinks back against the pillows and measures sugar into his cup. He glances around the room again, hoping to find a telephone. He must phone Jessica – he has to let her know that he's safe.

'Do you mind if I make a phone call?'

'You want to phone your wife?' asks Valentine, stealing a slice of toast and snapping at the crust with her teeth.

'Yes.'

'OK. Finish eating and get dressed. You'll find fresh clothes in the wardrobe. Your old clothes were disgusting. I told Webster to burn them.'

She gestures at a huge wardrobe, carved from oak and set with panels of stained glass.

'It's old. Genuine antique.'

She stands up, hands deep in her dressing-gown pockets, and swaggers towards the bedroom door, where she pauses to glance back at him.

'Have you ever been to Rangoon?' she demands, for no apparent reason.

Frank shakes his head, watching her turn and walk away disappointed, the silk washing against her shoulders, catching softly between her legs, shimmering where it catches the sunlight.

He waits until she has left the room and then looks down at the breakfast tray. He's hungry! He devours the eggs and toast, takes a second cup of coffee and plugs his mouth with a madeleine, before setting out at last to explore the wardrobe.

The doors are as heavy as tombstones. The handles are dancing skeletons, cast from copper, eyes made from polished ivory beads. But when the doors are flung apart, the wardrobe is turned from a funeral vault into a carnival attraction, a travelling tailor's window display. The interior is packed with fine underwear, shirts, suits and shoes, arranged according to season and colour. Everything is new. Nothing has been touched. The shirts, with their arms folded behind cardboard backbones, are still sealed in polythene wrappers. The shoes are gleaming from factory boxes. The suits of every weight and measure, paraded on polished wooden hangers, still wear their price tickets on their sleeves.

Frank steps back in surprise and stares. He'd expected to find gardening clothes, a few old sweaters, an assortment of boots and carpet slippers, cobwebs, mothballs and walking sticks. What's happening here?

He shakes off the pyjamas and searches his body for signs of damage. One shoulder is stained blue with bruises and a weal still smoulders against his neck. His elbows are grazed and there's a small cut beside his mouth. His penis, caught in the light, takes his interest for a moment and he gathers it into his hand where it fills his palm like a cow's teat. It's a queer sensation to be standing naked in a stranger's house. He takes a packet of underpants, breaks open the seal on the envelope and starts to dress, glancing furtively at the door. Expensive. Silk against the skin.

He chooses a pair of tartan socks, a plain white cotton shirt and a dark-brown suit. Everything feels too big for him. He spends several minutes trying to remove the price tag from the jacket sleeve but it's been secured somehow by one of those tiny plastic threads that he has to gnaw through with his teeth.

He selects a pair of brown Oxfords, rejects them in favour of heavy black brogues and has scarcely finished lacing them when Valentine returns to collect him.

'What do you think?' he asks hopefully, raising his arms

and turning a circle. He feels like a scarecrow dressed for a wedding.

Valentine shrugs. 'It doesn't fit. I bought all that stuff for my father.'

'I hope he won't miss it.'

'He doesn't know he's got it.'

She leads him from the bedroom, along a wide empty corridor and down a marble staircase. His shoes creak whenever he presses a foot to the floor. His sleeves dangle.

'I'll return these clothes as soon as I get home,' he announces, creaking carefully down the stairs.

'Forget it!' says Valentine scornfully. 'We don't want them now that you've worn them.'

She throws open a door, beckons Frank forward and plunges him into a tropical twilight. The heat makes him stagger and gasp for breath. Great palms rise from the ground and press themselves against the ceiling, their trunks sprouting curious epiphytes, flowers in the shape of painted skulls and grass like fountains of corpses' hair. Monkeys chatter in the canopy. Parakeets scream. A tiger coughs in the undergrowth.

Frank creaks down a twisting jungle path, trampling through tangles of ivy and jasmine, fighting through drifting green fogs of fern, until he reaches a sunlit clearing containing an ornamental pool.

There is a man standing beside the pool. He is wearing a printed cotton frock, a string of pearls and bright red shoes.

'What do you know about fish?' demands the man in the frock.

Frank creaks to the edge of the pool and stares down at the dark water. A dozen large fish are floating motionless on the surface, their fins fanned and their bloated stomachs turned to the sky.

'They're dead,' says Frank.

'Are they?' frowns the man in the frock. 'I thought there was something wrong.'

He's tall and softly spread with fat. His broad ugly face looks like a badly blemished potato. The folds of his ears and his big marbled nose are choked with quivering silver bristles. His eyebrows are brambles. His blotched brown eyes are full of sorrow.

The frock, a faded print of daffodils, strains at the seams, pulls at the buttons, as if it were trying to shrink from the horror of being held captive against him. His butcher's arms bulge from the little sleeves. His bony feet have broken the sides of the red leather shoes, forcing him to walk with a shuffle.

'What do you think of the house?' he asks Frank, surveying him with a mournful eye.

'It's big,' says Frank.

'Damn right, it's big! This is my house. I've got a luxury fitted kitchen, an indoor swimming pool, sauna, gymnasium, cinema, art gallery and jungle hothouse. This is the jungle hothouse. It has automatic climate control and random stereophonic wildlife. Do you want a sauna?'

'No. No, thanks.'

'You can have a sauna if you fancy one.'

'Some other time,' says Frank. The heat crushes him. He opens the jacket and yanks at his collar.

'The garden has a marble patio, a king-sized barbecue pit, ornamental Italian fountains, flowerbeds for all seasons and fantasy floodlights that dance to music. What's your name?'

'Frank.'

'I'm Conrad Staggers. This is my house. You've met my daughter.'

'Valentine?'

'That's right.'

An ape barks in distant treetops. Frogs are honking like motor horns. Conrad fondles his necklace and absently counts the pearls, a clicking rosary.

'I was raised in the gutter, Frank. Can you believe it? Look. There's the gutter. When they knocked down the street I had it removed and set right here in the hothouse floor.' He shuffles to the water's edge and stares at the worn granite slabs that form a kerb to the goldfish pool, emphasising his words by giving the stones a gentle poke with the tip of a scuffed red shoe. 'That's history staring back at you.'

'It's a shame about the fish.'

'Yeah. Maybe I'll get some terrapins.'

'I need a telephone . . .'

'Conrad.'

'I need a telephone, Conrad. I have to phone my wife.'

'You're married. That's good. A man needs a woman to call his own.'

25

'She'll murder me when I get home. I've been missing so long she probably thinks I've been kidnapped.'

Conrad smiles. He takes Frank gently by the arm and shuffles him deeper into the jungle. 'What's your game?' he asks abruptly, when they've walked a few yards along a narrow cobbled path. He catches Frank's elbow with his hand and gives it a confidential squeeze.

'What?'

'What's your racket?'

'Marketing.'

Conrad looks pleased. He grins and grinds the elbow between his fingers and thumb. 'My grandfather worked the markets. They were hard times. He made a living selling scratchings.'

'I sell fruit,' says Frank.

'Do you know how I made my money, Frank? Security. Staggers Security Holdings. People paid me to protect them. I'm worth a fortune. I started out forty years ago as a bouncer at the local dance hall. And now I'm worth a fortune.'

'Why did they need protection?'

'That's a very good question, Frank. A very good question.' Conrad blinks and looks amazed. 'That's what they often said to me when I offered them my services. "Why do I need protection?"'

'What did you tell them?'

'You have to know what frightens them, Frank. You have to look into their dreams. A lot of men think they're fearless, but they lack imagination! It's a wicked and dangerous world. You have to demonstrate the dangers. When you fire their imaginations they soon need protecting from themselves. They frighten themselves into buying life assurance.'

They push through the dripping undergrowth, into a glade of star-shaped flowers where butterflies as small as snowflakes scatter into the shimmering air.

'You threatened them?' ventures Frank. The hair

26

prickles against his neck. His scalp seems to shrink and pull on his skull. This is a dangerous conversation. This shambling bear in the pantomime frock is a gangster. A man who makes money from menaces. The sweat springs from his hands. He makes a little performance from peeling off the jacket and rolling the sleeves of his shirt.

'You've got it wrong, Frank,' says Conrad patiently. 'They paid me to look after them. I never did them harm. I never laid a finger on them. I left that to a man called Hamilton Talbot.'

'And he was your partner,' suggests Frank.

'Yes. We were partners. That's true. But I had a name for law and order and he was the devil for mischief.'

'What kind of mischief?'

Conrad wags his head and makes a sucking sound through his teeth as if tormented by memories. 'He was the prowler in the attic. The bogeyman beneath the stairs. The smiling stranger at the school gates. The burning rags pushed through the letterbox at midnight. The acid attack in the supermarket. The bacon slicer filled with fingers. He was nasty. Very nasty.' He shuffles forward to pick at a cluster of flowers and loses one of his shoes. It comes adrift from his foot and slithers into the shrubbery.

'And what happened to him?' Frank demands as Conrad tramples into the gloom.

'He went crazy when I retired. I couldn't control him. He still works a territory south of the river. But there's something wrong in his head. He's a very twisted man, Frank. He thinks I'm trying to persecute him.'

He bends to retrieve his shoe and the frock sags open at the throat, the necklace rippling under his ears. Frank glances quickly into the frock, half-expecting to catch sight of breasts, an old gorilla's dugs, dark and hairy as coconuts.

'The men who nearly killed Webster last night . . .'

'The Cockers,' says Conrad.

'Yes.'

'They're Hamilton Talbot's men. They've been hunting Webster for weeks. They're making his life a misery.'

Frank watches Conrad struggle to stretch the shoe to his foot, his weight balanced on one gaunt leg, using his fingers as ramrods to pack down the scruff of his heel.

'I have to find a phone,' he says softly, turning and blinking the sweat from his eyes. He feels scared and sick with heat. He doesn't know how to escape the maze.

'I can't let you loose, Frank. You're not safe on the streets. I wouldn't forgive myself if something happened to you . . .'

Frank swivels his head, scowling, defiant. 'Are you threatening me?'

'I'm protecting you, Frank. The Cockers are killers. They're professionals. Murder and mutilation.'

'Yeah? What do they do for fun?'

'They hurt dogs.'

'What's to stop me walking out of here?'

'I've got a ten-foot wall trimmed with razor wire, video surveillance and armour-plated security gates. I like to sleep secure in my bed without having some little nut-brained yobbo breaking into the house at night and pissing over the carpets.'

'Listen. I just went out to post a letter. I don't know what happened. I don't care what happened. I didn't hear anything. I didn't see anything. I just want to go home and change into my own clothes.'

'It's a dangerous world, Frank. Think about it. As soon as we turn you loose the Cockers will be waiting for you. They'll trail you home. They'll find your wife . . .'

'I don't believe you.'

'Do you know what they do to women?' whispers Conrad, clutching his necklace against his neck. He trembles. His mad eyes bulge with secret horrors.

Frank shakes his head. He doesn't want to be told but then, despite himself, he's seized with a morbid fascination.

'It would turn your stomach . . .'

Now Frank imagines Jessica forced to confront these evil bastards. He thinks of them breaking into the house, catching his wife alone, snatching at her ankles and wrists, grinning as they slash at her clothes, dragging her down, prising her open. He thinks of her naked, weeping, bleating, crawling from the house to the street.

'What?' shouts Frank the good citizen. 'What harm have I done?'

'You helped Webster,' Conrad says softly. 'You've done enough to get yourself turned into dogs' meat.'

A panther yawns like a thunderstorm. The monkeys scream and take fright, clattering through the canopy.

'What do you want?'

'I want to look after you, Frank. You could help Webster settle the score. He's not a young man. He'd appreciate your help. It should only take a couple of days. It's a simple street-cleaning operation.'

'I've got an important meeting with the chairman of the Gooseberry Guild this morning!' protests Frank. 'I've got to get to the office . . .'

Conrad pays him no attention. He spears his nose with a finger and squints at his jungle flowers. 'You thought you were going to die last night, Frank. What were your last thoughts?'

'I thought, Jesus, I'm going to die. And then I thought, thinking I was going to die was going to be my last thought and I tried to think of something else to keep myself alive.'

'That's right,' says Conrad. 'You didn't think, Jesus, I'm going to die – I wish I'd spent more time at the office.'

Frank shrugs and a butterfly spills from his shirt.

'This is an exciting opportunity for you,' Conrad murmurs peacefully, as if the matter is already settled. 'The chance of a lifetime. Webster is the last of the big-hearted bruisers. He's an artist. You could learn a lot from him.'

'What happens if I get killed?'

29

'We always look after widows and children.'

'I don't want to get involved!' insists Frank, chopping at the air with his hands. 'I just want to get back to my wife.'

Conrad says nothing, bored by the effort of conversation. He takes his guest by the elbow and silently leads him back to the pool.

'Valentine will give you a phone,' he says at last, gesturing towards the door. 'Ask her to buy me some terrapins. A couple of dozen. Different colours.'

Frank stumbles from the jungle to find Valentine waiting for him. She's wearing a simple cashmere sweater and a pair of sailor's canvas pants that balloon from a snakeskin belt. Her long black hair spouts from her head in a pony-tail.

'I want to talk to Webster!' he snaps, shaking out his crumpled jacket. Webster will explain this madhouse. He owes him something for trying to save his life. He punches a sleeve with his fist and pulls the jacket over his shoulders, groping for the second sleeve with his arm twisted behind his back, bent forward, getting tangled, spinning around in a ragged circle like a dog snapping at its own tail.

'I thought you wanted to talk to your wife,' says Valentine mildly. She steps back as he thrashes out and finally wins control of the jacket.

Frank, gasping for breath, his face and neck glazed with sweat, nods miserably.

She leads him across the marble hall and into a room with yellow walls and an intricate plasterwork ceiling freckled with sunlight from a single window. The room contains a massive Victorian ebonised bookcase filled to the brim with bumptious pot-bellied vases and bowls. There is nothing else in the room but a leather armchair and a heavy, old-fashioned telephone on a carved lacquer Chinese table.

Valentine makes a tour of inspection, following the edge of the carpet. 'You can use the phone on the table. Take your time. When you've finished I'll take you to Webster.'

Frank sits down at the carved lacquer table and waits for Valentine to leave him alone. She turns away, ignoring him; the pony-tail sweeps the curve of her neck. She walks the room with slow, kicking strides like someone wading through water.

The door clicks shut.

Frank springs from the chair and hurries across to the window. He brushes back the curtain and tries to force open the heavy oak frame. The window is locked. He slinks back to the table and picks up the telephone.

He dials the number and listens to the distant ringing tone, thinking of the telephone in his own living room, Jessica running to answer it, clambering into the sofa cushions, tilting her head, wedging the mouthpiece into her shoulder, pulling and stretching the flex with her fingers. She has a habit of curling around a phone call as if she's afraid the voice in her ear will flutter from her embrace and escape.

'Jessica?'

'Frank? Thank God! Where are you?'

'I don't know.' He sounds like a drunk who, falling asleep on the last train home, struggles awake an hour before dawn to find that he's marooned in the shunting yards.

'What happened to you? Are you OK?'

'Yes. I'm fine. I had an accident . . .' He tries to swallow the word but it slips out before he's had time to retrieve it.

'What kind of accident? Frank? Are you hurt? Where are you? Tell me what happened!'

'Nothing happened – there was a fight at the end of the

street when I went down to the post box – it was just some stupid argument – a couple of drunks – I don't know why I got involved.' He's making a mess of it, stumbling through an account of the Cockers, trying to make them sound like clowns instead of professional killers.

'What the hell are you talking about?' Her voice sharpens with resentment. 'I was so frightened I went to the police. I didn't get to bed last night. I've been ringing around the hospitals. Why didn't you call me? Are you hurt?'

'I'm not hurt, for Chrissakes! I'm OK. A few cuts and bruises. I had to take one of them home. He wanted me to stay with him.'

'You stayed with him?'

'Yes.'

'All night?'

'Yes.'

'Wait a minute, Frank. Let me get this straight. I'm tired. I didn't sleep. You went out to post a letter and decided to spend the night with some drunk that you happened to meet in the street. Is that the story?'

'I know it sounds crazy . . .'

She's tired and dazed and disappointed. Her relief at hearing his voice again, knowing that he's alive and kicking, has dwindled into irritation. 'Why didn't you call me? You could have been dead or anything!'

'I couldn't call you.'

'Frank, where are you?' She's growing more suspicious. She doesn't know if she wants to believe him. There's something wrong. It doesn't make sense.

'I don't know!' he shouts impatiently. 'I'm lost!'

'What the hell is that supposed to mean?' she yells back at him.

'I don't know the exact address. It's a house. A big house.'

'Well, are you coming home or what?'

'Jessica, listen to me. I want you to call the office and

33

tell Bassett to cover for me at the Gooseberry Guild meeting this morning. It's important. Tell him I'm sick or something.'

'Call him yourself!'

'Please, Jessica. I need your help.'

'Frank, are you in trouble?'

'No!'

'You're in trouble. For God's sake! What the hell is happening there?'

'You won't believe me.'

'Try me.'

'I've been kidnapped.'

'I don't believe you.'

The door opens and Frank glances up to find Valentine standing in the room. 'Forget it,' he says quickly, trying to smother the phone with his hand. 'I'll call again . . .'

'Frank, get back here!' Jessica screeches. 'Do you understand me? I want you home!'

'I'll call again —. .'

But the phone is dead.

'Feeling better?' Valentine asks him as he slams down the receiver. She smirks, watching his confusion, mocking him.

'Where's Webster?' he demands, grunting, pushing his hands against his knees to lever himself from the chair.

'We keep him locked away in the attic.'

He follows her from the room and through a series of corridors that lead to the back of the house. He has the sensation of strolling through an abandoned hotel. The silence presses down on him. Beyond these closed doors he imagines expensive, stagnant rooms, furniture wrapped in shrouds, carpets bearing no footprints. There is nothing to be heard but the creaking of his own shoes.

Valentine takes him to a servants' staircase tucked away at the end of the house.

'Ask him to give you a razor,' she says as she leaves him to climb through the dark to the roof.

34

Webster stands waiting for him at the top of the stairs. He's wearing a woodland camouflage shirt and battered corduroy trousers. He looks solid and reliable, like a prosperous city banker setting out on a camping trip. He smells of soap and spearmint toothpaste. His face has been scrubbed until it shines.

'Frank! How are you?' He reaches out and pumps Frank's hand as if he's recovered a childhood friend.

'I've been kidnapped by a man in a frock.'

'Is that right?' He grins and his big face glows with pleasure. His pale eyes are flecked through with copper. His teeth have been threaded with gold. 'Did he make any ransom demands?'

'He wants me to help you search out the Cockers.'

'That's an idea!'

'Do I have a choice?'

'No.'

'What happens if I don't oblige him?'

Webster wags his head. 'The Cockers are animals, Frank. They've built their reputation on senseless acts of violence. If you don't go looking for them, they'll come looking for you. There's a gang war down there on the streets and you've just been press-ganged into service.'

Franks looks at Webster and tries to imagine this strange old man storming through doors and somersaulting through plate-glass windows.

'I don't believe this is happening.'

Webster smiles, wraps an arm around Frank's shoulders and takes him into a small room with a bare scrubbed floor. There are framed photographs on the walls, foxed faces fading like ghosts into the brittle, varnished paper. The ceiling, slung from the window lintels, vaults to the whitewashed chimney-stacks in a sagging sheet of plaster, broken by beams and the stumps of rusty iron pegs. In one corner of the room a pair of chairs keeps company with a metal table.

'I wish I'd never tried to help you,' grumbles Frank.

He shrugs himself loose and moves away to one of the windows, pressing his face against the glass, squinting down through the rain at a high brick wall marking the edge of the garden.

'Don't say that, Frank.'

'Those bastards tried to kill me! They hit me so hard that I nearly swallowed my brains!'

Webster retreats to a chair and pulls a packet of biscuits from a pocket in his camouflage shirt. Ginger biscuits glazed with a shell of sugar. 'That's why you need protection. You're my responsibility. I know how to look after myself.' He carefully opens the packet and crunches a biscuit into his mouth.

'That's not how it looked last night, Webster.'

'That was different. They took me by surprise.'

'If it's all the same to you, I'd rather go home and take my chances,' says Frank. He's already late for work. He thinks of the crowded office, the cluttered desk, the smell of damp coats and dripping umbrellas. The thought depresses and worries him. If Jessica has delivered his message Bassett should already be preening himself for the meeting with the Gooseberry Guild.

'How do you fancy your chances, Frank? How do you fancy a fire bomb thrown through your kitchen window at three o'clock in the morning? How do you fancy the Cockers playing games with your wife?'

'What do you want from me?'

'Nothing,' says Webster, brushing sugar from his shirt. 'You're a civilian. I don't expect civilians to fight my battles for me. I'll be taking you along for support. You'll be my caddie.'

'What makes you think I won't get my brains knocked out again?'

'This time we have the advantage. The best defence is attack. We'll strike fast and we'll hit hard. They won't have time to spit.'

'What are you going to do to them? says Frank doubtfully.

'Nothing nasty.'

'You'll just scare them,' suggests Frank.

'Squeeze 'em. Scare 'em. Teach them a lesson.'

'Do you know where to find them?' says Frank, to humour him. It's plain there's nothing to be gained by trying to reason with him. He'll have to be patient. There'll be an opportunity to escape. When they leave the house. When they go in search of the Cockers.

'I'll put out the word. They'll be easy enough to track down.'

'How long will it take?'

'We'll have you home by the weekend,' says Webster confidently.

'But what happens if we get caught?' argues Frank. He likes to count the cost. He wants to know the risks.

'How exactly do you mean?' Webster frowns and probes a hollow tooth with his tongue.

'What happens if they call the police?'

'This doesn't concern the police! This is private family business. Do you fancy a biscuit?' He rattles the packet at Frank and covers his corduroy trousers in crumbs.

Frank shakes his head.

'They're Ginger Crumbles.'

'How did you get involved with a man like Conrad Staggers?'

'Don't be fooled by the frock, Frank. He's a very powerful man. He's dined with kings and presidents. He was sent an invitation to the coronation of the Emperor Bokassa.'

Frank gazes around the walls at the rows of fading photographs. Men in rented dinner jackets, grinning, grinding cigars in their teeth. Women standing, smiling, stranded, sucked into wonderful pyramids of fluttering black lace skirts.

'How long have you worked for him?'

'A long time. I met him during the scuffles that followed the Curzon Street Midget Murders. It must be twenty years ago.'

'Do you live up here in the attic?' asks Frank, tilting his head and staring at the pegs in the ceiling.

'I like it. I like the solitude.' Webster nods towards the chimney-stacks. There's another door, as narrow as a coffin lid, half-hidden in the whitewashed brickwork.

For a long time Frank stands silent, listening to the sound of the rain as it crackles against the slates and gurgles in the gutters beneath the windows. The room grows dark.

'Do you have a razor?' he says at last.

Webster grins and stuffs his packet of biscuits into the safety of his shirt. He takes Frank by the arm and leads him deeper into his kingdom of cobwebs and rafters.

At ten thirty Jessica phones the Fancy Wholesale Tropical Fruits Corporation and asks to speak to Hastings Bassett. His secretary, a sour blonde who is paid to guard him against intruders, recognises Jessica's voice and puts her through without argument.

'What's happening?' demands Bassett. He sounds angry. 'Frank has a big meeting with the chairman of the Gooseberry Guild in half an hour. Where the hell is he hiding?'

Jessica chokes back the tears as she struggles to blurt out her story. 'He's disappeared! He went out to post a letter yesterday afternoon and when he didn't come back I started to get worried and I went out to look for him and he'd just vanished and I called the hospitals and I called the police and this morning he phoned and told me he wasn't coming home . . .'

'Hey! Calm down!' Bassett says gently, afraid that she'll suffocate with fright.

'He's gone!' she shouts back at him.

'Do you want to come over here?' he says, raising an arm, snapping his fingers at the sour blonde and waving her from the office.

'No. I'm sorry. I'll be all right.' She snuffles and wipes

her nose on her sleeve. Her hand reaches down for the glass of Bacardi and Coke she's brought with her from the kitchen. She never drinks in the morning. It's Frank's fault. He's making her sick with worry.

'Are you still there?'

'Yes. I'm here.' She thinks of him sitting at his desk with the brass lamp casting its puddle of light over the big leather diary and already she feels more secure. She trusts this man's command of the world.

'What did he say when he called you?'

'I don't know. It was nonsense. He said he'd spent the night with some drunks he'd picked up in the street.'

'So why hasn't he come home?'

'I don't know!'

'Did he tell you anything else?'

'No. He wouldn't even tell me where he was hiding.'

'Hell! It doesn't make sense!' he complains and glances at his watch. He demands law and order in his life. Everything must have a purpose. Nothing must be wasted.

'Has he been acting strange at work? Have you noticed anything unusual about him?'

'You know Frank.'

'Anything *different* about him?'

'No. I've had him brainstorming baby grapefruits.'

'Well, did he seem peculiar to you last week when you came over here for supper? Did he say anything to you?'

It's nearly two years since she first asked Frank to bring his boss home for her inspection. She'd been anxious to get involved and take an interest in Frank's career. He was being considered for promotion. She'd thought it would help him. She'd taken a lot of trouble that evening preparing herself as the perfect, well-dressed, obedient wife. She remembers she wore the black stretch silk with jet studs and flat shoes.

Hásty had arrived late, flustered and grinning, bearing a box of fresh lychees, scented eggs in blushing, goose-pimpled shells. She'd thanked him, confused, whisked

40

them away, left them somewhere in the kitchen, served him sour grapes and cheese at the end of a long and difficult meal. But Hasty had been friendly, Frank had seemed relaxed and she'd been careful that evening not to pour herself too much of the wine.

The following day Hasty had sent her a spray of roses and the supper had been declared a success. Since that time he's become a regular visitor to the house. He eats with them once or twice a month. She feels easy with him. She trusts his advice.

'I didn't notice anything,' says Bassett.

'Well, something's wrong!'

They are silent for a moment. Bassett seems lost for words. Jessica gulps at her drink.

'Do you think there's another woman?' she says finally.

'Frank? No! Where would he find the time? He does nothing but work and eat and sleep.'

'These things happen . . .'

'They don't happen to Frank!' She frowns, rakes at her scalp, impatiently shrugging the telephone hard against her mouth.

'So perhaps he met a few old friends and they dragged him away for a couple of drinks and one thing led to another and he got himself rotten stinking drunk and now he's ashamed to come home.'

'You think I'm being stupid.'

'I didn't say that.'

'But that's what you're thinking.'

'I think you're wasting your time chasing after him. He stayed out last night. So what? It's not the end of the world.'

'But he's *never* stayed out all night. He's never walked out without a word.'

'Do you want to come over here to the office? I can always cancel the Gooseberry Guild. It's nothing important. We could go out and have some lunch.'

'No. No, thanks. I want to stay here.'

'Call me if anything happens.'
'Yes.'
'Call me whatever happens.'
'I'm going to kill him! I swear I'm going to kill him!'

Frank squeezes through the coffin door and finds himself standing in a great timber hall that runs the length of the house. The roof beams curve above him like the blackened ribcage of a shipwrecked galleon. Glass lamps hang from these beams on a system of silver chains. The walls twist beneath the weight of thick iron pipes that erupt from several water tanks, expand and divide, throw out cankerous flowers of rust and burrow into the floor. The tanks themselves are polished black cauldrons decorated with laurel wreaths and the grinning heads of demons. Beneath the first of these tanks, a sofa and a chest of drawers command a strip of Turkey carpet beside a tottering column of books balanced on a bamboo table. In the shadow of the second tank, a conspiracy of armchairs, hump-backed and huddled, filled with spidery horsehair cushions. Anchored to the timber blocks of the third and largest tank, a fleet of painted cupboards and chests. Beyond the tanks a buttress wall contains a bathroom no bigger than a confessional and beyond the bathroom, at the far end of the hall, in a nook of curtains, a hammock hangs from a cradle of pipes.

'It needs a lick of paint. But it's warm and secure and it smells sweeter since I killed the starlings,' says

Webster, hunting for towels as he leads Frank to the little bathroom.

Frank shaves and takes a shower, scalding himself with water from a bilious and belching boiler, while Webster makes a series of phone calls in search of Lloyd and Harry Cocker. He broadcasts threats and promises, collecting a debt, bestowing a favour, chasing his quarry from shadow to shadow.

'I've found them!' he says triumphantly, when Frank emerges from the shower. 'I spoke to a man who spoke to a man who says they were seen at the Golden Goose. I knew they wouldn't be far away – they're so lazy they wouldn't pull a soldier off their own mother.'

'What happens now?' Frank hangs the towel from his head like a cowl. He didn't know it would happen this fast and he's scared but he wants the Cockers caught for the sake of his own liberation.

'Nothing,' says Webster suspiciously. 'What did you expect?'

Frank shrugs. 'I don't know. I suppose I thought you'd go down there and sort them out.'

'It's raining!' says Webster. He looks appalled. 'We can't go out in this weather!'

Webster's reluctance to get his shoes wet strikes Frank as a trifle squeamish, but he isn't going to argue with him. So he settles into one of the hump-backed chairs and, while they wait for the skies to clear, Webster entertains him with a dog-eared scrapbook stuffed with snapshots and yellow press clippings. Tragic Beauty Found in Freezer. Six Dead in Banjo Bomb Blast. And here, between Mystery Blaze in Soho Nightclub and Kilburn Drug Gang Slaughter, a small, tobacco-coloured snapshot clings to the page like a pressed flower. The face that stares from the photograph is a blurred shadow, the eyes wild, the mouth pulled open in fear or surprise.

'Rinso the Human Torch,' says Webster. 'The man who

turned arson into art. An alchemist. A pyrotechnic genius. He could eat flames and fart the sparks.'

'What happened to him?'

'He drowned in his bath,' says Webster.

He licks his finger and turns the pages in his catalogue of crimes and pauses to glance at the true confessions of Garibaldi the Gorgon, the man in the animal mask.

'Remember the Beast of Baker Street?'

'The Mad Butcher?' says Frank. 'He murdered women and ate them and what he couldn't eat he buried somewhere in Regent's Park.' It must have been ten or twelve years ago. He remembers the story from the papers.

'That's it!' says Webster. 'That was the Gorgon. Poor devil. He used to live with his mother somewhere in Camden Town. They ran a little grocery shop. He found God when they locked him away. We always send him a Christmas card.'

'Did you know him?'

'I knew his mother. Conrad liked her home-cured bacon.'

He turns another page and Garibaldi the Gorgon surrenders to Hangman of Hanover Square who yields to Fat Turk in Torture Chamber who succumbs to Redhead in Bank Raid Blunder who resigns to Chinese Conjurer Killings: Fear Walks Abroad in Chinatown and there, beneath Panic in Park Street and Riddle of Head in a Hatbox, a photograph of Conrad and Webster, wearing Brylcreem and buttonholes, standing, smiling, disguised as young men.

'A rogue's gallery,' says Webster proudly, as he closes the book and presses it against his knees. The bandits and buccaneers. The spoilers and smudgers. He's lived through interesting times.

'Those bastards tried to kill me!' says Frank, haunted once more by his fear of the Cockers. 'I'm not going to give them a second chance. I must be crazy!'

Webster stands up and hugs the scrapbook to his chest.

'You made a lot of stupid mistakes, Frank.' He takes the book to a painted cupboard and carefully locks it away. 'You have to understand the basic rules of self-defence. And the first rule of defence is attack.'

'You've told me. What's the second rule?'

'Never get caught in an empty street. If you think you're being followed, change direction and mix into the crowd.' He sits down beside Frank and retrieves the packet of Ginger Crumbles from the pocket of his shirt. 'Killers hate working with an audience.'

'I'll remember that, the next time I want to post a letter.'

'Rule number three. When you're cornered, never try to engage your killers in the art of conversation. It's a common mistake, but it's fatal. You tried to reason with them, Frank. You can't reason with a man swinging a baseball bat at your head.'

'What should I have done?'

'Rule number four. Strike out. Hit hard and fast.'

'Thanks. You're full of bright ideas. I'll always make it a rule to keep a brick in my pocket.'

'Rule number five,' beams Webster, forcing a biscuit into his mouth. 'Don't waste time with a brick in your pocket. You've strength enough in your hands and feet. Pick a soft target. The eyes. The nose. The throat. The bollocks. Keep it simple. Hit him where it hurts.' He sighs and sucks sugar from his fingertips.

'Why?' says Franks in exasperation. 'What makes you do it?'

'Excitement,' says Webster, looking at Frank in surprise. He's honest enough to admit it. The reasons are obvious. 'There's nothing else like it. How much excitement do you get selling fruit?'

'I'm not looking for excitement,' says Frank and, all at once, remembers when he was eighteen and hungry for adventure, planning to join a two-year expedition to the mountain forests of Belize. Young and inexperienced,

46

with no particular qualifications, it had taken him months to win the trust of the team. The expedition leader, an authority on the jaguar and elusive jaguarundi, had finally agreed that Frank could join them as quartermaster at the base camp in Cockscombe Basin. Frank was jubilant. He'd spent the winter reading everything he could find on the region, studied jungle survival techniques, struggled to learn a few words of Spanish. And then, a few weeks before they were due to leave for Central America, he had unexpectedly been offered a job with the dried fruits and nuts division of Lotus Pitcher International. His friends congratulated him. His parents were absurdly proud. He was eighteen years old and still anxious to please the people who loved him. He surrendered his ticket. He felt like a man caught trying to shirk family responsibilities. Lotus Pitcher promised early promotion and the chance to work in one of their foreign outposts. So the expedition went to Belize and Frank stayed at home. He was never posted abroad. He found himself sharing an office behind the typing pool and working as assistant brand manager on Calypso Fried Banana Bites. He worked hard and rarely complained. We learn to regret the things we have done – we grieve for those things left undone. Years later he would still find himself startled awake at night by the sight of a beautiful jaguar, a spectre of sunlight and shadow, stalking the forest that grew in his dreams.

'But there must have been a time in your life,' insists Webster.

'What?'

'There must have been a time in your life when you nearly lost control. A moment when you wanted to push a chair through a window or screw a knife into someone's chest.'

Frank recalls the moment at an ill-fated Christmas party when Jessica, so drunk she'd become a stranger, had clambered onto a dining-room table to perform a queasy, shuffling striptease, dragging at her wine-soaked clothes

47

while a rabble of men had gathered around to encourage her with their shouts and whistles and he'd wanted to lash out at those stupid, leering faces and overturn the table and drag his wife home by the scruff of her neck.

'There must have been moments,' he admits.

'That's good!' says Webster. 'There's a monster sleeping in every man. It's dangerous to ignore your monster. What happened?'

'Nothing.' He shrugs. She'd fallen from the table and capsized into his arms. He'd taken her home and put her to bed and her vomit had fouled the sheets and pillows.

'That's bad,' says Webster, shaking his head. 'You shouldn't smother your desires. Anger turns to acid in your stomach. Hurts your head. Burns out your system.'

'If we didn't keep control we'd be sloshing around in our own blood. There'd be executions on the streets. The city would be a bonfire. There'd be no law and order left in the world.'

'That's true. And a life of crime depends on a sense of law and order. It's a world of goats and wolves, Frank. Goats and wolves.'

The rain crackles against the roof and snuffles in the throats of the soot-choked chimneys. Great gusts of wind try to lift the house away by the eaves, making the attic windows bulge and the silver lamp chains swing in circles.

The storm excites the water tanks, making them echo with distant thunder, their murky depths scoured by the raging of whirlpools, and then, with a rattle of rivets, they send a tumultuous surge of water screeching along the iron pipes and into the trembling floor. The pipes scream and bellow, banging themselves against the walls until, as night creeps into the attic, they create such a cacophony, such a battlefield of noise, that Webster conducts a smart retreat down the servants' stairs and now Frank finds himself at a long table where the Staggers are gathered for supper.

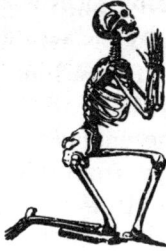

'Come and sit next to me,' says Conrad, waving Frank into the room. He's wearing a silk taffeta ballgown the colour of liver and diamond earrings as big as bull's-eyes that dangle from his bristling ears and flash in the candlelight.

Valentine, demure in a simple silk cardigan, is sitting at the far end of the table. She looks at Frank without a flicker of recognition. Her face is a perfectly painted mask. Webster sits down beside her and tucks a napkin under his chin.

The room is large and draughty, decorated with a series of gloomy oil paintings depicting a slaughter of animals, birds and fishes, heaped into banquets for castle kitchens. Frank gazes around the walls at the wreckage of pigeons, woodcocks and pheasants, dead rabbits hanging in chains, a fat-bellied hog on a butcher's block with a branch of oak leaves clenched in its jaws.

'I hope you're hungry,' says Conrad. He shakes a tiny crystal bell and four young women enter the room. They are lean and as lovely as ballerinas, dressed like French maids in brief black skirts, white lace aprons and caps.

These girls are employed by Conrad's cook, an ancient

Turk who is rarely seen but controls the house with a quiet and ruthless efficiency. He conducts the domestic affairs as if the days were battles in a war against the forces of anarchy. He orders fuel and food in quantities that would bring them, fat and victorious, through the cruellest winter siege. He launches attacks on the cleaning as if he were driving the enemy from battle lines in the furniture. Beating secrets from carpets, flushing snipers from cover in the giant laundry baskets. His days are long and bitter campaigns, fought with a courage born of endurance. At night he sleeps with the maids in a long basement dormitory. A pasha surrounded by concubines.

The maids come to the table at the same hour every evening bearing silver trays of extravagant delights. Lobster tails ablaze with brandy. Camel's hump with peppered snap beans. Smoked peacock stuffed with walnuts. They circle the table silently, deliberately, spoons clicking like castanets.

'What's this?' scowls Conrad, poking at a morsel of meat adrift in a pool of mud. He turns his mad eyes on the serving girl who is standing meekly beside his chair, head bowed, trembling with fright.

'Wild duck with truffles,' she whispers.

'It looks like a turd,' grunts Conrad the epicurean. He flicks up the back of her skirt and runs his hand against her legs, searching for the warmth of her thighs.

'Yes, sir,' she whispers. She looks alarmed but she dares not retreat. She stands, quivering, bobbing her head, like a beautiful ventriloquist's doll moved by her master's sleight of hand.

'It must be expensive,' he concludes, closing one eye and trawling the steam that drifts from the plate with the tip of his marbled nose. 'Is it expensive?'

'Yes, sir,' she whispers.

He looks reassured and absently slides his hand from her skirt. She blinks and seems to shrink, as if she's been standing on tiptoe. 'What's your name?' he demands, inspecting the pocket of her apron.

'Josephine, sir.'

'You're a good girl, Josephine,' says Conrad, very solemn, and he pulls a bull's-eye from his ear and presses it into her fist.

'Thank you, sir.'

'Compliments to the Turk.'

'Yes, sir. Thank you, sir.'

Conrad smiles and directs a friendly slap to her rump that seems to buckle her at the knees, sending her into a sprawling curtsey before she runs from the room followed by her startled companions.

'What's the news?' he growls at Webster, wrenching a stubborn cork from a bottle and splashing his knuckles with wine. He sucks at his fist like a toothless lion chewing a bone.

'They're at the Golden Goose,' says Webster.

'That's Crazy Larry's fun-house!' shouts Conrad, banging the table with the flat of his hand.

Frank misses his mouth with his fork and manages to spear his chin.

'That's right!' says Webster with a crafty grin.

'Remember the dog?' says Valentine.

Conrad throws back his head and explodes in great shouts of laughter. 'A few years ago I tried to conduct some business with Crazy Larry,' he says, turning to Frank. 'But I found I couldn't trust him. He was cheap. He was cunning. He had an unfortunate attitude. So I sent Webster out to have a few words with him.'

'It must have been something I said to upset him,' says Webster, as he shovels gravy with a spoon, 'because the next day he went out and bought a killer dog.'

'It was a Rottweiler,' says Conrad.

'A pit bull,' says Valentine.

'It was a bastard,' says Webster.

'He called it Castro,' says Valentine.

'Anyway, he kept this damn great dog running loose in his house,' says Conrad, 'squirting shit all over the carpets. And you couldn't get near Crazy Larry for the noise of that animal grinding its teeth.'

'So one night we stole it!' laughs Webster, spluttering bread crumbs over the table. 'We fed it raw steak seasoned with enough cocaine to knock down a buffalo and we brought it home and made it comfortable in the kitchen.' He picks at the crumbs with his fingers, returns them carefully to his mouth.

'It was no trouble,' remembers Conrad.

'It was no more trouble,' says Webster, 'because the Turk fed it cocaine cutlets. For three weeks it was curled in a blanket with its nose plugged into its arse.'

'And then we felt sorry for Crazy Larry, who was grieving for that dog like a mother grieves for a missing child. He was advertising a big reward. So one morning we delivered it back to his doorstep with a ribbon around its neck,' says Conrad.

'He was so pleased to see Castro again that he fell to his knees and wept,' says Valentine.

'But the brute was a slobbering junkie and without the comfort of a cutlet its nerves were getting jangled. Larry bent down to give it a kiss and that dog took off the bugger's nose, flipped it into the air and swallowed it down like a chipolata!' roars Conrad with another trumpeting shout of laughter.

'He was in hospital for months!' shrieks Valentine. 'Months! They had to make him a new nose.'

'It's clever,' reflects Conrad. 'You can't tell the difference except in cold weather.'

'But he's never been the same since it happened!' chortles Webster, wagging his head. 'It gave him a dicky strawberry.'

The company fall silent, breathless, exhausted by the sheer rapscallion fun of it. Conrad shakes the crystal bell and there is a brief interlude while the girls return to clear the plates and serve a selection of pastries and cheeses.

Josephine smiles at Conrad, brushes against him, presses herself against his chair, but no matter how she flirts with him she can't win another bull's-eye.

'When are you going?' Conrad asks Webster, when the girls have left the room. Frank senses a sudden shift in the old man's mood. Conrad leans across the table, pulls at the sleeves of his ballgown, lances a bowl of fruit with his elbow.

'Tomorrow morning,' says Webster, 'while the Goose is asleep.' He's talking of murder but looks as dangerous as favourite uncle plotting to play Father Christmas.

'Are you wearing armour?'

'No. They won't be expecting trouble.'

'What do they pack when they *are* expecting trouble?' asks Conrad.

'The Beast packs a customised small-frame snubby,' says Webster. 'He carries it on a bellyband.'

Frank abandons his pineapple tart as the pastry turns to straw in his mouth. He feels like a condemned man reaching the end of his last supper. He thinks of Jessica waiting for him, alone in the house, and Bassett waiting for him, alone at his empty desk in the office, and the meeting with the chairman of the Gooseberry Guild and the work waiting for him on the soft-fruit project and all the unfinished business of life.

'And Lloyd?'

'He wouldn't trust a wheelie. He wears an automatic. Probably a Glock with high-velocity combat rounds.'

'I'd be happier if you wore a vest,' complains Conrad, mauling a barrel of Stilton. 'I want the Cockers cleared out. We can't afford to lose respect by making another mistake. I won't have Talbot leaning on me with a couple of rented pillock-brains with too much shine on their shoes.'

'We'll take care of it,' says Webster.

'I want to drive,' announces Valentine, tossing an apple into the air. She catches it with a snap of her hand and rubs it against her sleeve.

'I don't know. You'll have to ask Webster,' says Conrad, stuffing his cheek with cheese.

'But he always lets me drive,' croons Valentine. She bends against Webster and nuzzles his neck, making a cockscomb of his hair by tweaking his scalp with her fingers.

'You can be the driver,' says Webster, flustered and grinning, stroking his skull.

'What about Tonto?' says Valentine suddenly, glancing across at Frank as she crunches on her apple.

Frank starts to open his mouth to protest but Webster is already speaking for him.

'He'll be fine. I've told him I want him to be my caddie.'

'I won't get involved with guns!' says Frank, pulling away in his chair and scraping the legs against the floor. He looks quickly around at the paintings on the wall as if, for a moment, he might vault across the table, clamber into a picture frame and bury himself in a soft heap of feathers or seek sanctuary in the hog's entrails.

'Sit down!' growls Conrad. He grabs Frank by the wrist and yanks him into the chair. 'You won't have the chance to get involved. We can't have civilians running around, shooting the mirrors like Tex Ritter and scattering the horses!'

He winks at Webster and grins. He glances at Valentine and sniggers. He clips Frank's head with the flat of his hand and his laughter rolls through the room like thunder.

The big green Bentley is launched through the security gates and into the shallow winter sunlight as a million men are rushing to work. They are swarming from stations, scrambling up holes in the steaming pavements, chasing each other along the streets. They are armed with newspapers rolled into cudgels. They are hauling briefcases stuffed with confetti made from order books, handbooks, rule books, diaries, ledgers, receipts and requests to feed the demented paper tigers that lie in wait beneath their desks.

Frank is sitting in the back of the Bentley with Webster beside him. They've been fitted with charcoal business suits and immaculate pin-stripe shirts. Frank is guarding a Gladstone bag. They look like corporation generals on the way to a boardroom battle.

'The Golden Goose is a fun house and massage parlour,' says Valentine, as she nudges the car through the rush hour traffic. 'Have you ever been to a fun house, Frank?'

Frank shakes his head.

'No imagination,' snorts Valentine, scowling at him in the driving mirror.

'Crazy Larry owns a string of them,' says Webster,

checking his pockets for peppermints. 'They're cheap and nasty. Pink mirrors and nylon sheets. He gives the racket a bad name.' He frowns and slaps his jacket like a man about to burst into flames. When they're out together on active service Valentine likes to place peppermints somewhere about his person.

'The Goose is managed by a woman called Uncle Joe. But don't let her bother you. She's all meat and no potatoes,' says Valentine.

'She's slow on her feet but she bites,' adds Webster cheerfully. He's found the roll of peppermints in the pocket of his pin-stripe shirt.

'Are you going to tell me the plan?' demands Frank. He presses his nose against the window, searching the streets for familiar landmarks. He calculates they've been holding him captive somewhere north of King's Cross and Euston and now, bearing west on the Marylebone Road, they are turning south towards Marble Arch.

'What plan?' says Webster, peeling the paper roll and working a peppermint loose with his thumb.

'Don't tease him,' says Valentine.

Webster leans back in the seat, plucks at his sleeve and checks his watch. 'The Goose is a two-storey house, narrow but deep, with a door to the street and a small backyard. They keep the front door guarded but the back of the house is unprotected. An alley runs down the side of the house and takes you to the kitchen yard. The yard is surrounded by a wall. We'll go through the kitchen, check the stairs and then start searching the bedrooms. If we're quick we'll catch the Cockers asleep.'

'What happens if something goes wrong?' says Frank.

'If anything goes wrong,' says Valentine, 'you get out fast and wait for me to pick you up again. Whatever happens, don't panic and don't try to make a run for it.'

'There's nothing to go wrong,' says Webster peacefully, admiring the shine on his shoes.

The Bentley is trapped at a set of lights. They gaze

around at the sales clerks and scribblers pouring towards them from the pavements, swilling around the limousine. They are bent into ragged question marks, marching like refugees from the onslaught of some catastrophe on the distant edge of the city, and Frank the truant, knowing he should be marching with them, watches them pass with a thrill of excitement.

'How long do you need?' says Valentine, as the lights change and the Bentley pulls away.

'Ten minutes,' says Webster. 'If we're not out in fifteen, you'll know we've got into trouble.'

They turn towards Notting Hill and enter a maze of neglected backstreets, leaving the office workers behind them.

'This is it,' says Webster, as the Bentley whispers to the kerb on the corner of a decrepit square.

Frank peers out at the Lazy Launderette and the Red Hot Pepper Chicken Parlour. The launderette has been gutted by fire and boarded against intruders. The chicken parlour, scorched to its brickwork, sulks behind galvanised iron shutters. A crust of rain-blown rubbish has set like a scab against the blistered and padlocked door.

'Ten minutes,' says Valentine.

They clamber from the safety of the car and start walking towards the far side of the square. Here, under canopies of crumbling stucco, are Chinese grocers, wreathed in incense, squatting on piles of wrinkled fruit; Arab butchers crouched in kiosks, hawking skewers of peppered meats; Indian tailors, Turkish traders, herbalists and hypnotists. The streets are filled with a fractious rabble of touts and thieves, babblers, junkies and fighting dogs.

Webster steps out in long, easy strides, as confident as a slum landlord bearing eviction orders. Frank chases after him, clutching the Gladstone bag. He glances back at the Bentley as it disappears from view. This is the moment to make an escape but there's nowhere to run and nowhere to hide.

The Golden Goose is a shabby bed-and-breakfast hotel with a No Vacancy sign in the window. The sign is faded and rimy with rust. Webster turns abruptly and disappears down the alley that leads to the hotel kitchen.

In the shadow of the yard, sheltered from the eyes of the street, he takes the bag from Frank's hand and sets it down on the cobbles.

'We want to make a good impression,' he says, snapping it open, unscrambling boiler suits, masks and gloves.

And now Frank follows Webster's instructions like a clumsy automaton, pulling the boiler suit over his shoes, fumbling with the rubber buttons.

The masks are knobbly, knitted hoods, tight as balaclavas, with holes cut out for the eyes and nose. These soft hairy skulls have been knitted from hideous stripes of colour: taupe and tangerine, turquoise, puce and acid green. They look like the scarecrow heads of men pickled and painted by cannibals.

'I can't breathe,' mumbles Frank, searching for his nose with a glove. He claws at the mask, wrenching the wool, stretching the holes to fit his eyes.

'You get used to it,' snuffles Webster, hiding the empty Gladstone bag in the rubbish along the wall. He looks like a tribal demon, a flea-pit phantom, the tap-dancing clown of death.

'Are you ready?'

Frank is confused. He is waiting to be armed with a stick or a stone, a rubber club or a tin whistle. They can't confront the Cockers without something to protect themselves. But there's no time to argue because Webster is already leading him to a small window set high in the brickwork beside the kitchen window.

When he presses his face against the glass and peers through the gloom he can see the figure of a young woman standing, motionless, in the darkness of the scullery, lit by a solitary beam of light. The woman is wearing

58

camiknickers and a pair of rhinestone cowboy boots. A cigarette, clenched in her teeth, sends a twist of smoke floating through her tangled hair. The sunlight pours from a tall refrigerator, a veteran Sno-Queen, the door hanging open, the shelves trapped in dirty pack-ice. The light stains her skin with a saffron glow, turns the camiknickers to gold, catches the front of the cowboy boots, firing the rhinestones into diamonds.

While Frank gawps, the woman seems to come to life, spurts smoke through her teeth, plunges an arm into the shaft of freezing sunlight and pulls out a carton of orange juice. She tweaks open the spout and holds the carton under her nose, scowling, chewing the cigarette, kicking the fridge door shut with her boot.

'What's happening?' whispers Webster.

'There's a woman!' marvels Frank and he sounds astonished like a mariner in some tropical sea who catches sight of a mermaid.

'What's she doing?' Webster demands impatiently, trying to pull Frank away and take command of the spy glass.

'She's coming out!' hisses Frank, jerking back his head and colliding with Webster. He turns to take flight but Webster has caught him by the arm and presses him against the wall.

'Don't move!' he whispers through his woollen bandage as the door chains rattle and a key scratches the lock.

They flatten themselves against the wall, imitating invisible men, as the door creaks open and a large ginger cat is pitched abruptly into the yard. The cat is an ugly, venomous brute with tattered ears and a broken tail. It bristles and spits and twists around but the door is quickly slammed in its face. For a few moments, screaming with indignation, it bangs its head against the door and then, gradually losing interest, forgetting the cause of its grievances, slinks away to explore the drains.

'She's gone!' whispers Frank, returning to the window and searching for his mermaid through the dirty glass.

Webster opens the kitchen door and the masked intruders enter the house. The silence settles upon them like dust. The air stinks with the smell of old food. A dozen empty pizza cartons neatly stacked on a metal table. A bowl of cats' milk on the floor.

Beyond the deserted scullery they find themselves in a large room filled with armchairs clustered around a TV set the size of a cocktail cabinet. The armchairs are filled with bags of knitting, torn copies of *True Romance* and books of crossword puzzles. A paper balloon for a lampshade. A fruit bowl for an ashtray.

They pick their way across the room and reach a flight of stairs dimly lit by a murky red light where, peering through the balustrades, they catch sight of the girl in the cowboy boots vanishing into a bedroom. Webster leans against the newel post, turns to Frank and points a finger to heaven and then they begin to climb up through the crimson twilight.

At the top of the stairs a Chinese lantern casts a feeble blush of light along a narrow corridor paved with a strip of purple carpet. The walls are lined with framed photographs of fantastic big-breasted women dressed as pixies and Roman slave girls, like a small-town picture palace advertising future attractions.

Webster creeps forward and pauses beside a bedroom door. He turns the knob with a twist of his fist and furtively peeks through the gloom. He beckons Frank and grants him a view of a giantess, wrapped in a nightmare of chiffon, slumped asleep on a brass bed. A long wig of nylon hair hangs like an animal pelt from a mirror.

'That's Uncle Joe,' whispers Webster, gently closing the door again and moving along the corridor.

They pick another room, prising open the door, leaning forward into the shadows and there, sprawled naked on a ruined bed, with his head submerged in the mangled pillows, one leg trapped in the sheet, one leg dangling overboard, they find Harry Cocker. He's asleep beside a half-dressed woman. She is young and skinny in boxer shorts, shoulders hunched, turned away from him, curled in a ball like a petulant child. They are snoring.

Frank follows Webster into the room and they tiptoe slowly towards the bed. The floor is littered with clothes, bottles, satin cushions in the shape of hearts and a circus of stuffed toy animals. A pink plush hippo with button eyes, a brown bear and a lion cub; a chimpanzee in a bowler hat, a giraffe and a kangaroo.

Now he stands next to Webster, staring down at the Beast, and waits for something to happen. At any moment the vampire will open its blood-bloated eyes, bare its fangs in a bellow of rage, throw out its arms and drag him down through the gates of hell. Frank feels the room start to move around him. The sweat seeps through his knitted hood and collects in the fingertips of his gloves. The girl moans softly, her legs twitching as she runs through her avenue of dreams towards the beckoning daylight.

At the far end of the room light is pouring through a crack in a door. Webster weaves a pantomime with his hands, instructing Frank to guard the bed while he sets out to invade the bathroom. He picks an empty champagne bottle from the carpet and weighs it in his fist, hesitates, twists on his heel, sprints forward, catapults through the bathroom door and is lost in the luminous fog.

Lloyd is sitting in the bath with his legs wrapped around a fat, freckled girl armed with a sponge the size of a skull. She is staring vacantly at the ceiling, her arms raised, the sponge held high above her head, while Lloyd supports her breasts in his hands, grinning at them, licking his mouth, as if he might eat one for breakfast.

As Webster storms through the door the girl shouts, drops the sponge and tries to escape Lloyd's embrace by yanking him apart at the knees. Lloyd roars in pain and surprise. The bath erupts in a plume of green foam as the girl clambers out and scampers to hide herself in a corner, wrapping her face in a towel.

Lloyd explodes from the bath and turns to confront his assassin. The water spills from his shoulders, a beard of bubbles hangs from his chin. Webster raises the bottle and slaps it against the palm of his hand. Lloyd grins, stamps the floor with his wet feet, snatches at the girl, struggles to pull her into his arms, spreading her into a shield. But the girl is slippery with soap. She screams, wriggles loose and plunges into the bath again, trying to hide beneath the water.

The bottle bounces against Lloyd's head. He whistles and turns away, leans like a drunkard against the wall. Webster hits him again and this time Lloyd makes a queer little grunting noise in his throat and slithers from the wall to the floor. The blood spurts from his ear and tumbles in tiny crimson beads.

Webster lets the bottle slip through his fingers and watches it roll against the bath. The girl in the bath is sobbing loudly, her knees drawn against her chest, hiding her face in her hands. Lloyd stays on the floor, his mouth clicking open and shut, his head in a shining pool of blood.

Now the Beast awakes, snaps open his eyes and stares at the man in the knitted hood who is looming over the bed. He springs to life with a terrible shout, kicking the skinny girl to the floor, as he plunders the pillows in search of his gun. He snatches at a small, blunt revolver, wraps the gun in a fist and punches the fist at Frank's head.

Frank is so surprised that he simply stands and stares. He looks down the barrel of the Smith & Wesson and he remembers the spud gun he carried as a boy, the smack and sting of potato pellets as he fought long duels in the dusty heat of late summer afternoons and the smell of the percussion caps that came on peppery, pink paper rolls to fit his silver Colt .45 and the penknife he wore with the bent blade and the Captain Fantastic atomic stunner and for a moment it's as if his entire life will parade before his startled eyes.

The Beast fires at Frank's head but the skinny girl in the boxer shorts, clutching the sheets as she tries to haul herself from the carpet, throws herself over the edge of the bed like a drowning sailor reaching a life raft and the mattress groans and sinks beneath her weight, knocking the Beast askew as his finger squeezes the trigger.

Frank staggers, stunned by the noise, blinded by the muzzle flash, as the chimpanzee in the bowler hat jumps from the floor and explodes in a snowstorm of feathers. The hat cartwheels across the carpet in a trail of glittering sparks. The girl screams and the Beast, cursing, turns to her in a rage and clubs at her head with the gun. The girl shrieks and squirms and tries to gaff him with her fingernails as Frank recovers his wits, scrambles across the bed, locking his hands around the Beast's neck.

The Beast falls back, hoping to shrug Frank loose, but Frank is quick to seize the advantage and knocks the gun from his fist. He's scared and dazed but angry enough to fight with reckless courage. He has the Beast by the throat and is trying to corkscrew his head from his shoulders when the girl, jumping for the safety of the floor again by using the bed as a trampoline, grinds the Beast's testicles under her heel, making him shriek and kick out his legs, cracking her in the groin with his knees, knocking her down against Frank's shoulders, driving him forward over the Beast with his hands still locked around his neck, and the three of them slither to the carpet in a helter-skelter of fear and loathing.

For several moments they roll, one upon another, as spiteful as brawling children, until the Beast pulls away, stretching an arm across the bed, growling with pain, groping in the sheets for the gun. Frank is wrestling with the girl who, more by accident than design, has managed to master a hammerlock. She is sitting astride him, concentrating the last of her strength in pulling his arm from its socket, when the bathroom door bangs open and Webster stumbles forward. He's blowing like a wounded walrus and his boiler suit is spattered with blood.

The Beast grabs the revolver, launches himself across the bed and fires three shots towards the light. But he's too late. Lloyd Cocker, armed with the empty champagne bottle, has joined the fight again and clubbed the back of Webster's head. When Frank flings the girl against the wall and turns in search of his partner he finds him slumped on the floor with Lloyd standing over him, swinging the bottle.

Lloyd is grinning and staring at the wisps of smoke that drift from the holes in his chest. He raises one hand and dabs at a hole with his fingers, sighing softly as if lost in admiration for some wonderful conjuring trick, while his legs buckle and his spine turns to rubber making him concertina into the bathroom and the arms of his fat and freckled companion.

The Beast is flabbergasted. He stands up and wipes the hair from his face. He looks lost. He stares at Frank, the gun in his hand, the broken bed, the feathered floor, the girl with her face pressed into the wall. Then he starts slowly across the room, moving like a sleepwalker, perched on tiptoe, probing the air with his outstretched hands, stepping carefully over Webster and locking himself in the bathroom where he lets out a series of terrible screams.

Frank hauls Webster to his feet and navigates him from the room.

'Have we finished?' he shouts above the uproar around them.

'It's time to go home!' wheezes Webster.

They are sprinting along the corridor, clipping pictures from the walls, shaking dust from the Chinese lantern, and have almost reached the top of the stairs when Uncle Joe springs from the shadows, a monstrous genie wrapped in chiffon and waving a wicked carving knife. She swings the knife above her head, screws up her eyes and plunges the blade at Webster's heart but finds herself swept away, as if a whirlwind had filled her nightgown, and falls to the ground, shouting and stabbing the floorboards. Before she has time to recover, Frank and Webster are through the kitchen and into the yard, shivering in the cold morning air, removing their hairy scarecrow heads, peeling their hands and shedding their skins into the Gladstone bag.

The fat girl is choking, the thin girl is wailing, the Beast is moaning, his brother is bleeding, Uncle Joe lies stranded like an upturned turtle, the girl in the rhinestone cowboy boots hangs from a window, hoping to shimmy down a broken drainpipe, and Frank and Webster are walking with careful, measured strides away through the crowded and dirty streets. Frank swings the Gladstone bag in his hand. Webster pulls out the peppermints.

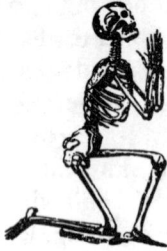

Conrad, looking lovely in a white silk blouse and a pleated blue crepe skirt, is sitting in a gilded chair the size of a sultan's throne. He's wearing black stockings. His big feet, bulging from their high-heeled shoes, are planted slightly too wide apart, the skirt in a swag between his knees. He sits, with a silken elbow propped on the arm of the chair and his chin in the palm of his hand, listening to Webster describe the defeat of the Cocker brothers at the Golden Goose Hotel.

Webster paces the room, waving his arms, snatching words from the air with his fingers, jerking his head towards Frank who stands patiently beside the window watching Valentine in the garden, strolling and smoking a cigarette. He transforms the ugly bedroom brawl into a whirling waltz of death, praises Frank for his courage, crowns his own battered head with glory, describes in exquisite detail the damnification of the brothers and finally, exhausted by his account of their triumph, swaggers across to Frank and shakes him by the hand.

'He's a killer!' he shouts, laughing, slapping Frank's shoulder and knocking him against the window.

Frank grins and pulls himself from the curtains. He feels like a pirate in seven-league boots. The world is a thigh-slapping pantomime of devils, boggarts and cannibals. He's a villain with eye patch and badger moustache.

'You deserve a drink!' declares Conrad. He looks amazed. His nostrils flare, his eyes are huge, the tufts of his bristling eyebrows twitch into fantastic curlicues. He steps down from the throne and clip-clops to a crystal table loaded with bottles.

'What's your poison?'

'Do you have a beer?' says Frank.

'I've got everything,' says Conrad, peering into the rainbow of bottles and decanters. 'Scotch whisky, Irish whiskey, Russian vodka, Polish vodka, Dutch gin, London gin, cognac, calvados, white rum, Navy rum, tequila, schnapps, rice wine, palm wine . . .'

'I'll have a beer,' says Frank.

'I can't find the beer,' grumbles Conrad, growing impatient, shaking the table.

'Give him a brandy,' says Webster.

So Conrad opens a bottle of cognac and fills three tumblers to their brims and they drink once for the healing power of the grape, twice for the scouring strength of the spirit and a third and fourth time because they've acquired the taste for it.

'You'll want to phone your wife,' says Webster confidentially, poking Frank with his thumb.

'I'll drink to that!' says Conrad.

Frank smiles, confused, his senses saturated, and tries to remember the reason he wanted to talk to his wife. He's forgotten his fight with Jessica and the bickering Bassett and the chairman of the Gooseberry Guild and all the fiddle-faddle of life. He's become the great Apollyon. Beelzebub in a balaclava. The laughing larrikin. He's drunk with excitement. He can still taste the gun smoke in his mouth.

'It can wait!' he says carelessly, draining his glass.

So they have another drink and one bottle leads to

another and Frank sleeps the afternoon away, slumped in the sultan's throne.

When he wakes up it is dark and the room feels cold. His eyes hurt and his bones feel broken. He falls from the chair and staggers in search of his companions, roaming the silent corridors of the house until he finds himself at the gates to the Turkish pavilion containing a marble swimming pool. The pavilion is lit by a thousand candles. The flames jump and flare on the walls and dance in the glittering water. In the centre of the pool floats Webster, beefy as a Smithfield bummaree, soaking his bruises. At the far end of the pavilion Conrad and Valentine are sitting in wooden deck-chairs, sharing a hamper under a giant parasol.

'Come over here and sit down!' shouts Conrad, waving Frank forward with a sickle of pie crust. 'It's too late to get you home tonight. We'll make a fresh start in the morning.'

'I'll drive you,' says Valentine as he sits beside her in the shade of the parasol. She's wearing a black swimsuit and smoking a cocktail cigarette. 'Are you hungry?'

Frank looks at the eggshells and salmon bones, the fruit skins and pastry crumbs. He shakes his head.

'This is for you,' says Conrad suddenly, wiping his hands in a napkin and pulling a briefcase from the darkness beneath his chair.

'What is it?' frowns Frank, catching it with outstretched hands, letting it slip, surprised by its unexpected weight. He imagines the briefcase packed with explosive, an intricate death trap of cut wire and nails.

'Open it,' prompts Valentine. 'Don't you want to open it?'

Frank hesitates, strokes the knubbly crocodile skin, gently prints his fingertips against the polished brass lock.

'It won't bite,' growls Conrad.

So Frank snaps open the clasps and swings back the lid

upon bundles and bundles of crisp, new twenty-pound notes.

There is silence. Conrad grins and grinds his teeth. Valentine pulls on her cigarette. Webster drifts to the side of the pool and hauls himself from the water.

'I can't take your money,' Franks says at last.

'What's wrong with it?' grunts Conrad. He leans forward to check the notes for fear he's packed roubles, rupees or zlotys.

'There's nothing wrong with it,' says Frank quietly. 'But I can't take it. There's more money here than I could hope to earn in a year.'

'Are you kidding?' says Conrad, looking at the money again with fresh interest. He's impressed.

'So what?' demands Valentine impatiently, grinding her cigarette into the eggshells.

'How could I explain it away?'

'Tell 'em you got lucky!' Webster shouts from the water's edge. 'Tell 'em you had a big win on the horses.'

'I don't play the horses.'

Valentine snatches a bundle of notes from the briefcase, leans forward and stuffs it into Frank's jacket pocket.

'Buy something for your wife,' she says flatly.

'You're a strange bugger!' grins Conrad, slapping his knees. And he lets out a great shout of laughter.

Frank hurries home to surprise his wife. He buys her a dozen roses, wrapped in a crackling paper cone, and a box of pastries, fragile pillows of sugar stuffed with a fragrant almond paste.

The streets are greasy with rain. The house, as he turns through the gate, looks empty and dark. He doesn't need to ring the front bell but unlocks the door with his own key, pulls off his coat and walks to the kitchen.

His wife is sprawled on the kitchen table. She is naked. Her mouth is open and her eyes are closed. Her arms are hanging loose and her bent legs raised against her chest. Bassett is slumped against her body, his fingers clutching the edge of the table, his shoulders wedged between her knees. His face has been contorted in death, the blind eyes bulging, the nostrils flared, the lips pulled away from the grinning teeth. His buttocks look grey in the dull winter light. His scrawny legs, bracing table and floor, have a cheesy, mottled appearance.

Frank stops breathing. Walking into the room, at the moment of impact, he translates the scene as the consequence of some freak car crash where the victims, hurled from the tumbling wreckage, have been blasted through the kitchen window to fall, tangled and stripped

70

of their clothes, on this polished pitch-pine table. The bodies are locked together, embracing dreadful, internal wounds, impossible to prise apart without tearing muscles or breaking bones. In his horror, blundering into this mortuary, he checks the desire to step forward and compose the twisted limbs of his wife, close her mouth and cover her nakedness with a towel.

Nothing moves. Nothing makes sense. He is still holding the cone of flowers and the box of sugar pastries.

He looks around the kitchen, as if seeking alternative explanations to the violence that confronts him. He divides the room into sections and cuts these sections into squares. He picks a square at random. He makes a list of everything he can find between the edge of the wooden window frame and the corner of the wall, extending from ceiling to floor. He counts the bottle of vodka and two glass tumblers containing slops of melted ice; an old-fashioned chrome toaster, a carton of Quaker Puffed Wheat, a plate of sandwich crusts, a perforated steel ladle, a spilled nest of plastic measuring spoons, a pair of scissors and a rind of cheese. No blood. No knives. No suicide note.

He tries again, concentrating on a line between the brass clock on the far wall and the base of the kitchen cupboards. This line is broken by the edge of Jessica's naked foot. His attention is drawn by the curve of her foot, the curled buds of her toes. He stares at the knub of her ankle bone, the flexed calf, the pale slope of her thigh. An artery sews a seam down her throat. Her head, tilted over the table's edge, seems suspended in a halo of hair.

Bassett blinks and his body jerks free from the table top. He has seen the intruder at the door, felt the danger, shovels his body into a crouch. His open hands congeal into fists. His feet slap the floor. His glistening penis swings like a baton under his belly.

'What the hell are you doing here?' he barks in alarm.

'I came home.' Frank raises the cone of wilting roses. It sounds absurd. It sounds like an apology.

Bassett, standing there, stark bollock naked, senses that Frank is stupid with shock and quickly starts working to seize the advantage. 'What makes you think you can come home?' he shouts. 'You walked out, dammit! You can't come walking back again!' He scowls and slaps at his bristling chest, like a wrestler mocking his opponent.

Jessica rises from the grave. She struggles to sit upright, straddles the table top, jumps to the floor. Her face is flushed. Her eyes are pebbles of dull blue glass. Her voice, when she finally works her mouth, sounds thick and slurred by sleep.

'Oh, Christ! Frank, what are you *doing* here?' She digs her fingers into her hair and then strokes her legs, as if smoothing down an invisible skirt. She dare not look him in the eyes.

Frank ignores the questions. He stares at his wife and glances again at Hastings Bassett.

'Perhaps you should get dressed,' he advises him quietly.

Bassett smiles. He pulls back his shoulders, swaggers past Frank and strolls down the hall towards the living room.

As soon as they are alone, Jessica starts moving around the kitchen, walking in circles, talking at him in nervous spurts. 'You could have been *dead*! I didn't know what to think. I didn't know what was happening.' She yanks open the fridge door, searches for nothing, kicks it shut. 'Where the hell were you? Why are you doing this to me?' She finds the cheese rind, picks it up and drops it on the plate with the sandwich crusts. 'I was going to tell you, Frank. You never gave me a chance . . .'

She stops talking and bites her lip. She is making it sound like a birthday surprise. She can't find the words. She is trying to make him understand that, no matter how she screwed up her life, she wanted, at least, to spare his feelings. Despite everything that's happened she didn't want to hurt him. But even as she confronts this pain, she feels a surge of relief begin to rush through her own body. It's finished. This is it. Everything she had dreaded for months has happened in the last few moments. It's all here and it's finished. She is going to survive.

'I was going to tell you, Frank.' Her voice cracks and breaks up in a snuffling gasp of misery. She begins sobbing, raising pink knuckles against her face, huddles behind her arms.

'I don't believe this is happening,' he says softly, shaking his head as he looks around the familiar kitchen. His mouth tastes bitter, as if an aspirin had caught in his throat.

'I don't believe it either,' she whispers. She finds a tea towel to mop her face and stands before him, a contrite and trembling child.

He throws the gifts of flowers and pastries upon the table. The pastry box with its scarlet ribbon slithers across the polished surface and falls to the floor. There's no reason to retrieve it. He stumbles towards Jessica, reaching out with his hands, trying to wrap her in his embrace, and is startled when she shrinks away with the quick suspicion of a cat. He realises, in a panic, that she feels self-conscious before him, is ashamed of her nakedness, as if they were suddenly strangers. What does she think is going to happen? Is she afraid that he'll go berserk, burst his brains and hack her to death with a bread knife? He feels so hurt that he wants to punch her in the mouth.

'I can't find my fucking shoes!' Bassett bellows from the living room.

Frank turns, abandons his wife and goes in pursuit of Bassett who is sitting on the living-room carpet, sweeping the floor in search of his shoes. He is already dressed in his Savile Row suit and a slightly crumpled cotton shirt. Impossible now to think of him naked with his sour, grey skin and that ugly penis like a goose neck hanging from a bristle collar. He stands up when Frank

73

walks into the room and straightens the sleeves of his jacket.

'You're making a big mistake, Frank,' he says mournfully, wagging his head. 'You ought to look after that sweet little wife. You should have paid her more attention.' His shoes are hidden behind the sofa. He creeps forward, takes them by surprise and spears them with his feet.

'What are you?' sneers Frank. 'God's gift to women?'

A pair of Jessica's soft silk panties are hanging from the shade of the lamp. The matching brassiere is spilled on the floor. Her dress, a wrinkled fan of dainty green and yellow flowers, has been thrown against the skirting-board.

'Yeah, something like that,' says Bassett. He sits down in a chair to tie his laces.

'Get out!' shouts Frank. He looks at Bassett sitting there in the chair, shoulders hunched, fat hands straining to touch his shoes, and he wants to kill the bastard, bring down his fists and break his neck.

'Take it easy, Frank. I'm going.'

Now Frank is aware of Jessica standing beside him, stooped forward, trying to dangle her breasts into the cups of her brassiere. She straightens up, hooks the straps together with a deft twist of her fingers. She patters about the room, collecting the rest of her clothes, while Frank and Bassett stare at each other, silent, frozen, not daring to peek at her while she's half-dressed.

'Are you ready?' Bassett asks her as soon as she seems safely hooked and buttoned.

'Yes. No. I need my coat,' she says, frowning, raking her hair. She turns and hurries from the room, the thin dress flicking against her calves.

'Don't take it so hard, Frank,' says Bassett as the two men stand together waiting for her return. 'No one's to blame.' He stuffs his hands in his pockets, rocks gently back and forth on his heels. 'These things happen,' he adds philosophically and purses his lips as if he's about to whistle a tune.

'How long?' demands Frank.

Bassett sucks a tooth and makes a big performance from a little mental arithmetic. 'Remember the first time I came over here for supper? I don't remember the exact date.'

'The first time she saw you? Jesus Christ! The first time?'

'Don't blame Jessie. It's my fault. Blame me. I should have stopped before it started getting serious. And then, when you disappeared . . .'

Frank flinches. Nobody calls her Jessie. They're not talking about the same woman. Bassett is taunting him, hinting at pet names and lovers' secrets. This bastard has been sitting down to supper with them, once a month for the past two years. Eating his food and fucking his wife. Guzzling wine, telling Frank pointless jokes while he fondled Jessica under the table. He can't believe it. He doesn't want to hear these confessions.

'You should have stopped before it got *started*!' he yells in a sudden explosion of anger.

'Take it easy, Frank.'

'Don't tell me to take it easy, you bastard! Don't tell me anything!' He is shouting, chopping at the air with his hands. He must get away before he does Bassett some serious damage.

He turns and narrowly escapes colliding with Jessica, dressed in her cashmere overcoat and clutching a heavy overnight bag. It's the old scuffed bag of Spanish leather, the one she bought on their honeymoon. A glance at the bag tells Frank that she's walking out on him.

'I need some time to think, Frank,' she says anxiously, wanting to make it easier for him. 'I'll phone you when I'm settled. I'll keep in touch.'

'Where are you going to stay?' He takes a step forward and seems to stagger. The room shifts around him.

Jessica shrugs. 'I don't know. I'll find a hotel for tonight. You'll find ham in the fridge and try to finish the tomatoes and we've still got eggs and mushrooms if you want an omelette and tins of stuff but you'll have to buy some more bread . . .'

'I'm not hungry!' he blurts out impatiently, trying to stem this shopping list.

'You have to eat,' she says stubbornly.

The three of them are moving gradually from the room, edging sideways as they talk, bracing themselves for separation.

At the front door Jessica suddenly turns to face him, reaches across and pecks him lightly on the cheek. Her lips are cold. Her blue eyes bubble with tears.

'Forget about me, Frank. I'm no good. You'll find someone else,' she whispers, smearing mascara with the back of her hand.

Is that supposed to make a difference? Is that supposed to help? Christ, what a stupid thing to say when you're walking out of someone's life!

Frank sags away, props himself against the wall. The front door opens in a draught of darkness and winter rain.

As they step through the door Bassett pauses, with Jessica beside him, and nails Frank with a crafty grin.

'Hey, Frank,' he calls softly. 'Do yourself a favour. Save yourself some embarrassment. Think about finding another job.'

The door slams shut.

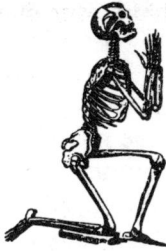

It is midnight. Frank, wrapped in a blanket, slumped in a sofa, nursing an empty bottle of vodka, is master of nothing but dreams. He falls asleep in the cushions. The dreams are filled with blood.

1. He bursts upon Bassett in the bath and strikes him down with a thunderbolt. Catch! The electric fire somersaults into the room and melts through Bassett's soapy fingers. He screams. He vomits sparks. He sizzles as he starts to sink beneath the blue, fluorescent waves.

2. He collars Bassett in the street, swings him against a plate-glass window. The glass cracks apart and falls like a whistling guillotine, taking Bassett's head from his shoulders. The body slumps into Frank's open arms. The head hits the pavement and rolls away in a wheel of bright blood.

3. He breaks into Bassett's office, topples the chair and overturns the tyrant's desk. Bassett crawls away on his hands and knees, pleading for mercy, trying to hide in a crack in the floorboards. The axe splits his spine. He flounders like a butchered animal.

4. He bombs Bassett's car. The dynamite drives him through the roof, still clutching the stump of the steering wheel. He rockets into the sky, smoke belching from blazing buttocks. He flutters back to earth as flakes of white ash.

The phone is ringing. The noise startles Frank from his scarlet sleep. He jerks himself from the cushions and plants his feet on the floor. The vodka bottle drops from his hand and plunges into the darkness. What's the time? It must be late. The room is so cold that when he lurches from the sofa his breath is a soft explosion of steam.

He grabs the phone in his fist, punches it against his skull.

'Jessica?'

The floor seems to tilt beneath him. He shuts his eyes, braces himself against the sofa as he feels the house begin to turn like an empty carousel.

'Frank? This is Webster. Conrad asked me to call you. He wants to see you again . . .'

'Leave me alone!' raves Frank. 'I don't want to talk to him!' The carousel spins, flinging him into a whirlpool of shadows and flying furniture.

'Frank? He wants to talk business.'

'Tell him to go to hell!' Frank roars at his clenched fist. He jumps up, shrugging off the blanket, tugging the telephone from the table. The phone jangles as it hits the carpet and bounces back on its rubber coils, dragging the mouthpiece from his face. 'Tell him I hope he rots in hell!'

'Frank?'

He throws the receiver at the wall and lashes out with his foot as the flex wraps around his leg. He tramples across the room, trailing the telephone like an anchor, and kicks at the table, making it jump and spill its tray of ornaments. How she loved cheap china ornaments! Cats wearing tail-coats. Geese in poke-bonnets. He stamps them into the carpet, crushing them down, rubbing them out until, sobbing and exhausted, he stumbles against the fallen table, picks it up in his arms and batters it against the wall.

He turns, rushing from the room and finds his way upstairs to the bedroom. Her dressing gown hangs from the hook on the back of the bedroom door. The air is still sweet with her perfume. He storms her wardrobe in a rage, dragging open the doors and pulling down clothes from the rattling hangers. Jackets throw out their sleeves in alarm. Skirts and trousers fall at his feet. He flings her shoes across the carpet, pulls her pillows from the bed and sweeps the contents of the dressing table into the wickerwork laundry basket.

The basket creaks beneath the weight as he drags it protesting across the room, raises it against his chest and tries to launch it from the window. But the frame is stubborn and he can't force it open. The basket slips through his arms and rolls away. He follows it across the room, kicking it like a dog, making it splinter and skitter, casting its cargo over the floor.

He comes to rest against the far wall, sweating and breathing hard. A silk slip is wrapped to his leg, clasping his foot as if pleading for mercy. Face powder hangs in the air like smoke. Tomorrow he'll clear the room and scrub away the sorrows. Tomorrow he'll set fire to the house. He trudges downstairs, falls back into the sofa and sleeps.

When he opens his eyes again there is sunlight seeping through the curtains and the stale air is spiced with peppermint. He turns his head in the cushions and finds Webster staring back at him from the armchair beneath the window.

Frank groans and rakes at his scalp.

Webster grins and shakes out a fat bunch of skeleton keys. 'It's time you changed your locks, Frank,' he says brightly.

Frank struggles from the sofa, turns to the door and finds Valentine standing there, watching him. She is wearing a long black coat and holding a pair of evening gloves.

'Is this really where you live?' she asks in amazement, flicking at the wall with her gloves.

Frank nods and wipes his face in his hands, suspecting that he might be a castaway in someone else's dream.

'Jesus!' mutters Valentine, looking around at the broken table and the trail of shattered ornaments. 'What happened?'

It's early in the morning when Frank is carried off to the jungle hothouse and thrown once more upon Conrad's mercy. He's obliged to describe the night's events down to the smallest detail, including Jessica's underwear and the colour of Bassett's shoes.

'We'll have his guts for garters!' says Conrad, rumbling with indignation. 'I'll ask Webster to skin him for you. We'll have his scalp made into a purse with a string to hang from your belt.' He tightens the cord of his dressing gown and pulls a bone-handled pruning knife from the trunk of a sago palm.

Frank gulps at his coffee and sits down on a granite slab half-buried in trailing jasmine. 'I'm in enough trouble. I don't want to be charged with murder,' he says quietly.

'You're too soft!' grumbles Conrad. 'This is a crime of passion. I'm surprised you don't want to blow out his brains. Tip me a wink. I'll make the arrangements.' He swipes at the air with the knife, hacking the dripping undergrowth.

'She wasn't dragged away from me kicking and screaming,' says Frank, trying to explain. 'She walked out. She must have been thinking about it for weeks. And I couldn't see it. I didn't suspect. I didn't pay her enough attention.'

'You kept your nose to the grindstone!' shouts Conrad. 'You can't expect to have eyes in your arse!'

'I don't know,' grieves Frank. 'I should have sensed that something was wrong . . .' Women can do it. They have some kind of instinct. They can smell deception and cunning in men. They use the same instinct to measure the dangers of other women, guarding their own men from predators.

'Family?' asks Conrad.

'We don't have any children . . .'

'That makes it easier. It's always hard on the children, Frank. Are your parents still alive?'

'My mother died five years ago. It scared my old man so much that he sold the house, cashed a couple of pension plans and disappeared.'

'A death in the family – it tears your life apart,' whispers Conrad.

'The last time he wrote he was cleaning motel rooms in New Brunswick. Jessica never liked him.'

'Is this the first time she's played around?'

'Yes!' says Frank indignantly. She flirts when she's drunk but he knows he's supposed to shrug that off as high spirits.

Conrad cannot be mollified. 'It's not natural. A woman doesn't abandon her home. It's against her nature. My wife would never have run away with the first little smarmy tosspot who slipped a cucumber into his pocket. And she had some admirers, Frank. She was a very beautiful woman . . .'

He stops, his eyes blurred with pain, haunted by terrible memories. He cocks his head, harking to ghosts that seem to come whispering into his ear. He trembles. He blows through his nostrils and rolls his eyes like a wild horse. Then he turns abruptly and tramples into the undergrowth where, to Frank's great alarm, he bursts into floods of tears.

When he returns he wipes his face in his dressing gown

and lets out a thick, phlegmatic bark before sitting down on the granite slab and staring at his carpet slippers.

'She was young and she was beautiful and God snuffed out her flame in the glorious brightness of youth,' he says softly. 'It must have been one of God's little jokes that passeth all understanding . . .' He stops, his voice strangled into silence, and pulls at his nose with his hand. Monkeys gibber and mock him from their perch in the distant canopy.

'What happened?' says Frank.

'Valentine was six years old,' says Conrad, rolling his eyes to blink out the tears. 'We sent her away to school and I was taking Dawn on a second honeymoon. It was something we'd always promised ourselves. Dawn worked hard and she needed the rest. She'd complained that she was feeling tired. Breathless. Pains in the chest. I thought she needed a tonic. We were going to forget everything for a couple of months. We were going to swim and sit in the sun. And she had a heart attack on the flight to Barbados. There were three doctors on board that flight. When the captain asked for help they came forward to the first-class cabin and stretched her out in the aisle. They pulled off her blouse and took it in turns with the kiss of life and the massage of her heart. They were dedicated, Frank. I can't deny it. She had them sweating on their hands and knees. They even accepted the help of a priest and a semi-retired dermatologist . . .'

'Horrible!' says Frank.

'I haven't finished!' barks Conrad, aggravated by the interruption.

'What happened?' says Frank.

'Nothing,' says Conrad. 'It was a miracle. The colour came rushing back to her cheeks and she looked as right as ninepence. She wouldn't go to the hospital in Bridgetown. The next day she went out swimming and a wave caught her up and swept her away. She demised alone in the deep,

Frank. Stolen by a jealous God and carried to the bottom of the sea.'

Frank turns the coffee cup in his hands and gazes stubbornly at his knuckles. He doesn't know what to say in response to this high-flown tragedy.

'We had a plantation house with a view of Pelican Bay. Do you know it? I never liked it. I could never manage the dago food. But Dawn couldn't get enough of it. She was a woman of the world. A woman of the world. She was a star. She knew how to handle a knife and fork. We used to have houses everywhere. Spain. Morocco. South of France. When Dawn demised I sold 'em. I don't go out. Sometimes I sit in the garden. I don't have the stomach for it.'

He falls silent and stares around at his tropical acre's breadth, a capsular kingdom of steam pipes and glass.

'Why did you call me here?' asks Frank, watching Conrad sink away into melancholy.

'What?'

'Webster told me you wanted to talk.'

'It can wait,' says Conrad, brushing the question aside with a flick of his hand. He becomes agitated, scowling and sucking his teeth.

Frank drains the dregs from his coffee cup and sets it down in the damp earth beside the granite block.

'I've something I want to show you,' Conrad says at last. He beckons Frank closer, leans against him. 'I want you to see something wonderful.'

'What is it?' whispers Frank.

'I want you to see my wife,' he confides in a trembling voice and his eyes sparkle again with tears.

'Here?' whispers Frank, looking around, searching for the site of her grave beneath the dark spread of forest trees.

'Downstairs,' breathes Conrad, winking and tapping the side of his nose. 'We can see her downstairs.'

So they leave the forest and follow a flight of stairs into

the basement of the house, where Conrad bullies open a door that leads to a square room with several rows of quilted armchairs. The chairs are turned towards the wall, gawping at an empty cinema screen.

Frank feels chilled, plunged from the heat of the jungle into this subterranean chamber. The room with its curved ceiling and whitewashed walls has been decorated with a brass pot containing a bunch of wilted flowers. Bronze and gold chrysanthemums. It's cold and sparse with the lonely smell of a private chapel.

'Sit down,' snuffles Conrad. He jerks a handkerchief from his pocket and snorts an oyster from his nose.

'Dawn made dozens of pictures, Frank. But *Rude & Ripe* was one of her first and I think it was her favourite.'

He settles down beside Frank and gropes for the box of controls beneath his chair.

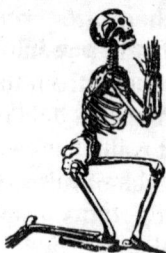

The lights dwindle into dead stars.

The magic window in the chapel wall opens into a sunlit orchard, a garden of crooked apple trees with their branches loaded with fruit. Music wafts from an orchestra hidden somewhere among the trees, flutes like fluttering songbirds trapped in a sticky web of strings.

A young woman is standing on a ladder, plucking at the apples and filling a basket slung from her arm. She's a dark-eyed Juno with her hair wrapped in a red silk scarf. She is wearing a simple summer frock printed with bunches of daffodils.

Frank stares. He recognises that frock! It's the same design that Conrad wore to greet him on the first morning beside the goldfish pond.

Conrad groans in the darkness and mauls his handkerchief as his wife seems to lose her balance, clinging anxiously to the ladder, while a breeze balloons her petticoats and reveals the length of her legs gleaming in old-fashioned nylon stockings and a fancy black suspender belt. She leans against the ladder, slapping at her skirt with her hands, and the apples go bouncing from the basket. She twists, cries out and tumbles from the rungs, falling into a tuffet of grass at the base of the tree, rump reared, hair slipping loose from the red silk scarf, the frock hanging loose from her shoulders, exposing her breasts in their flimsy black lace harness.

At the first joggle of those pendulous titties Conrad is howling and chewing his hankie. Frank reaches out in the dark and squeezes the old man's hand. It's terrible. Dawn is heaving, the apples are rolling and Conrad is bawling so hard there's a danger he'll swallow his tongue and choke to death on his grief. But there's no time to attend to him since Dawn's late fall has brought a stranger into the orchard.

The scrumper is a thin young man with the face of a hungry pangolin. He stares at the windfall under the tree and, without a word of introduction, pulls his penis from his pants and sinks to his knees before the sight of the whiskery cleft in Dawn's unbridled buttocks. For a moment he hesitates, staring, grinning, rolling his balls in his fist, then he slips his hand around her waist and pulls her against him, splitting her pouting cunt on his pike.

Dawn looks more than a little surprised, her eyes wide, her breasts spilled and shivering. She struggles and squirms but there's no escaping this violation.

Conrad squelches his nose into the sodden handkerchief as the eager young pomologist reaches out to pull Dawn's fruit. Her breasts bulge in his hands, her nipples very dark and erect. Frank looks away, dizzy, excited, lights popping in front of his eyes.

When he turns back to the screen, Dawn has lost her frock and the shreds of her underwear. She is flat on her back with her legs apart and her knees pressed hard against her chest. The man must have dipped his wick in some enchanter's potion – the thrust of his attack is sending Dawn into raptures. She gurgles and groans and rolls her head in a swoon. The music has slipped to a slobbering of saxophones and the muffled heartbeats of keyboard and drums. And then, at the height of her delight, the devil withdraws his favours, straddles her waist and slowly takes his penis in hand, strokes Dawn's mouth with its glistening bulb, her throat, her shoulders, the tips of her breasts.

She wriggles and moans, trying to clasp him again with her thighs, knocking him forward, catching his quivering shaft with her hands and guiding the length of it into her mouth. He shivers, held fast between her teeth and the slithering of her tongue until, at last, with a desperate shout, he jerks himself free from the embrace, his head thrown back, his spine arched, the music in a thumping finale triumphant while his penis fires strings of pearls through her dark and tangled hair.

As the lights come up again Conrad is wheezing and wiping his face in his dressing-gown sleeves.

'That's poetry!' he whispers proudly. And Frank wraps an arm around him, trying to give him comfort.

Valentine is waiting for them at the top of the stairs. She's wearing some kind of star-spangled cocktail dress and a pair of red shoes with impossible pencil heels.

'What the hell happened?' she demands angrily, hands on hips, scowling at the voyeurs as they grope their way to daylight. It looks bad. Conrad is still sobbing and leaning on Frank for support.

'It's nothing,' he snotters, avoiding her eyes. 'Frank was telling me about his marriage. He's had a very difficult time. We shall have to be kind to him.'

'You've been looking at mother again!' shouts Valentine.

'A glimpse. No more than a glimpse!' protests Conrad, wagging his head. 'I wanted to show her to Frank.'

'Why can't you leave her alone, you stupid man! You know how much she upsets you.' She takes his arm and leads him back towards the warmth and security of the jungle. He shuffles away like a frail old man, trailing his dressing-gown cord behind him.

'You're staying here, Frank,' he shouts, before retreating into the mist. 'Webster will make you comfortable. Tell Valentine to take you up to his quarters. I want you to relax and make yourself at home. Remember you're part of the family. When you're ready we'll have some lunch and talk about your future.'

Frank follows Valentine in silence as she takes him through the house towards the servants' stairs. A gloom of Gothic cupboards. A fat chintz sofa. A bandy rococo armchair wreathed in fruit and gilded flowers. A chipped Chinese vase large enough to drown a child.

'I didn't know she was family,' he says at last, breaking into the silence.

'So what?' snaps Valentine, without turning to look at him.

Frank shrugs. She has reason to hate him. He's just had a ringside seat at the ceremonial shagging of the woman she is pleased to call mother. He feels ashamed, assaulted by the spectacle, thrilled and horrified at the same time, like a man at a public hanging.

'I couldn't refuse. I think it would have insulted him.'

'He's a crazy old man.'

Frank scowls at her heels clicking on the polished floorboards. Nothing seems real. Nothing makes sense. It's as if he's been plucked from the world and is now condemned to watch life continue without him. A flickering film running in an empty cinema where he sits alone, a prisoner in darkness. Jessica and Bassett. Dawn and the Unknown Scrumper. Scratchy hardcore action between the cartoons and newsreels. He wants to explain to Valentine but she isn't listening to him.

A maid appears, running along the corridor, her face flushed, her arms filled with laundry. She shrinks at their approach and presses herself against the wall, punching the linen in her fists like some demented pastry cook pounding a lump of tumescent dough.

'I can find my own way from here,' he says, as they reach the staircase. 'You don't have to come with me.' He reaches out thankfully for the big oak baluster, wrapping his hand around the pineapple crowning the column.

'I wasn't offering.'

90

'It wasn't my idea!' he says in a final attempt to plead his innocence. 'I wouldn't have watched if I'd known what he wanted to show me.'

'Oh, yeah?' The contempt pinches her face, reducing her eyes to slits, twisting her mouth in a sneer.

'I didn't know!' He slaps the pineapple with his hand, making the newel posts rattle.

Valentine turns on him, whipping the hair from her face with a scornful shake of the head. 'What's wrong? Don't you like to look at women? Didn't she give you a cheap thrill? Didn't you enjoy yourself? Didn't you think she was beautiful?'

'Yes. Beautiful.'

'Hah! What would you know about my mother!' she shouts triumphantly.

'I think I'd recognise her again,' he says quietly. He's been introduced to the woman by having his nose rubbed under her belly. It's the kind of encounter he isn't likely to forget.

'You're so stupid!' she says impatiently, striding forward, trapping him, glaring into his startled face. 'Whenever she stepped from her clothes she became invisible. Her body was her disguise. Do you really think you can know a woman by looking between her legs? You didn't meet my mother. You were shaking hands with your own fantasies.'

Frank flinches, thinks of Jessica, flagrante delicto, kicking her heels on the kitchen table, under the rule of Bassett's thumbs. One man's dream is another man's sorrow. He feels sick to his stomach, poisoned with drink and jealousy. 'So why do you let him watch it!' he barks back at her, humiliated and angry.

'He's got every film she ever made down there in the basement. Thousands of photographs. Dozens of boxes of old love letters. He kept everything. He saved her clothes, her shoes, her make-up, the hair from her combs and brushes.'

91

'Why? For God's sake, why?'

'Fucking is the poor man's opera,' she hisses, stabbing her finger into his chest. 'And my mother was a diva!'

Frank climbs to the attic where Webster makes him welcome with pastries and strong sweet coffee. He's cleared a corner of the long room and assembled a hospital bed, set square on a Persian carpet beneath a narrow window.

'There's a wardrobe for your clothes and somewhere to keep your personal effects,' he says, nodding at a metal locker wedged in the crook of the iron pipes that snake through the timber beams.

Frank sits down on the edge of the bed and chews morosely at a pastry.

'I'm sorry about your wife,' says Webster, turning to the window, hands in his pockets, staring at clouds as dark as bruises in a bright band of yellow sky. 'Do you want me to fetch her home?'

'That's not the answer,' says Frank.

'Did Conrad have any suggestions?'

'No. We went to the movies.'

'He took you down to see Dawn?'

'Yes. Does he always make his guests watch his old home movies?'

'He's very proud of 'em. They're not home movies, Frank. Dawn was a big star at the time. Her films sold

93

around the world. Some of them are classics. She had a regular photo-feature in a couple of magazines. A successful mail-order business. The works.'

'But how can he want to watch them – his wife making love to other men?' demands Frank. It's enough to drive you crazy and he's talking from bitter experience.

'That's acting, Frank!' chuckles Webster, amused by Frank's bewilderment. Theatre imitates life. A mockery of love and death. Reality is suspended. The law of gravity denied. 'She'd been to drama school. She was a proper actress. She could sing and dance. She'd once had a part in a pantomime.'

'How did they meet?'

'Conrad saw her by chance one afternoon in a little theatre in Soho. She was starring in a movie called *Hungry Housewives*. Did you ever see it? Conrad fell in love the moment she appeared on the screen. He tracked her down to an address in Ladbroke Grove and besieged her with diamonds and flowers.'

'And she fell into his arms,' suggests Frank. The prince of thieves and the gypsy dancer. A song from the chorus and the curtain falls to a storm of applause.

'No. It took a long time to win her trust. She was deeply suspicious of men bearing gifts. But Conrad was a young man and full of energy and determination. He was already rich and influential. He always took what he wanted and her resistance only served to excite him. He took her out to big society parties and introduced her to film producers, photographers and all the rest of the hoi-polloi. It took time but he had to be patient.'

'Did they have a big wedding?'

'The biggest. As far as he was concerned she was the most desirable woman in the world. A goddess adored by millions of men. The creature that other men saw in their dreams when they turned in the dark and reached out to make love to their small, ugly wives. Think of the sense of power that gave him! He possessed the object of other men's dreams! It was like owning their souls!'

Webster turns and walks to a big wooden chest, wrenches at the mouldering leather straps and throws back the lid. The chest has been packed with bundles of letters. The envelopes are tattered and curling, like bundles of faded leaves, neatly tied with yellow silk ribbons. He pulls an envelope from a bundle, plucks out the contents and gives it to Frank.

'The object of other men's dreams,' he says gently, as he watches Frank unfolding the letter.

Dear Dawn

Whenever I see you're massive busty endowments in my favourite mag I have an uncontrollable urge to yank forth my capacious carnal column, plunge it into the creamy curvacious cleavage of you're ponderous protuberances and explode like an atom bomb swamping you're ample acreage with sweet spurts of sticky love lava. Then I'd tumble you onto you're back, pull apart those tremendous temptatious thighs and stroke the shaggy abundance of bountiful bush that shelters you're squelching love tube. Lunging forward, hands massaging those mountainous mammaries, I'd launch my throbbing torpedo between those curling petals of pinkness and glide into the sweet squeeze of you're silky sex shaft – spurting as I enter, gushing as I pump with my love thrusts, drowning you in delicious oblivion as you're screaming climax shatters the mirrors. Please find enclosed snap. I am available most evenings.

The letter has been composed on an old typewriter with a faded ribbon. The signature is a small squiggle of blue ink. Eric Something. There is a Polaroid with the letter. A smudged portrait of a naked middle-aged man grinning

95

at the camera and sporting an erection, dark as a smoked sausage, beneath a rumpled paunch. His hair has been plastered against his skull and his eyes, scorched by flashlight, are crimson holes in the white of his face. He's standing randy and ready for action, in some corner of his own parlour. The curved back of an armchair. The pole of a standard lamp. A light switch on the wall behind his left shoulder.

'Everybody loved Dawn,' says Webster. 'They were always writing her begging letters, asking for pictures in special poses or items of underwear.'

'How did she answer them?'

'Answer them? She never bothered to open them! They went straight through to the office where Conrad employed a couple of girls to send out catalogues. There were Dawn to Dusk pyjama sets. New Dawn vibrating ticklers. Inflatable rubber Dawns . . .'

'She wasn't a woman,' protests Frank. 'She was a trade mark.'

'That's right!' beams Webster, very impressed by this observation. She became a living icon and people paid for the privilege of possessing anything she had touched or blessed.

'How many of these do you keep in that trunk?' asks Frank, returning the letter to Webster.

'I don't know. I've never had time to count them. These are the letters that came to the house in the weeks that followed her death. But nonetheless it's a big collection.'

'Why didn't she retire when they married?' Frank wants to know as Webster buckles the leather straps. The spoils of war. A dungeon for other men's fantasies. A legion of forgotten prisoners, snared by their short-and-curlies, locked in the dark and rotting to dust.

'It would have been a crime to have stopped her exercising her talents,' says Webster, surprised by the question. 'She loved it. She was a natural born performer.

Conrad became her agent and manager. He sank a small fortune into her pictures.'

'You mean he rented her out for exhibition like some sort of circus freak.'

'That's no way to talk about another man's wife, Frank,' says Webster mildly, remembering that Frank is still in a state of deep shock. 'He was a broken man when she died. He locked himself away and grieved.'

Frank scratches his chin and stares around the attic. 'Why did he ask you to bring me back here?'

'We like you!' says Webster cheerfully.

'I wish someone would tell Valentine.'

'I'm worried about that girl,' Conrad confides to Frank when they meet again for a picnic lunch beside the goldfish pool. He's wearing a floral cotton two-piece with a sagging, empty cross-over top that ties on the hip with a sash. It looks faded around the armpits and the hem is badly frayed. 'I've given her everything. A good home. A fine education. And what does she do with her life? Nothing. She spends her time shopping and watching TV.' He takes a linen napkin and tucks it into the top of the dress where it hangs like a furled flag.

'It sounds harmless. If it keeps her out of trouble . . .' says Frank.

'She's wasting her time. It's criminal. You can buy almost anything, Frank, but you can't buy time.'

'What do you *want* her to do with her life?'

'I want her married while she still has her teeth. She could marry anyone. She's fit for royalty. She could have power and influence in affairs of state. That's why I've sent for you.' He picks fastidiously at a lobster salad taken from the willow hamper beside them on the paving stones. The basket is packed with salad, fruit and cheese, bottles of mineral water and wine.

'How can I help?' says Frank, watching Conrad spear the lobster meat with a polished silver fork.

'Look after her for me, Frank. She likes you.'

'What makes you think that?'

'It's obvious!' says Conrad confidently. 'And she needs an escort. I can't stop her shopping but I won't have her walking around town without the benefit of my protection. The streets are crawling with vermin. Hoodlums. Bum-suckers. Junkies. Filth. Kids throwing fire bombs at grocery stores. Fourteen-year-old rapists! Did you read about that in the papers? Children raping their mothers! What's going on out there, for Chrissakes! When I was young we had some respect for law and order. You could walk anywhere in the territory, day or night, and never feel afraid for a moment. We kept the streets clean. We were born in the gutter but we were proud of the neighbourhood. You see these granite kerb-stones?' he says, slapping the ground with his hand. 'I used to sit on them as a boy. I had them removed when they knocked down the street.'

'I know,' says Frank.

'Who told you?' scowls Conrad.

'You told me,' says Frank and thinks, you're as mad as a moon-calf.

'I don't remember,' says Conrad sadly, twirling the fork between his fingers.

So Frank gently reminds him of their first conversation and reminds himself in the process that Conrad wants turtles for the pond.

'They were hard times,' continues Conrad proudly. 'But you didn't need chains and window locks before you felt safe in your bed at night. You could walk the streets. You could swim the canals. Valentine doesn't understand. The world has gone bad but she's too young to have seen the changes. She doesn't know the difference. She doesn't understand the dangers.'

'What about Talbot?' ventures Frank. He thinks again

of the room in the Golden Goose Hotel, trembling in the stinking twilight while the Beast ferments from the bedclothes like a genie with a gun in his fist; Lloyd standing naked and grinning, his fingers sunk to their knuckles in the blood that spurts from his chest. They were Hamilton Talbot's rented bruisers. Talbot must be an angry man.

'He won't crawl out of the woodwork again,' says Conrad. He picks a quail's egg from a little porcelain dish and squeezes it between finger and thumb while he dusts it with celery salt from a shaker no larger than a silver thimble. 'There's nothing to be feared from Talbot.' He sucks the morsel into his mouth and squashes it against his teeth.

'Why can't Webster do it? He's got the experience,' argues Frank, suspicious that Conrad is playing a subtle and devious game.

'She's too clever for Webster,' he grins, pleased at the thought of his daughter's cunning. 'She always gives him the slip.'

'If she can outwit Webster she'll run circles around me.'

'It's different. You'll be more of a companion. You can take her out and keep her entertained. You'll be paid for your trouble, you'll continue to live here and it will occupy your mind while we decide how to tackle your other problem . . .'

'I just want to forget,' says Frank quickly. He takes an apple from the hamper and gives it a shine by rubbing it against his sleeve but he's not hungry and the fruit, when he bites through the skin, tastes sour.

'Are you planning to join the Foreign Legion or what?' says Conrad. 'You can't bury your head in the sand, Frank. Believe me, you can't forget a wound by leaving it to fester. Dawn met a lot of men in her career. A lot of men. Actors. Producers. Politicians. All kinds of poisonous riff-raff. She never looked twice at one of them.

We had trust. That's important. When you break trust it can't be repaired.'

'I don't see what I can do to change anything.'

'You can't change what's happened. That's true. Life plays cruel tricks. A man has nothing but his wife and his work to help him make sense of the world. And you've lost both of them.'

'Thanks for putting it into perspective.'

'You can't change what's happened but you can change how you feel about it.' He pulls the napkin from his dress and dabs at the corner of his mouth.

'How's that?'

'When someone hurts you, Frank, you hurt them right back.'

'When I found them together I wanted to kill them. I wanted to break his neck.'

'That's crude, Frank.' He shakes his head and stares across the black pond where a group of waterlilies are beginning to unfold their flowers.

'It felt right at the time,' says Frank softly.

'Leave it with me. We need to think about it. I'll talk to Webster. You look after Valentine. And tell her to skip the turtles. I think I'll have some more fish.'

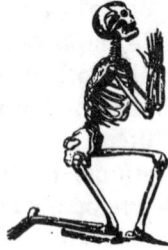

Frank's first task is to take Valentine on a trip to Harrods and she wastes no time in making him feel unwelcome. She insists on driving the Bentley – despite his offer to be her chauffeur – and maintains a stubborn truculence as she struggles to weave the limousine through the gridlocked London traffic.

It's a crisp February morning, frost in Hyde Park and diesel smoke in the streets like rolling banks of blue fog. Valentine, cursing, takes them to Knightsbridge and finally gains the sanctuary of a private car park in Basil Street. The attendant, a tall young man wearing a hooded tracksuit and a pair of wrestling boots, runs from his cabin to greet them and gives the driver a brilliant smile as she drops the car keys into his hand.

This morning she looks demure in a pillbox hat and a huge black overcoat but the coat kicks open when she walks to allow the world to admire her legs in a skirt so short it leaves the young man mesmerised. He winks at Frank, throws the car keys into the air and catches them with a slap of his fist as he saunters back to the warmth of his cabin.

Frank follows Valentine into the street and towards the department store. Hans Crescent is crowded. She jostles and elbows a passage between a group of indignant women and slips through number four door into the menswear department.

Frank is left behind on the pavement, takes a wrong turning through the door, hurries away from the department towards the escalators and catching no sight of her on the staircase is forced to retrace his steps and finally tracks her down among the suits and overcoats. He grows breathless and prickly in the torpid warmth of the store. Valentine looks at him, her face blank, standing there with her hands in her pockets, pillbox perched at a jaunty angle, a remote and beautiful stranger.

'Measure him!' she snaps at the first assistant who glides towards them over the floor. She raises one hand and points a lazy finger at Frank.

The assistant, sleek as a greyhound, wreathed in vapours of fancy cologne, unrolls a tape measure and slips it around Frank's neck, working swiftly from collar to cuff, catching him in a loose embrace to gauge the size of his chest and waist.

'What the hell are you doing?' Frank hisses at Valentine when the assistant briefly disappears behind a marble pillar.

'If you're going to follow me around like a bad smell you could at least change your shirt,' she says, wrinkling her nose.

Frank is painfully aware that he's still wearing the clothes he was given for the raid on the Golden Goose. The shirt looks dirty under the pin-bright ceiling lights and the suit has wrinkled like cheap wrapping paper. He jerks at his sleeves and buttons the jacket.

'He'll take a dozen white cotton shirts. A couple of suits. Three pairs of good leather shoes and a decent overcoat,' she tells the assistant on his return.

The assistant blinks and pulls nervously at his fingers, making the joints crack like firewood. He moves his weight from one foot to another in a queer little shuffling dance.

'He can choose his own underwear,' adds Valentine, in a very superior tone of voice.

The assistant makes several obsequious bobbing movements with his head, glances furtively at Frank, and retreats. Valentine watches him slip away through the maze of stands and cabinets, borne upon his errand towards the distant shelves of shirts.

'I can't afford this stuff!' protests Frank. He has nothing in his pockets but the bundle of twenty-pound notes that Valentine pressed upon him before he made his last trip home. His wallet, his cards, his passport, everything that gave him a sense of himself, have been left behind in the house. There's no way he could prove his identity except by the fillings in his mouth.

'Relax. We have an account,' murmurs Valentine. 'Why don't you pick a couple of sweaters?' She strolls away, kicks open her coat and flaunts her legs at a group of gormless mannequins dressed in paisley silk dressing gowns.

Now Frank has been dressed in the proper manner, Valentine returns to the serious business of spending money for her own pleasure. In the following few days she buys sixteen pairs of shoes: five pairs black leather, four pairs red leather, three pairs yellow silk, two pairs green lizard, one pair copper velvet, one pair in soft pistachio suede; a feather skullcap, a lipstick, twelve pairs of stockings, a handbag, a set of brocade pyjamas, a pair of antique ivory chopsticks, a scarf and several strings of beads. She also remembers to buy Webster a ration of chocolate and finds Conrad a dozen ornamental carp.

She is dedicated to department stores. They are mansions of mirrors and soft illusions. She listens, with serious concern, while thickly painted shopgirls twitter over the latest miracles in shampoo and skin cream, pauses at every opportunity to be anointed with perfumes and precious unctions, attends fashion shows and demonstrations of steam irons and patent potato peelers. She loves these rambling emporiums with their tunnels and bridges, high ceilings and stuffy, old-fashioned restaurants. She roams the endless corridors like an enchanted child while Frank trudges behind, waiting for the moment when, seduced by a skirt or a set of elaborate underwear, she will vanish behind the curtains of another changing room and he can sit down to rest on one of the painted bamboo chairs they provide for abandoned husbands.

At such moments, sitting like a tired sentry, he finds himself tantalised by the sounds of shuffling silks, the clink of a buckle, the click of hangers against hidden mirrors, and tries to imagine her naked with no more than the fragile curtain between them. She is taller than her mother and more angular but they share the same strange sloe-eyed beauty. Did she inherit those heavy, dark-tipped breasts? The thought of it stirs him and makes him nervous. Jessica with her cropped blonde hair would be a shadow beside this woman. His wife is cold and detached. Her eyes hold a frosty blue light. Naked at night she seems reduced to a slender sprite with her neat breasts, the pink bud of her cunt peeping through its pale tuft of thistledown, her cool skin shining like moonlight. A fairy princess who likes to be fucked on the kitchen table.

Sometimes the curtains will blow apart and Valentine emerges, unbuttoned and flustered, asking him to choose between a linen suit or a silk jacket, a pattern of poppies or cornflowers; and he's flattered that she wants his opinion, happy to pretend that it makes a difference, as if she were buying these clothes to please him.

At other times, but rarely, she'll send out for him and when the sales assistant beckons from the changing room, taking them to be man and wife, he does nothing to correct the mistake but allows himself the pleasure of slipping behind the forbidden curtain where Valentine waits impatiently to be admired in her underwear.

105

'Do you think the colour suits me?' she says, scowling into the long, bright mirrors.

'Perfectly,' says Frank. A blackberry satin bra with matching French knickers. A camisole in apricot silk.

'Do you think it looks cheap?' she demands, daring him to challenge her choice of silver beads and ribbons. A cabbage rose made from taffeta. A bunch of rubber grapes. And it's true, she has a knack of looking cheap, despite all the time and money she invests in her appearance.

'Elegant,' says Frank with studied nonchalance and is careful to slip a secret smile to the loitering sales girl. What's to be done? He's been asked these questions a thousand times. The young and impetuous wife. The patient and indulgent husband.

At the end of the week Frank is called to account by
Conrad who takes him into the gallery to admire his
collection of paintings.

'Has Valentine been buying your clothes?' he asks
suspiciously, glancing at Frank's new wardrobe.

'Yes,' says Frank.

'You look like a flaming shirt-lifter.'

They are strolling through a long marble gallery of
empty picture frames. Magnificent carved and gilded frames
encrusted with fruits and curious shells. A small green
typewritten card has been pinned beneath each of them
and Conrad pauses now and then to read their legends.

'Gustav Klimt. 1913. "Kneeling Semi-Nude Bending
Forward",' he recites proudly. 'It's a pencil picture of
a woman showing her backside. Nothing vulgar. Very
artistic. He worked in Vienna. Lived with his mother.'

Frank confronts a carved mahogany frame inlaid with
marquetry bands of ivory, brass and satinwood, the margins embellished with stylised pear trees.

'Claude Monet. 1919. Untitled. Oil painting. Looks
like pond life,' says Conrad, squinting at the card. 'Big
beard. Blind as a badger,' he adds by way of historical
background.

Frank considers the faux-bamboo frame containing a band of embossed leather with margins of gilded wood carved with cockles, winkles and grove snails.

'Did she get you into mischief?' enquires Conrad casually as they stand to admire the phantom canvas. 'Where did she take you?'

Frank describes the department stores, the fashion shows and demonstrations, tea-rooms and restaurants.

'Did she talk to anyone?' says Conrad, walking away, trying to hide his disappointment. He's hoping for intrigues and lovers' trysts. He wants to hear that Valentine has lost her heart to a playboy prince.

'No,' says Frank and shrugs his shoulders. He doesn't feel inclined to list the sales girls, waiters and doormen, buskers, beggars and acrobats. Valentine talks to everyone.

'Toulouse Lautrec. 1896. "Woman Removing Her Stockings". Crayon drawing on foxed paper. He was a dwarf. Lived in a brothel,' says Conrad, retrieving Frank and leading him forward by the arm.

'Does she have many friends?' says Frank. He contemplates a polished walnut frame with a carved cornucopia of fruits finished in glass and mother-of-pearl against bands of gilded gesso decoration.

'None,' says Conrad. 'She had some playmates when she was small. She once brought her school chums home for Christmas. Stephanie and Charlotte. They laughed like screech owls. Ate like sparrows. I don't know what happened to them. Probably married into the gentry . . .'

'Did she like school?'

'It cost enough! I never went there myself, of course, because of my singular circumstance. But I sent Webster down several times. Concerts. Sports days. He said it was the sort of establishment where they cut the crusts from the sandwiches. He said Valentine was popular with the other girls. But she never kept in touch with them . . .'

'It's strange to be so solitary.'

'It's easy enough to buy friends,' says Conrad, rather defensively, and hooks a nostril with a fingernail.

'She must have broken one or two hearts . . .' suggests Frank.

'She's breaking *my* heart,' says Conrad. 'I want to see her get married to someone with a respectable fortune.'

This fails to answer Frank's question but succeeds, nonetheless, in reminding him of Conrad's ambitions for his daughter. She's required to hoist the old devil into the aristocracy by giving herself in wedlock to one of its favourite sons.

'Did anyone approach you?' enquires Conrad darkly, pulling and bending his mighty nose.

'No,' says Frank. He frowns. A young Jamaican stopped them on the pavement near Liberty's, whistled at Frank and flicked his tongue at Valentine, whispering obscenities as he slouched away through the crowd. Walking down Jermyn Street a gang of workmen mewed and moaned, stamping their boots on the scaffolding as Valentine passed beneath them. She offers no acknowledgement to these rude salutes. They never fail to startle Frank but Valentine seems not to notice them. Waiters linger at her table, loom on her shoulder, hoping to peek down the front of her dress as they make suggestions from the menu. Salesmen crouch beneath her skirt, stroking her legs with fluttering fingers, helping to fit her with shoes and sandals. Valentine pays them no attention.

'Paul Gauguin. 1893. "Sister of Anna the Javanese". Brown girl in red armchair with blue monkey,' continues Conrad.

Frank cranes his neck at an ebonised wood frame with incised and painted ecclesiastical decoration finished with a Chinese porcelain panel set in a polished brass mount.

'He was a postman. Died of the pox,' says Conrad helpfully.

'Where are they?' says Frank, at last. 'Where are the paintings?'

'Bank vault!' shouts Conrad, pulling away and marching around his gallery. 'It's obvious! You can't hang a Monet on the wall like a Royal Lifeboat calendar!'

'It's a waste!' declares Frank, refusing to be bullied by the bellowing curator of this empty and worthless museum.

'I know that!' growls Conrad impatiently. 'You think I like it? I thought it would be different. I thought the money would make life easy. Do you know how much these paintings are worth? Millions. They're worth millions and I can't afford to look at them for fear of some little fart who can't tell a Braque from a lavatory wall stealing them from under my nose. I'm worth a sodding fortune and I spend all my time trying to hide from the riff-raff. It was different when Dawn was alive. It made sense. Now I only have Valentine . . .'

'I'll watch her for you,' says Frank and hopes to conceal his infatuation from the baleful stare of her father by moving briskly away and pretending to ponder Pablo Picasso. 1920. 'Still Life with Violin'.

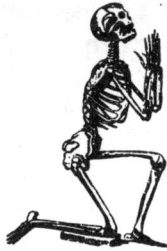

The days slip away and Frank's interest in his new career quickly becomes a fascination. He tries to conceal his feelings, even from himself, and takes great care not to give Conrad doubts about the wisdom of renting friends. But he's bolder with Webster and coaxes him to talk of the past, enduring the stories of blood and thunder in the hope that he'll think of happier times when he dangled Valentine from his knees and made the pilgrimage to school to watch her tumble in the egg-and-spoon race.

His patience is rewarded one night in the attic when Webster, holding court from his hammock, begins working his way through an alphabet of crimes and punishments. A is for Arson. B is for Blackmail and Buggery. C is for Corporal Punishment – Dawn made several spanking movies. *Discipline Dormitory* and *The Mississippi Paddle Screamer* are Webster's particular favourites.

Frank is fighting to stay awake, comfortable in a hump-backed chair, picking at the bowl of biscuits that Webster makes the maids provide against the dangers of night starvation.

D is for Drugs. E is for Embezzlement, Extortion, Embowelling and Execution. F is for Flogging and Forgery.

Frank closes his eyes and lets a biscuit slip through his fingers. He drifts on the edge of sleep when Webster reaches K for Kidnap and suddenly thinks of Valentine.

'I remember a time when we thought she'd been kidnapped from school!' he says with a grin. 'She must have been eight or nine years old. Dawn had been dead for a couple of years and Conrad was still in mourning.'

'Was she snatched?' says Frank, awake again and wiping his hands on his knees. He imagines a black Mercedes screeching away down a gravel drive with the tiny, terrified face of a child screaming for help at the rear window.

'No!' grins Webster. 'She was hiding in the boiler room. She'd sent the ransom note herself – the letters had been cut from her school history books. We never found out why she wanted the money. They said she was seeking attention – the death of her mother must have left its mark. The school matron took a special interest – she'd studied Freud at some evening class. She was a very handsome sort of woman with a lot of freckles and the habit of wearing her hair in a braid. I don't remember her name. The older girls called her Bunty. Conrad sent me down there to sort her out . . .'

'She must have been a difficult child,' suggests Frank.

'Valentine?' says Webster, still dreaming of his afternoon with the matron. 'Hah! She was a demon!' He rummages for his wallet and offers Frank a tiny snapshot of Valentine the schoolgirl.

Frank takes the tattered picture and holds it tenderly in his palm. Here is the kidnap victim, dressed in a drab school uniform, trailing a satchel by a broken strap. A dark and precocious nymphet, gangly as a cranefly, with her hair held in place by a length of white ribbon.

M is for Murder, Mickey Finn and Mutilation. N is for Nark. Webster continues the alphabet, rocking slowly in his hammock, as Frank slips the photograph into his pocket.

'Have you ever feasted by starlight in the mountains of Turkistan?' Valentine asks, without warning, one afternoon as they pause for coffee and pastries in a half-empty restaurant at the top of her favourite department store. She is sitting flanked by shopping bags, elbows propped on the table, nursing a cup in her hands.

'No,' says Frank.

Valentine snorts with contempt and looks around the restaurant as if seeking more interesting company. 'Tell me about your wife,' she demands, settling on him again.

The question takes him by surprise. He glances up from his plate and tries to read her eyes. Her hair has been pulled from her face and sculpted into a snail resting against the back of her head, revealing the shape of her ears and the pale stalk of her neck. Her eyes stare back, dark and unblinking, over the rim of her cup.

'What do you need to know?'

'Where did you meet?'

'Does it matter?'

'I'm just taking a friendly interest.'

'We met at a charity dinner organised by the Citrus Growers Guild,' says Frank. She was with a man called Charlie Collins who was something special in marmalades.

Jessica ditched him the following week but for the first few months of Frank's courtship Charlie was writing Jessica letters in which he threatened to kill himself unless she married him. Jessica saved the letters and used to read them aloud to friends. Everyone laughed except Frank who felt depressed by her cruelty, glimpsing something of his own fate if he should ever fall from favour. Charlie, as Frank remembers it, met and married the winner of the Miss Marmalade contest the following summer and Jessica threw the letters away.

'An office romance!' mutters Valentine with a scowl of general disapproval. 'I should have guessed it was an office romance.'

'We never worked together. She was helping to raise money for the Ethiopian famine-relief appeal.'

'Did she ever visit Ethiopia?'

'No.'

'Were you in love?'

Frank considers the question. We all like to think we're in love. It's a social obligation. Falling in love makes you ordinary, respectable, demonstrates that you're not a threat to the rest of the rookery. Falling in love is a cheap song, a novelty sweatshirt, a TV game show.

'We were married,' he says simply. And, yes, he was in love with his wife and she was in love with him.

'So why did she run away with another man?'

'I used to get drunk and knock her around,' says Frank, to keep her quiet. He's tired of this interrogation. 'I like to hear her scream.' He picks up a little fork and cracks open his pastry, lifting the flaking crust to inspect its slippery, scented fruit. He's disappointed. It looks like sweet, boiled apricot.

'You're not the kind to get drunk. You like to keep control. You probably hogtied her to a chair or made her walk on a leather leash.'

'How did you guess?'

'You look like a manacle man.'

'Shut up and eat,' says Frank.

'Do you want her back again?'

He pauses. 'I don't know,' he says quietly. He feels like a man who is stirring from an anaesthetic and, despite the pain and the shock of the light, he's reluctant to be submerged again.

'You don't want her back,' she declares triumphantly, taking his hesitation as doubt. 'She can't be trusted. It wouldn't work.' She picks up a fork and mutilates her own choice of pastry, a peculiar whipped-cream concoction smothered in toasted almond flakes.

'Thanks for the advice.'

Valentine sucks her fingertips and kisses the corner of her napkin. 'You'd be all right for a couple of weeks while she acted the part of the cute, repentant little wife and baked your favourite puddings and took extra care while she ironed your shirts and all that other stuff . . .' She stops short for dramatic effect and folds the napkin into a square.

'And then?'

'And then, just when you thought you were safe again, you'd wake up in the middle of the night and catch her calling his name in her sleep. Or she'd cry out the name of some other man that you didn't even know existed while she was getting her Saturday poke. And you'd never know what she was thinking when she stared at you over the branflakes in the morning and you saw that dreamy, faraway look in her eyes and pretty soon she'd start driving you crazy and you'd want to beat out her brains.'

'That's very encouraging.'

'It's true,' says Valentine. 'You'd start looking for bruises and love bites when you caught her in the bath. You'd get paranoid when she tried out new little tricks in bed. You'd go crazy!'

Frank pushes away his plate, spilling his fork, scattering crumbs, and looks around the room. He feels awkward and out of place in this hushed atmosphere surrounded

115

by knots of whispering women pecking at pastries and preening themselves.

'What do you suggest?'

'You've got to do something for your own self-respect. You've got to show them how you feel about letting them crap all over you. You're walking around like a corpse that can't find a comfortable coffin . . .'

'What am I supposed to do, for Chrissakes!' he shouts impatiently, surprising a group of elderly women at the next table. 'You want me to kick down the door to his office, drag him downstairs and break his nose?'

'Yeah!' grins Valentine. 'Something like that.'

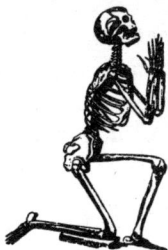

They are sitting in the Bentley, trapped in the early-evening traffic, heading north towards the Marylebone Road. A fine freezing rain drifts through the beams of the headlamps. The pavements are crowded with workers, escaping computers and counters, bodies bent to the rain like sickles, their faces pinched with a cold despair. They've been sitting in silence for several minutes, staring out at the darkness, when Valentine opens the glove compartment and slowly pulls out a gun. It's a stainless-steel Colt Mustang, big enough to kill a man but small enough to fit her fist. She weighs it in the palm of her hand, curls her fingers over the barrel.

'What's happening?' says Frank. His heart skips a beat and his shoulders tighten, pulling him away from the seat.

'I'm looking for cigarettes,' she says innocently, squinting into the glove compartment and finding a pack of Silk Cut. She takes a cigarette, lights it and sucks greedily on the smoke. The automatic remains in her hand.

'Do you know how to use it?' he says, trying to call her bluff, uncertain why she's chosen this moment to show him that she carries a weapon.

Valentine tilts back her head and grins, flicking her tongue against her teeth. 'It's easy. You pull it out of your handbag and total strangers wet their shoes. It isn't loaded,' she adds wistfully. 'Webster wouldn't give me the ammo.' She drops the Colt carelessly into her lap and snaps shut the glove compartment.

'Remind me to buy him a drink,' says Frank thankfully, sinking into the seat again.

'Cigarette?' she says, holding out the pack and flipping the lid with her thumb.

Frank shakes his head and peers anxiously into the street, staring through the windscreen at the floating beads of rain. 'We turn left at the next junction and the office is a couple of hundred yards beyond Huckleberry Hotdog and Bagel King . . .'

The traffic begins to bump and grind forward and the Bentley, jumping a set of lights, swings left, clips the kerb and slithers to a halt against a bollard.

'I'm coming with you,' says Valentine as Frank starts to climb from the car.

'You're staying here,' growls Frank.

Valentine leans against him and catches him by the wrist. 'Take the gun,' she says urgently, pressing the weapon into his hand.

'It's empty.'

Valentine smiles and snorts smoke. 'So what? You can't shoot.'

Frank tries to restore the gun to its hiding place but Valentine pulls it from his hand and pokes it into his jacket pocket.

'I don't need it . . .' he protests.

'Take it,' she whispers, sealing his mouth with her fingertips. 'You might learn something.'

He leaves the warmth of the car and walks quickly towards his target. The rain stings his hands and face. The gun in his pocket pulls him along, drags him forward and starts shouting warnings into the street. 'Take cover! Run for your lives! This man is crazy and dangerous!' No one but Frank is listening.

A few yards from Bagel King a mad old woman with bird's nest hair is clasping a skeleton youth by the neck as he pukes capaciously into the gutter. She shakes him gently, muttering words of encouragement as nervous people slosh around them, tilting their umbrellas like shields. Frank hurries past, the gun in his pocket cursing and broadcasting muffled threats.

The Fancy Wholesale Tropical Fruits Corporation is a plain block of concrete and glass, wedged in a terrace of shanty shopfronts. A flight of marble steps to the door. A polished brass plate on the wall.

He clatters up the steps and strides through the door into a brightly lit arena where a young woman sits at a glass reception desk reading *Hello!* magazine. She's wearing a thin white shirt and a grey skirt. A black cardigan hangs from her chair. She turns her head and scowls at the draught sweeping in from the street, glances vacantly at the gunman, recognises him, smiles briefly and returns to her magazine.

Frank watches her for a moment, head bent forward, dark hair hooked behind one ear, her red mouth softly popping and pouting as she struggles to follow the magazine story. He's been away from the place for two weeks and she probably didn't know he was missing.

'Freeze!' shouts the voice in his pocket. 'Don't move and you won't get hurt!'

'Is Bassett still here?' says Frank cheerfully, knocking the rain from his sleeves. He takes a step forward, gazing down through the glass desk at the pale curve of her legs. She has kicked off one shoe and curls the bare foot around her calf, absently stroking herself with her toes.

'I think he's in his office,' she says, leaning sideways to reach for the phone. 'Shall I check for you?'

'Nah!' sneers the beast in his pocket. 'Stand on the chair and pull up your skirt! We wanna take a look at your legs!'

119

'No, thanks,' says Frank. 'I'm already late for the meeting.'

She sighs, exhausted by the effort of shifting her weight across the desk, and drops the receiver into its cradle.

Frank hurries towards the lift, changes his mind at the last moment, collides with a frazzled palm in a heavy Romano-plastic tub, glances back at the girl, grins, twists on his heel and disappears through a door to the stairs. On this cold winter's evening the building already feels deserted. The broad corridors are empty. A few lights still shine through the frosted-glass doors. His own office is dark and the door closed against him. He stifles the urge to check his desk and presses forward in search of his quarry.

These corridors have a particular smell that he's never quite identified. It's like a mixture of stale food and damp linen and the dusty, flea-bitten velvet you find in old theatres. It seems to seep from the walls and the worn industrial carpet. He's spent seven years of his life walking these corridors, sitting at the same desk in the same office with the gloomy fluorescent ceiling panels and the window that's rusted shut and the framed print of Turpin's 'Urpflanze' hanging above his head; sweating out flow charts and progress reports, harvest potentials, market predictions; sticking his hand up the coffee machine, groping for the little cup that always gets caught in the same position.

'Hey, Frank!'

Frank swings around, startled, to find Horace Larkson standing at the end of the corridor. Larkson from Soft Fruits and Summer Berries and the man most likely to succeed in the battle for the bottled bilberry market. He's wearing the same old familiar blue suit and the pair of horn-rimmed spectacles that neatly divide the polished peanut shape of his face. He's clutching his raincoat and a bulging briefcase, reluctant to abandon his work for fear it will vanish overnight.

'Did you finish the pineapple project yet?' he calls down the corridor in a voice loud enough to raise the dead. 'I'd appreciate some help on that report for the Gooseberry Guild if you can spare the time.'

'It's finished,' says Frank, forcing a smile.

'Roast in hell, sucker!' sniggers the voice in his pocket.

'Fine!' Larkson looks pleased and slaps the belly of his mock-pigskin briefcase. 'Can we talk tomorrow?'

Frank salutes the question with a wave of his hand.

'Have you been away?' says Larkson, hoisting the raincoat over his shoulder. He loiters. He frowns. His eyebrows look stencilled above the horn-rims.

'I took a few days,' admits Frank.

Larkson nods and smiles goodnight, creeps away with the briefcase held against his chest, cradled like a sleeping child.

Bassett's private office is a large room furnished in chrome and black leather with an oatmeal carpet on the floor. The blinds have been drawn against the windows to shut out a view of rooftops and rain. The captain's table stands at the far end of the room, bathed in the butter-coloured light from a heavy brass lamp. Behind the desk a serving trolley with wire shelves serves as a cocktail cabinet. The walls are decked with the framed awards and qualifications beloved of pint-sized tycoons. President of the Plum Crazy Club, 1990. Award of Excellence from the Brazilian Mango Shippers Association, 1985. Guava Guild Order of Merit, 1987. Chairman of the World Candied Fruit Peel Conference, 1979.

Frank slips into the room like a thief, pressing the door shut behind him. The President of the Plum Crazy Club (retired) sits at his desk, his face in a circle of yellow light, his mouth puffed out like a man sucking pebbles.

'Where the hell have you been?' he barks at the intruder. He doesn't look in the least surprised to find Frank standing before him. He spreads his fingers out on the edge of the desk and taps out a tune with his fingernails. 'Why don't you answer the phone, for God's sake! Jessie must have called you at least a dozen times.'

'Drop dead, punk!' shouts the quick-tempered pocket oracle.

Frank hesitates. He wants to vault across the room and knock Bassett from his chair. But the moment is lost, Bassett already has the advantage and there's too much oatmeal carpet between them.

'Is she all right?'

'Jessie? Fine. But you've got to talk to her. She needs to know what you're planning to do about the marriage. You must have guessed that she wants a divorce.' He pauses, waiting for Frank to make pitiful protests. Nothing happens. He tries again. 'Why don't you come to some arrangement? Sell the house and share the money. Maybe give her a small allowance. Whatever you think. I won't interfere. But if you want a fight, then I'm warning you, Frank, the way the law works they'll have the shirt off your back.'

'I don't care what happens,' says Frank, pushing away from the door, moving deeper into the room.

'That's not the answer, dammit! She wants to get into the house. She needs her clothes. She's entitled to claim a few personal effects.' He stops playing the piano with his fingernails and bangs his fists on the desktop. The lamplight flickers. The diary flutters its pages.

'Kiss goodbye to your kidneys, wise guy!' growls the voice in Frank's pocket.

'Tell her to help herself,' says Frank.

'When?'

'Whenever.'

'Tonight?'

'It makes no difference to me. I haven't been back to the house since she left,' says Frank, edging closer to his prey.

'Where are you staying?'

'None of your damn business!' shouts Frank.

'None of your damn business!' shouts the devil in his pocket.

Bassett begins to look uneasy. This doesn't feel right. Frank should have come here to plead with him for the safe return of his wife. He should be wailing and gnashing his teeth. What's wrong with the fool? Doesn't he care what's happening? Does he like the idea of another man groping inside his wife's pants? Does he enjoy this humiliation? Bassett feels insulted. He expects the game to be played by the rules. He demands law and order in his life.

'Whaddya want?' he says suspiciously as Frank stops in front of the desk. 'You think I'm going to let you work here again? Forget it! I don't need you creeping around like Marley's ghost, wringing your hands and sobbing into your sandwiches. You're fired. That's official. And there's no golden handshake. Jessie walked out on you and you walked out on me. That's fair and square.'

He leans back, tilting his chair, and plants his feet on the captain's table. He rocks himself gently, clasping his hands to the back of his neck. His eyes flit from the shine on his shoes to the gloss of sweat on Frank's face.

'I know how you feel, Frank. Believe me. She's a lovely girl and it's tough when a marriage doesn't work out. But it's finished. Finito. You've got to face up to the facts.'

Frank smiles and takes Bassett firmly by the ankles, wrenching the feet high and wide above their owner's head. Bassett looks bewildered and tries to kick out with his legs but Frank pushes forward and throws him over the back of the chair.

Bassett bellows and disappears.

Frank is so surprised that he laughs as he leans across the desk in search of the toppled dictator. He feels himself transformed. His limbs seem to stretch to impossible lengths, his blood thickens to molten lava, his shadow billows against the walls.

'I'm warning you!' bawls Bassett, scrambling from the carpet. 'Piss off or I'll have you charged with assault!' He hauls himself over the edge of the desk and finds himself staring into the barrel of a small, grey Colt automatic. And now it is Bassett's turn to experience a transformation. He blinks. He gulps at the air like a bullfrog and whistles thinly through his nose as he plunges into the shadows again, searching for shelter beneath the desk.

Frank lashes out at the desk and hurls it aside, casting its contents over the room. Bassett is crouched on the floor with his hands on his head and his head pressed between his knees.

'Stand up!' shouts Frank.

Bassett yelps at the command and pulls himself tighter into a ball. His fingers are laced together against the crown of his head as if he's afraid that his brains will explode. The fingers are purple with blood.

Frank places a foot against the back of Bassett's skull and sends him sprawling over the carpet.

Bassett rolls against the wall and scrambles into a sitting position, pulling his knees against his chest. He finds a pencil lodged in the carpet and holds it out, waving it at Frank like the stump of a crucifix.

'Stand up!' shouts Frank. He towers victorious over his prey, legs braced, arms outstretched, clasping the gun in both hands the way he's seen it done in the movies.

'This won't change anything!' whines Bassett. He looks mad with fear. He stares around the floor at the debris from his desk. There are pens and pencils everywhere, scattered across the carpet like a game of Chinese sticks.

'You're wrong,' says Frank.

'That's right,' sings the gun.

'Let's talk,' pleads Bassett. He climbs unsteadily to his feet, shaking his head and wringing his hands, like a man dragged drowning from a frozen lake. Oh, it's cold! He can feel the frost in his heart. He can barely talk through his clacking teeth. 'I didn't mean any harm. It's a mistake. You took me by surprise. It hasn't been easy these last weeks. Believe me. It hasn't been easy. Why don't we go home and talk to Jessie? Put down that gun. I know that she wants to talk to you. It hasn't been easy these last few weeks. Put down that gun. Let's talk to Jessie.'

'You think we'll fall for that old trick?' sneers the gun.

'You're staying here,' says Frank.

'She was worried sick. When you found us in the kitchen. It wasn't as bad. It wasn't as. The first time. Believe me, Frank. I wouldn't do anything to hurt your feelings. Christ, we're old friends. Jessie was drunk. I only stayed there for comfort. It was you, Frank. We were worried. Put down that gun. Let's go home. Let's talk to Jessie.' As he continues to jabber he seems to be growing smaller, his head sinking into his shoulders, the flesh shrinking against his bones. He's growing old before Frank's eyes, withering into a wall-eyed goblin.

'Walk over to that chair.'

'Anything you want, Frank. Relax. It's all right. Put down that gun. Let's talk to Jessie.' He offers his executioner a positively demented grin and shovels deeper into his clothes. His ears are bending against his collar and his fingers vanish into his sleeves as he shuffles across the room.

'Stop!'

Bassett stumbles blindly against the edge of a chrome and leather chair, bleating with fear and wrapping himself in his arms.

'One mistake, Frank. First and last. Honest to God. It was nothing. Comfort like brother and sister. Believe me. I didn't know. You disappeared. What could I think? Wanted to look after Jessie for you . . .'

'Drop your pants,' says Frank.

'What?'

'Drop your pants!' roars the gun.

Bassett begins to whinny as he fumbles and fools with his belt. His fingers seem to be turning to rubber. The belt breaks apart. His trousers fall in a shivering heap over his shining shoes.

'And the rest!'

He huddles over his hands, prising at a pair of black satin underpants that he drags down to cover his quaking knees. He trembles. He cowers. He looks pathetic. His penis, that treacherous charger, pugnacious beard-splitter, God's gift to women, has shrunk to a winter acorn stuck in a spidery mulch of leaves.

'Sit down.'

'I don't want to die, Frank. Please! God Almighty! Don't do it, Frank. I don't want to die!' He buries his hands between his legs, squirming and grinding his heels in the carpet. His teeth look huge in the wizened face. His eyes roll in their sockets.

Frank stands over the chair and pokes the barrel of the gun into Bassett's protesting mouth, tapping it against his teeth to prove, if there be any lingering doubt, that it hasn't been carved from prison soap.

Bassett gurgles and screws up his eyes. His hair crackles with horror. His skin fades to the colour of dust.

click

Bassett screams so loudly that the force of it blasts the gun from his mouth. Frank jerks away and drops the weapon into his pocket. Bassett curls into a ball, rolls from the chair and hits the floor, his face buried in oatmeal carpet.

Frank stands frozen and stares. He wants to turn and take flight. He's scared of this gibbering animal that snuffles the ground at his feet. But when he tries to move, he seems to be floating, drifting in circles around the room. He has taken no more than two or three steps away from the killing chair when the door bursts open and Horace Larkson comes scampering into the room.

'Oh, my God!' he shouts, jerking his briefcase under his arm and throwing himself to the wall. 'What happened? What have you done to him?' He peers at the overturned desk, the wreckage scattered over the floor and Bassett, poor Bassett, plum crazy and half naked, with his buttocks still pumping the air.

'What happened?' wails Larkson, turning to Frank. He can't believe his eyes. It's the end of the world. He keeps tapping the horn-rimmed spectacles into position against his nose.

'He fell off his perch,' explains Frank. There's no time to waste in small talk. He turns to escape but now finds himself trapped by a sentry standing guard at the door. She's standing with her hands thrust deep in her overcoat pockets, grinning and staring into the room.

It's Valentine.

'How did you get here?' demands Frank, lurching forward, trying to keep her from the scene of the crime by stretching his arm like a chain to the door.

'I bought a ticket downstairs,' she says with a radiant smile, leaning against the chain, stretching on tiptoe to view the battlefield over his shoulder. Her eyes glitter with excitement. Her hair is still filled with the cold air of night.

'You're too late,' says Frank, finding his arm around her waist. 'You missed the show.'

'What did you do to him, Frank?' she says proudly, her face pressed against his neck. 'He looks like you nailed his tongue to the floor and pushed the hammer up his arse!'

'I didn't touch him.' He turns her around in his arms to guide her back to the stairs and the street.

'Let's go home, tough guy!' chuckles the voice in his pocket.

'Where are we going?'

He stares through the rain at the terraces of narrow houses. They've driven north through Maida Vale and are lost in the sprawl of dark streets beyond the squalor of Kilburn.

'We're going to celebrate!' grins Valentine, swinging the Bentley from the road and stopping at a pair of iron gates set in a high brick wall. Beyond the gates, caught in the headlamps, a series of empty paths lead through a maze of tombstones to a distant grove of cypress trees.

'This is a graveyard!'

'It's the North West London and Metropolitan All Saints Garden of Rest,' she corrects him. 'Unlock the gates.'

'Are you kidding?'

'Here's the key.'

He steps from the car, clutching a key the size of a sword, and walks down the beams of the headlamps, towards the cemetery gates. Above him, perched on their lofty pillars, a pair of slumbering marble lions. Beneath his feet, caught in the filigree skirt of the gates, a crust of blown newspaper. Coke cans, hamburger wrappers, Lucozade bottles, fruit juice cartons, pizza boxes, fruit peelings and clots of Kleenex. The key clatters in the rusting lock. The gates drift apart and the limousine rolls forward, turns left and stops beside a small flint cottage propped among the buttresses of the wall.

The cottage is a Gothic gatehouse with arched windows of dressed stone supporting turrets of fishscale slates. The windows are dark. A broken sarcophagus, filled with sour earth, spreads ivy against the flint walls.

Frank waits patiently in the rain while Valentine gathers her cigarettes, hat, gloves and the day's collection of shopping bags, before leading him to the cottage where a deep, lugubrious porch hides an oak door embellished with stained-glass panels and a pock-marked verdigris knocker in the shape of a human skull.

'Isn't it beautiful!' she whispers, unlocking the door. 'Webster found it for me. It's the perfect hideaway.'

'It's cold!' complains Frank, blinking as she snaps on the lights.

'I'll fix the heating and then we'll have something to drink.'

They are standing in a room no larger than a family mausoleum, crowded by a sofa and a rusted cast-iron stove. Cobwebs dangle from a plasterwork ceiling. A rug laid against the chill of the floor. There is a kitchen tucked under a staircase that leans against the opposite wall.

Frank walks as far as the sofa and sits down among faded needle-point cushions. Valentine throws her coat on the floor, strides to the kitchen and starts banging cupboard doors. She's wearing a black silk jacket and a pleated skirt that swings open and shut like a fan when she walks. Her shoes clink on the flagstones.

'It's vodka,' she says, returning with a bottle and two crystal glasses balanced on a battered metal tray. 'I forgot to order champagne.'

She places the tray on the floor and curls into the sofa beside him, sitting side-saddle, tucking her skirt beneath her knees.

Frank pours the drinks. It's a darkly flavoured Polish vodka that gloops from the bottle like cooking oil. The heating comes to life with a muffled roar from one of the cupboards in the little kitchen. Beneath the windows, elderly radiators start complaining and pulling against their moorings.

'It tastes like paint stripper!' chokes Valentine, sipping suspiciously from her glass. She seems delighted by the discovery.

Frank gulps at his drink and settles deeper into the cushions with his mouth and throat on fire. He keeps thinking of the bare-arsed Bassett, bleating and chewing the carpet. This small act of senseless violence has worked wonders for Frank's self-esteem. He's balanced the books, adjusted the columns of profit and loss. He is no longer obliged to play the victim, betrayed and alone, nursing his wounded pride in a corner. When someone offers you poison, drink from the cup and spit in their eye. It won't bring Jessica home but at least he can live with himself again.

'What's that?' Valentine flinches and frowns at him, stretching a long white hand to her throat.

'What?'

'Did you hear something?' She twists around to scowl at the window but catches nothing more than her own reflection, deformed by the ripples in the ancient glass.

Frank holds his breath and listens to the grumbling of the central heating, the fizzling rain, the scratching of mice.

'You're crazy!' he grins, shaking his head.

'Why?' She sinks into the sofa again, runs her fingernails over her collar, flicks a strand of hair from her neck.

'We're sitting in a graveyard!' The absurdity of the idea brings laughter bubbling into his throat. He shifts his weight in the cushions and feels the hard knub of the automatic pressing against his ribs.

'It's got character,' protests Valentine. She glances

quickly around the room, her eyes flitting from shadow to shadow, as if she expected skeletons to erupt through the flagstone floor.

'Doesn't it give you the spooks?'

'Yeah!' She grins and leans forward, pulling her shoulders into a hunch.

'Does Conrad know you come here?' he says softly. He pulls the Colt from his pocket and places it carefully in her lap.

'It's a secret,' she says, pushing the gun beneath a cushion. 'Every girl needs a secret.'

'I'm supposed to look after you.'

'So what? This must be the best-guarded patch of turf in London. They keep the gates locked to stop crazy people smashing the graves. Can you believe that? Mad people used to come here at night and try to dig out the corpses! Jesus! Are they sick or what!'

'And the gatehouse?'

'It was empty so I bought it.'

'How?'

'How what?'

'How did you manage to buy your way into a locked graveyard?'

'If you have enough money you can buy your way into the Kingdom of Heaven,' she says scornfully and she believes it.

A silence settles between them. The radiators tick like clocks. In the darkness beyond the windows, angels stretch their dripping wings.

'It's getting late,' says Frank, turning the empty glass in his hands.

Valentine jumps up and plucks at the pleats in her skirt. 'We don't have to be home until midnight,' she says quickly. 'You know the rules. Have another drink while I go upstairs. I want to try my new outfit.'

'Aren't you afraid to go up there alone?' he asks, rolling his eyes at the ceiling.

She hesitates. 'I'll scream if I need you.'

She gathers together her shopping bags, retrieves her fallen overcoat and staggers up the staircase to the cottage bedroom.

Frank puts down his glass and walks to the window. A thousand graves out there in the rain. Pillars and crosses. A crooked marble obelisk shining in the winter darkness. Men, women and children. Buried deep in the mud and forgotten. Nothing left of them but their names, fading on tablets of stone. The stones themselves get eaten away, decay like teeth, leave nothing but stumps in the ground. No one believes it will happen. No one believes in their own death. Impossible to imagine. Eternal sleep. Oblivion. Is that why they've started locking the grave-yards? Blaming the dead for spreading the curse. Mortality held in isolation like some contagious disease.

'Frank!'

He swivels, turns to confront the staircase.

'What is it?' he shouts at the ceiling.

'Come here!'

He runs up the stairs, punching at the wooden banister, sensing the cottage shiver around him.

The room contains a narrow brass bed covered by a quilted eiderdown. An old-fashioned enamel bath stands in one corner, sheltered by a folding screen. There are shopping bags and clothes scattered across the bed and the floor. Candles flicker around the walls.

Valentine stands beside the bed and watches him enter the room, pausing, staring about him, surprised by the candlelight. She's wearing a full-blown satin ballgown with a bodice tight as a swimsuit that flows into thick, voluptuous skirts. The satin is a crimson so dark it looks black in the candlelight. She fills the room like a fantastic moth trapped by the dangerous flames.

'What do you think?' She turns on tiptoe, a dancing movement, making the skirts swirl under her hands.

'Beautiful,' he says simply.

'Jesus. I dunno.' She looks doubtful, cups the bodice with her hands and gives it a violent twist that drags at her breasts and ruffles the skirts against her hips. 'I think it makes me look cheap.'

There is no answer he can find to challenge her low opinion of this unexpected miracle. His mouth is dry. His chest feels squeezed by desire.

'Help me out, Frank,' she says finally, impatiently clipping the skirts with her fist. 'I think I'm beginning to suffocate.'

Frank steps forward and she turns her back, presenting herself to the window. After so many years of married life he's become a master of hooks and buttons, tangled knots and broken zips. He studies the tight scoop of the bodice beneath the wings of her shoulder blades, looking for the trace of a seam.

'I can't find the buttons,' he says at last, but continues to finger the satin skirt, reluctant to abandon his search.

'It doesn't have any buttons, stupid! You're supposed to lift it over my head.'

He drops to one knee, dainty, fussing, a haberdasher with pins in his teeth, gathers the hem in his hands and draws the ballgown around her waist. For some mysterious reason she's discarded her shoes and pantihose. As he rises from the floor, the skirts lifting into his arms, his eyes follow the map of her legs, the long muscles in her calves, the sharp cords of the hamstrings, the faint popliteal hollows where she's placed a little of her poisonous perfume, the swelling convexity of her thighs, until he straightens up again and the bundle of satin obscures his view.

He hesitates, breathing hard, excited by her sudden captivity in this sagging crimson hoop, while she patiently stands and stares at the rain with her arms raised above her head. A witch calling out to the dead. This dark-haired phantom. This woman who is not his wife.

'Hey, take it easy!' she complains, as he tries to wrench

her loose at the waist. He fumbles, spilling some of his precious cargo.

Valentine snorts impatiently, turns in a circle and twists from the bodice, conceals her breasts in her hands, tilting at him with her elbows, bending her head to pull the ballgown over her shoulders. The skirt slithers the length of her arms and falls from her fingertips.

She stands for a moment and stares at him, her arms still held against her breasts, the gown sinking on the floor between them. 'Are you going to fuck me?' she whispers, so softly that Frank thinks, at first, he imagines it. He's amazed by the sight of her standing there naked; the way the candlelight dapples her face, the brittle bones on her bunched knuckles, the long belly, the tuft of black hair in the fork of her thighs. His heart is pounding. The blood roars through his head.

'That's what you've been waiting for, isn't it?' she says quietly, unfolding her arms in surrender and watching him concentrate on her breasts. The dark nipples harden to berries against his obsessive scrutiny.

He steps forward in a trance, trampling through the puddle of satin, and reaches out to take her hands. She draws him closer, pushing out with her hips in an effort to close the distance between them. He places a kiss on her neck, tasting the bitter flavour of perfume, pecks quickly along the line of her jaw towards the corner of her mouth that opens, without hesitation, to the darting tip of his tongue.

He pulls back his head, breathless, excited, wanting to look at her again, but she sucks him back to the heat of her mouth. She is peppery with vodka, slippery with lipstick. Their tongues coil like serpents against her teeth. She has pinned his hands against her waist but he now feels her grip begin to slacken and reluctantly she releases him, setting him free to explore her skin. He traces her spine with his fingers, shapes a saddle to fit her haunches. He makes love to this strange and beautiful woman in the simple way that he courts his wife. But she feels so foreign in his embrace. She is taller than Jessica, broader at the shoulders and cushioned around the hips. She becomes huge to his senses, an unknown continent. He measures her body with floating hands, searching for a pulse, the kick of a nerve, some small response to help guide him forward. He ventures as far as her belly but her thighs snap shut against his advance, trapping his fingertips in her bristles.

'Fuck me against the window,' she whispers urgently. 'I want you to frighten away the ghosts.' She kneels down in the heap of crushed satin and clings to his belt while she works with one hand at his buttons. His trapped penis swings from his pants, stiffens slowly for her inspection.

He stumbles forward, clumsy and ridiculous, his penis rolling like a happy drunkard as he follows her across the room. She stops before the window, grasps the wooden frame in her hands and stands, arms stretched and legs braced apart, tilting her backside towards him. She is luminous in the candlelight. His shadow is a leaping cat.

She cries out at his penetration, jerking forward and making the windowpanes rattle. Her hair unrolls against her neck like a rope of liquorice. He buries his face in its darkness, closing his eyes, feeling her big breasts sway in his hands.

'Do you know what my father would do to you if he caught you?' Her voice has grown small, the words catching against her throat.

A gust of rain against the slates. A candle gutters. Beneath them the field of gravestones is a crumbling coral reef.

'I can imagine,' gasps Frank.

'He'd kill you!' she says with relish. 'He'd make Webster kill you!' She throws back her head and squirms against him with her slapping buttocks.

'Slow down!' he begs as she bumps and grinds and, in a moment of confusion, Jessica springs from his memory, bucking her bones, determined and nimble-fingered, fighting against his caress, impatient to be rid of him.

'If he finds out that you gave me a fucking, he'll *kill* you!' she growls. But she stops pushing, giving him time to pull from the brink. He trembles with fever, his breath in short blasts of steam on the window.

'How will he find out?' he says, nuzzling her neck. He imagines microphones under the bed, cameras concealed in knots in the woodwork, everything on video tape reduced to a gritty black-and-white peepshow. The thought of it cools his ardour, reminds him of Valentine's mother, crawling around on her hands and knees, mocking attitudes of desire, a pornographic pantomime. Turning tricks for the camera. Worse than circus animals.

'You might tell Webster,' she suggests. She levers herself from the window frame, twists around and cradles his face in her hands. His penis plops loose, slapping her thigh, leaving a snail's trail against her skin. 'Men talk!' she adds indignantly.

'Silent as the grave,' says Frank, rubbing her arms and making her shiver. Already he feels that the room is too crowded. He senses Jessica's ghost, intent on mischief, conducting his hands upon Valentine in memory of her own body; Conrad's spirit, brooding and violent, the eye of a storm above their heads; and somewhere in Valentine's upturned face the ghost of her mother, a shadow of distant tragedy.

Another candle crackles and gutters, whipping shadows around the room. He wants to drive out the ghosts and demons by purging himself to the core in her heat. He grabs her by the waist and tries to turn her towards the bed but she stumbles over the clothes on the floor and falls back, shrieking, bouncing against the mattress, digging down with her elbows and kicking out with her feet.

'You're paid to look after me!' she shouts with her

voice edged with fear. Her eyes are blurred. Her black hair scribbles across her shoulders.

He stands above her, catching her ankles in his hands, watching her pump and thrash in the stirrups. 'I'm paid to do as I'm told.' He contemplates her joggling breasts, her sleek belly, the powerful pistons of her thighs. He wants to stand here for ever, frozen by some marvellous spell, and do nothing but luxuriate in the sight of this wonderful, sprawling beauty.

Her struggle subsides and she grins. She stops pedalling. When his hands relax their hold she pulls back one leg, stroking the ball of her foot against his stubborn erection, supporting it, kneading the shaft with her toes.

'Come here,' she whispers, wrapping both legs around his waist and pulling him down towards her embrace. He topples forward, buckles against the bed and finds himself on the floor with his face pillowed between her thighs. She moans and shuts her eyes. The arms, held out to catch him, scissor together and tumble helplessly over her face.

He kneels like a man in prayer, lapping at her cleft with his tongue, drinking the bittersweet sap, anointing his nose and chin with her spices. Her legs straddle his shoulders. She arches her spine, rubbing herself against his face, offering grunts of encouragement and prodding him with her heels. He feasts until she pouts open, a bubble of heat against his eager mouth, and feels himself melting into her body.

'No . . . !' She cries out. Her thighs lock against his skull, shaking him loose and landing his face aboard her belly.

'Come and lie beside me.'

He opens his eyes, unravels his aching limbs and throws himself on the bed. While he lies there, fighting for breath, she sets to work undressing him, wrenching his arms from his jacket sleeves, yanking down his pants, crawling over his chest to prise him from his shoes.

'He'll kill you!' she mutters gleefully, tossing the shoes at the wall.

'That's if I survive the night,' he wheezes as she turns to sit astride him and the last candle flickers out, leaving a ribbon of smoke curling softly against the window.

'What happened to you last night?' says Webster, bright as a button, wearing a natty new camouflage shirt, as he joins Frank at the breakfast table. He pours coffee from a glass pot. A brilliant sunlit morning flooding the windows brings the first teasing promise of spring.

'Nothing happened,' says Valentine sharply, before Frank can clear his throat of toast. She sits beside Webster and scowls at a carton of yoghurt, set down on her plate with a napkin and silver spoon. She's wearing her long silk dressing gown with the heavy embroidered sash. Her hair has been tied in a ponytail.

Webster smiles softly and spoons sugar into his cup. One. Two. Three. Four. 'So where d'you stay until three o'clock in the morning?'

Frank wipes crumbs from his mouth and searches the walls for inspiration. He feels as guilty as a schoolboy. Webster must have seen them come creeping home, watching from his perch in the rafters.

'Don't tell him!' warns Valentine, snatching the sugar bowl from Webster's hand.

'You know Conrad likes you home before midnight,' he says, smiling, stirring his coffee into a whirlpool.

'I'm not a child,' complains Valentine. She prises the

lid from the carton of yoghurt and licks it clean with her tongue. 'Did he get angry?'

'He didn't know you were missing. He watched a couple of your mother's old movies. *Hanky Spanky* and *Gusset Groaners*.'

'Yuk!'

'He was so upset that I put him to bed about ten o'clock with a mug of hot milk and whisky.'

'Did he cause any trouble?'

'He slept like a baby.'

'You're lovely!' she says, grabbing the back of his head in her hands and kissing him hot and hard on the mouth, making Frank flinch and turn his face towards the window.

Webster grins, suddenly embarrassed, drains his cup and reaches again for the coffeepot. 'He wants to talk to you,' he says absently, belching and looking at Frank.

'When?' Frank glances at Valentine who quickly looks away, avoiding his eye, making him feel uneasy. A few hours ago he was holding her by candlelight, naked in a haunted gatehouse on the edge of a rain-swept graveyard. This morning they're strangers. He's hungry for a sign that something has happened between them, anxious to believe that something has changed in their lives. Don't flatter yourself, Frank Fisher. You're just here for their amusement. You're Johnny the jolly gigolo.

'He's waiting for you in the hothouse.'

'Finish your breakfast,' commands Valentine as Frank pulls back his chair and launches himself from the table.

'I've just lost my appetite.'

He strides from the breakfast room, narrowly avoiding a maid with a tray, and hurries towards the jungle lair.

He finds the old man sitting in the branches of a fallen tree in a damp glade of mosses and sword-edged grasses. He's wearing a primrose cotton frock and a pair of gold earrings the size of walnuts. A shapeless blue cardigan hangs on his shoulders. His legs, in black stockings,

140

dangle through rustling petticoats of curled and brittle leaves.

'Frank!' he shouts and grins as Frank comes trampling down the forest path and wades towards him through the field of swords. 'Is this the tosspot who stole your wife?' He produces a cardboard folder, flips it open and pulls out a black-and-white photograph which he hangs between bony knees.

It's a picture of Bassett with his arm wrapped around a girl in a corset and fishnet tights. Bassett is wearing a dinner jacket and smoking a fat cigar, a dark turd poking between his teeth. The girl is sporting a smile and a sash with the legend Golden Delicious warping over one breast. They're posing for the camera at some annual fruit shippers' dinner and dance.

'That's Bassett,' says Frank, plucking the picture from Conrad's fingers. 'How did you get hold of it?'

'Simple,' says Conrad. 'Fancy Wholesale Tropical Fruits is part of Pelican All Star Foods.'

'I don't get it.'

'You haven't heard of Pelican?'

'Well, I knew there was some connection . . .'

'Pelican is a flag of convenience for Trojan Imports and Trojan is part of Staggers Security Holdings.'

'You mean, you *own* Tropical Fruits?'

'Yeah. That's about the size of it,' beams Conrad. 'Small world.' He places a finger against the side of his big, marbled nose, squeezing one nostril, and winking at Frank with a blood-chilling smile.

'Well, don't look so surprised!' he bellows when Frank is slow to recover from the shock of this revelation. 'I'm more important than you. I've got more money.'

'How long has he worked for you?'

'I dunno, Frank. I didn't know I owned Fancy Fruits until I made some enquiries. It's difficult to keep track. But now that I've found him, it's a pleasure to lose him for you.'

141

'What have you planned?' says Frank suspiciously. He can't tell Conrad about his late brawl with Bassett because of Valentine but, as far as he is concerned, their dispute is settled.

'I'm sending down the accountants to look at his paperwork.'

'That should wipe the grin from his face,' says Frank, holding out the photograph. It's a most bizarre revenge but Conrad seems pleased enough with it. Frank had half-expected him to have Bassett shot in the back of the head, the corpse skinned and boned, the flesh flaked and fed to his goldfish. He's mad enough to do anything.

'You haven't heard the rest of it,' says Conrad. He reaches down for the photograph and restores it carefully to the folder. 'I'm closing down the company!' He sniggers softly to himself, watching Frank through the chinks of his eyes. 'I've told Pelican All Star to fire the Fancy Fruit staff, strip out the assets, destroy the records and put the building up for sale.'

'Can you do that?'

'Damn right!' explodes Conrad, shaking the branches of his tree. He's the king of the jungle. Mr Mumbo-jumbo. The high and mighty Boogaloo.

He starts to erupt with laughter. It begins as a growl in his stomach, runs up through his chest and rushes into his throat, choking him, making his eyeballs bulge in their sockets, until he throws back his head and roars, his jowls set dark and trembling like the wattles on a mad old turkey cock. His grey face, swollen with so much blood, ripens into a varicose gourd.

'You can't shut down the company! You'll hurt a lot of innocent people!' argues Frank, shouting to make himself heard through the uproar. 'They shouldn't suffer because of Bassett!'

Conrad stops laughing and wipes his nose. 'You think it's too crude?'

'A trifle elaborate,' says Frank diplomatically. 'He

doesn't deserve anything so grand. He's really not that important . . .'

'Perhaps you're right.'

'Why don't we leave it alone?'

'No! Why don't we burn down his house, wreck his car and shoot the dog?'

'I don't like it!' complains Frank. 'It's dangerous.'

'Don't turn soft on me, Frank!' Conrad bellows down at him. 'Where's your killer instinct?'

'I don't want anyone hurt!' Frank shouts back, picking at the leaves in his hair.

'He hurt *you*, Frank.'

'I don't care. It's not worth the risk.'

'Come and sit beside me,' says Conrad, reaching down and clutching him by the wrists. Frank finds himself yanked from his feet and hauled into the tree where he scrambles onto the branch beside the old man.

'I'm here to maintain law and order,' Conrad tells him gently as he holds him fast with a mighty arm. 'I've a reputation to protect.'

'I know that.'

'You can't steal another man's wife, Frank, and expect to get away with it. What would happen if everyone tried it? Think of the pain and suffering. The broken homes. The abandoned children. The wasted years. The empty dreams. Terrible. Terrible consequences.' The shadows flitter across his face, staining the folds and creases, filling his eyes with darkness.

'Everything has its price,' says Frank quietly, thinking at once of his intrigue with Valentine.

'That's right!' exclaims Conrad, in great delight. 'Everything has its price. And I'm the bugger who sets the prices!' He smirks, he splutters, he laughs until he suffocates, cock-throppled and struggling, gasping for breath and fanning his face with his skirt.

Frank falls from the tree and makes his way back to the breakfast room, his shoes splashed with mud and cobwebs hanging from his sleeves. Webster is still at the table, bent to a plate of fried eggs, bacon, sausage and mushrooms, a slice of bread and butter folded into his fist.

'Where's Valentine?'

'She went swimming,' says Webster, smiling up from his plate. 'Want some more coffee?' He points at the coffee-pot with his bread-and-butter truncheon.

Frank shakes his head and retreats, picking his way through the puzzle of silent corridors towards the Turkish pavilion.

The water dazzles him, making him screw up his face to protect his eyes against the glare. The walls are glittering cliffs of blue-and-white Moorish tiles. The glass ceiling, filled with sunlight, is draped in fantastic clouds of muslin. At the far end of the pavilion, beneath the canvas parasol, fresh towels have been heaped on a deck-chair.

He enters in silence, careful on the marble flagstones, squats at the edge of the pool to watch Valentine kick through the sparkling water. She's wearing an old-fashioned swimsuit, speckled with green and red rosebuds and trimmed with a little skirt at the waist. When she catches sight of him she turns and glides to the side of the pool.

'What did he want?' she demands, treading water and wiping a hand across her mouth. Her face streams with sunlight. Her eyelashes are jewelled spikes.

He shrugs forward, leaning over the precipice, and tells her of Conrad's plan for revenge, the breaking up of the company and the burning down of the house, a string of comic disasters designed to destroy the victim by pulling his life apart at the seams.

'Isn't there anything we can do to stop him?' he says at last, hoping for a promise of miracles.

'Nothing,' says Valentine, pulling herself from the pool. She stands beside him on the marble ledge, water spilling from the skirt of the swimsuit, spreading puddles around

144

her feet. 'He enjoys making mischief. Don't worry. He'll have forgotten it tomorrow.

'But someone could get hurt.'

'You mean your wife could get hurt. That's what you're thinking about it, isn't it?' she says with irritation, squeezing the water from her hair by twisting it into coils that snake against her neck. The wet swimsuit sucks at her breasts, pulling greedily on her nipples. The skirt hangs heavy, dribbles against her thighs. 'If someone cheated on me I'd make his life a misery. I wouldn't rest until he was down on his hands and knees pleading to be left alone. I'd teach him a lesson he wouldn't forget. Will you fetch me a towel?'

He walks across to the parasol, dipping into its shadow to pull a towel from the deck-chair. He thinks of Jessica trapped alone in a blazing bedroom, black smoke spurting through crackling floorboards. The walls blistering with heat. Flames streaking through shattered windows. 'He's crazy! I can't stay here!' he blurts out angrily, returning with the towel held like a cloak, draping the cloak around her shoulders. 'It's time to quit!'

'You can't quit,' she says bluntly. 'Don't be so stupid.' She hangs her head to scoop the hair from her neck as he works the towel along her spine like a butler polishing silver. 'Do you think he'll let you just walk away from here? You know too much about his business. You're family. You can't walk out on the family.'

'And you?' He slides the towel to her waist and carefully places a kiss against the chill of her shoulder, looking down the front of her swimsuit. The blazing bedroom is soon extinguished.

'I don't want to lose you,' she whispers.

Encouraged by this confession, he kisses her again and slips his hands around her waist to draw her tighter against him. But she pulls quickly from the embrace.

'Be careful, Frank,' she says, shivering, stepping aside and pulling the towel from his hands. 'It's dangerous.'

He retreats as far as the parasol and throws himself into the deck-chair, knocking its cargo of towels to the floor. 'Where do you want to go today?'

'I don't know.' She shrugs, looking at the sunlight in the muslin clouds. 'I'm tired of shopping. Let's go to the zoo.'

Later, standing in the sweet stink of the elephant pavilion, Valentine reaches for Frank's hand, lacing her fingers and leaning softly against him. She looks so happy to be here on this empty winter afternoon as they shuffle from building to building, searching for signs of life in the heaped nests of dung and straw. Frank smiles, dips his face in her hair, brushing her neck with his mouth. She says nothing. They stand together in silence, watching the lonely elephants rocking and treading their chains.

In the twilight of the aquarium, before a brilliant window of water filled with a shoal of milky fish with eyes as bright as blue glass, she lets Frank turn her face to be kissed, sighing as she yields beneath him, pulling him down to her mouth. An octopus floats from a flowerpot and hangs suspended above their heads.

Returned to the daylight, walking a cold, deserted terrace in search of bison or mountain bear, they link arms, their footsteps measured and falling together, and he feels elated, drunk with desire for this beautiful and elegant woman.

But then, on the way to the giraffe house, with ice on the water of the moat and a chill wind chewing his nose and ears, he dares to suggest that they sneak away to the warmth of the graveyard cottage and she becomes angry, pulling away from his arms, and in a moment the spell is broken.

'I'm not that cheap, Frank!' she says, turning her back and sulking into her overcoat collar.

Her anger startles him. 'Who said you were cheap?'

'That's what you're thinking, isn't it?' she demands, turning around to challenge him. 'You think I'm just like my mother. Easy pickings. The tart with the heart of gold.'

He scowls at her in confusion. What is she trying to tell him? He shuffles from foot to foot, apologetic and wretched. 'I don't remember having to kick down your door to get at you last night,' he says, hoping to hurt her.

She hesitates, sensing his bewilderment, already regretting her outburst. She feels vulnerable. She wants him to understand. 'Look, last night was a mistake,' she says gently, reaching out for his arm again. 'I'm sorry. It shouldn't have happened.'

'Are you telling me to forget it?'

'Yes,' she says. 'No. I'm just asking if we can start again.'

'Where do we begin?'

'Christ, I dunno. I'll think of something,' she says, pulling on his arm to lead him back through the west tunnel.

A troop of children trudges past, led by a woman in a tartan cape. The children are wrapped in scarves and mittens, clutching crayon drawings of rabbits.

'What went wrong?' asks Frank, prompting her to talk again, wanting everything explained.

'It wasn't wrong, exactly, Frank. It was just too fast. When it happens I want it to mean something . . .'

'So last night was nothing special for you?' he demands, afraid of the truth and yet vain enough to hope that she'll contradict him.

'That's not what . . .' But she stops short and stares along the path.

'What is it?' He follows her gaze as far as the reptile house where the figure of an elderly man is creeping slowly into the sunlight. He's tall and thin with a face as sharp as a steel blade. He's wearing an overcoat with an astrakhan collar and a pair of yellow kid gloves. His shoes are crepe-soled suede the colour of crystallised ginger. There's a young girl dragging on his arm, pulling him down, making him walk with a heel to starboard.

'Holy shit!' whistles Valentine. 'You see the old guy with the blonde midget? That's Hamilton Talbot!'

'Your father's old business partner?' whispers Frank. The acid attack in the supermarket. The bacon slicer filled with fingers.

'Yeah. The one who set the Cocker brothers on Webster. The one you've been hired to protect me against.'

'Fine. Let's go home,' says Frank the man of action, twisting away towards the main gate.

'No. Wait. I want you to meet him.'

'I'm supposed to keep you out of mischief.'

'Whaddya think is going to happen? He's not going to eat you,' says Valentine scornfully.

'Why go looking for trouble?'

'It's important to know your enemy, stupid!'

Frank turns a circle and tries to pull her away by the sleeve but it's too late. The enemy is standing before them. A corpse in an overcoat.

So this is Talbot the Torturer. The prowler in the attic. The bogeyman beneath the stairs. The smiling stranger at the school gates. The man who, thirty years ago, spread himself like a plague across London. Conrad's peculiar partner in crime.

'Ah, Valentine!' he croons with a deeply cadaverous smile. 'It's been a long time . . .'

'You haven't changed,' says Valentine, nodding at the hellion dangling from his arm.

149

'I'm far too old to break bad habits,' he says with a creaking sigh. He looks down at his diminutive courtesan and ruffles her bleached-blonde curls with his hand.

She's no more than twelve years old, a painted child, a rented poppet, wobbling in a pair of scuffed white high heels and wrapped in a fake fur coat. She wipes her nose on her sleeve and looks suspiciously at Valentine who smiles sweetly in her direction like a matron admiring a friend's toy poodle.

'Where's your mother?'

'Go fuck yourself.' The cherub snuffles and scowls.

'What a charming little creature!' Valentine exclaims. 'Have you taught her any tricks?'

'How's Conrad?' says Talbot, ignoring her question. His emaciated smile reveals a set of expensive crowns. His skin, stretched tightly against his skull, is a mask of finely crazed porcelain. His lips and nostrils are purple. 'I trust there's still hope he'll recover his wits. It must be such a trial for you to have a vegetable for a father.'

'He's fine. I'll tell him you asked,' says Valentine. 'He'll be so amused to hear that I saw you in the zoo.'

'Have you heard?' says Talbot in a stage whisper. 'They're threatening to close it down and turn the contents into meat pies!'

'Yeah, I know.'

'It's terrible how everything changes,' he complains. 'London! These days I barely recognise it.'

Valentine smiles. 'How is the Old Kent Road?'

'It used to have a certain charm that I always found rather amusing. But the neighbourhood has lately become disgusting. I miss the old days. Do you suppose it's my age? The streets seem to be swarming with ghastly juvenile delinquents. Child criminals. Schoolboy racketeers. Sandpit junkies.'

'Is that where you found your little friend?'

'I see *you* have a new companion,' says Talbot, blinking his pale grey eyes at Frank with a mocking flirtatious intensity. 'Tell me, whatever happened to the old one? What was his name? It was something queer. I never could remember it. I heard he's grown rather accident-prone. I hope I haven't missed his funeral. I should like to pay my respects.'

'Oh, Webster is still alive and kicking. He's here somewhere . . .' says Valentine absently, glancing across her shoulder as if she expected to see him come lumbering up through the tunnel towards them.

Talbot stops smiling. His eyes flicker. His fingers pull at the astrakhan collar, drawing it tighter against his throat.

'Shall I send Frank to look for him?' suggests Valentine helpfully. 'I know you both have a lot to talk about.'

This invitation to meet his old adversary has a most remarkable effect upon Talbot. He becomes, all at once, flighty and nervous, shuffling in his ginger shoes and blowing steam through his nose. He's ill-equipped to deal with trouble without the benefit of his bruisers.

'I fear we must postpone the pleasure,' he says briskly, gathering his fractious nymphet into the folds of his overcoat and sweeping her urgently to the gates. 'Make haste, my little scampo, before the windigo catches you.'

'Hey, where are we going?' she complains, trying to yank herself free of him. 'I wanna see the rest of the animals. You promised! I wanna go see the monkeys screwing.'

'Shut up!' snarls Talbot, twisting her arm until she yelps and stops pulling away. 'I've had enough of this flea-pit. I'm freezing my pecker off.'

'Can we go to McDonald's?' she whines as he bundles her through the gates. 'You promised! You promised!'

Frank watches them retreat. The child molester and the pygmy temptress. 'Why did you threaten him with Webster?' he says, turning back to Valentine.

'Well, he didn't look very scared of *you*,' she says disdainfully.

'He doesn't look scared of anything.' They begin walking along the east path towards the African aviary. The sun fades into dismal twilight. Strings of gulls float overhead, gathering for a raid on the pelican pool.

'Oh, he's scared of Webster,' smiles Valentine. 'That's why he hired the Cockers to kill him. Hell, it's cold!' she adds, blowing into her hands. 'I think we should have gone shopping.'

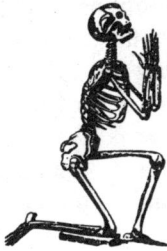

That night Conrad arrives at the supper table wearing a pastel summer dress, cut very low at the neck, with short puffed sleeves and a skirt ballooning with petticoats. His wrists clatter with Dawn's best bangles. The bodice sags in memory of her late departed breasts. Conrad sits down slowly, smiling, dreaming, pulling at the petticoats and, when he's made himself comfortable, rings the little glass bell to summon forth the maids.

Frank and Valentine sit together, confronting him through a curtain of brilliant candlelight. Webster sits marooned at the end of the table.

'Where did she take you today?' says Conrad, peering at Frank and waving a silver fork at his daughter. His breath is pickled. His eyes are bleary with afternoon brandy.

'We went to the zoo,' says Valentine quickly, before Frank has time to open his mouth.

'Let him talk,' says Conrad, without taking his eyes from Frank.

Valentine pulls a face and slumps against the back of her chair. She's wearing a long black slip with scarlet satin evening gloves. Small chains glitter and swing from her ears.

'We went to the zoo,' agrees Frank.

'That's very educational,' grins Conrad showing his teeth. 'You can learn a lot from the animals.'

But when Frank tells him of their brief encounter with Hamilton Talbot the old man suddenly looks forlorn, wagging his head and tapping his knuckles against the table.

'That bugger needs a stick of dynamite screwing into his arse,' he tells Webster.

'He's harmless enough if you leave him alone,' says Webster, tucking his napkin under his chin and smiling down at his plate.

The maids circle the table in silence, prancing on tiptoe, delivering baby quails in nests of ginger and carrot shavings. Webster picks up his nestling and sucks it bravely into his mouth, chewing thoughtfully on the bones.

'He's a child molester,' says Valentine, pushing her plate away in disgust.

'It keeps him out of mischief,' says Webster, neatly disgorging bones from the corner of his mouth. He arranges the bones on the edge of his plate. Tinker, tailor, soldier, sailor.

'He's a nasty piece of work!' complains Conrad, crunching quail as he tries to throttle a bottle of wine. 'And he won't be satisfied until he's seen you buried.'

'What did you do to him?' demands Frank.

'Oh, he blames me for everything!' Webster smiles vacantly and returns to shovelling shreds of bird's nest from his plate.

'Talbot was my partner in the old days,' Conrad starts to explain. He thrusts an arm through the candle flames and fills Frank's glass with wine, splashing his hand and puddling the tablecloth. 'But we had a difference of opinion. When I retired he made certain threats against my person . . .'

'He threatened to kill you,' says Valentine.

'That's right,' agrees Conrad. 'So I felt obliged to send Webster along to have a little talk with him.'

'What happened?' says Frank, turning again to Webster.

'I believe I broke his legs,' says Webster.

'Actions speak louder than words,' says Valentine.

'It was nothing more than he deserved,' says Conrad, charging his glass and draining it with a single swipe, making the bracelets chime on his wrist. 'But Talbot never forgave him.'

'He never forgave *you* for cheating him out of a fortune,' Valentine reminds him.

'He never had a head for business,' belches Conrad. 'He's an egg roll short of a picnic.' He smiles, raises a hand to his head and tenderly strokes his scalp, dreaming of distant days.

'Whatever the reason,' says Valentine, 'since that time he's directed all his anger at Webster.'

'He's no trouble,' says Webster modestly.

'No trouble?' shouts Conrad, reaching again for the bottle. 'He could have killed you that night in the Garter Club when he caught you in the thunderbox!'

'He was lucky,' admits Webster, licking gravy from his fingers.

'He nearly finished you with the Cocker brothers.'

'They took me by surprise,' says Webster.

'I want it finished!' shouts Conrad, banging his fists on the table and making the maids take flight. 'Damn and blast him! Go out and fetch me his head on a plate. Take Frank with you. I want Talbot strung by his short-and-curlies. When the world is rid of that man we'll all sleep sweeter in our beds at night.'

'Haven't you had enough to drink?' says Valentine, watching him drain the dregs from the bottle.

'A few glasses of wine!' roars Conrad indignantly. 'There's nothing wrong with a few glasses of wine!' He lets the bottle drop from his hand and roll across the table. 'I'm an old man. I need the comfort.'

'You look like you've been boozing all day,' Valentine accuses him.

'You've never seen me drunk!' explodes Conrad. 'Never!'

He pulls himself from his chair, looming large in the candlelight, and struggles to keep his balance on the treacherous and billowing carpet that makes him plunge from foot to foot in a clumsy, mocking dance.

'Dawn never begrudged me a drink!' he burbles, now fast dissolving into self-pity. The blood drains from his face. His bangles clatter. He grabs at the table for support as he feels the floor disappear beneath him.

'Catch him!' shouts Valentine.

But it's too late.

Conrad hits the ground with a roar of surprise and a flurry of petticoats and then, unable to find his feet, is content to remain in a heap and glare at the distant ceiling.

'Bugger it,' says Webster, stuffing his mouth with bread. He leaves the table and kneels beside Conrad, slipping a hand down the front of his dress to feel for the old man's heart.

'Put him to bed!' orders Valentine, helping the maids clear the table. The meal is promptly abandoned. The candles are snuffed. The dishes are whisked away to the kitchen.

Frank volunteers to lend a hand taking the drunkard away. Conrad is spread on the floor with his legs thrown apart like a ravished matron. The dress, pulled up to his waist, reveals a pair of torn lace panties and the snags on his nylon stockings. His eyes are closed. A string of spittle shines on his chin.

'There was treacle tart for pudding,' grumbles Webster as they pull the old man to his feet. Conrad moans and rocks on his heels. Webster folds him over his shoulder, where he hangs like a set of saddle-bags, his arms and legs loose, his cocktail slippers hanging by the hooks of his toes.

'Fetch his handbag,' wheezes Webster.

Frank finds a small beaded bag lurking under Conrad's chair, retrieves it with a sweep of his hand and follows Webster from the dining room.

'I want to talk,' whispers Valentine, catching his arm as he reaches the door.

'Where?' He pauses briefly but she slips past him, eyes downcast, flicking her hair with a quick movement of her satin fingers.

'I'll be in the hothouse.'

Frank overtakes Webster shuffling up the marble staircase. 'What does he keep in this bag?' he says, turning it in his hands as he fiddles with the clasp. It feels as heavy as a brick.

'The last time I looked,' puffs Webster, 'he carried an attack alarm, an automatic and a can of Mace.'

'Why?'

'He's afraid of being molested.'

The master bedroom is hot and dark with a stifling smell of mothballs and perfume. The bed is a high brass contraption, decked with flags and canopies, elaborate as a funeral carriage. The lamps that flank the bed are fashioned from coloured glass moulded in the shape of urns containing bundles of garden flowers. The room is stuffed with flowers. The carpet is a field of crimson leaves overlaid with ribbons of marigolds. The curtains are printed with roses the size of cabbages.

On the wall above the bed a portrait of Dawn rising, naked and tumble-haired, from a heap of brocade cushions. She grins at the camera, eyes half-closed, head tilted back, and fondles her breasts in her hands. She's wearing an old-fashioned corset and a rope of polished fake pearls. She is sprawled on her back, feet raised, kicking the air, inviting the viewer between her fat thighs, as if her cunt were a chart of the heavens, a cannibal's whiskery mouth, a witch's mad, mesmeric eye. The photograph has been coloured like some Victorian valentine. Smoky shades of rose pink, amber, jade and amethyst. The gilt wood frame has been decorated with swags of carved anenomes.

Webster leans forward and spills Conrad onto the bed, laying him out like a corpse on the floral counterpane.

'I don't like to see him so drunk,' he says sadly. He pulls off the cocktail slippers, unclips the stockings, dismantles the petticoats, unwrapping his unhappy employer with the brisk efficiency of an undertaker.

'What made him start drinking?' says Frank. He turns away from the sight of Conrad's belly as it rolls loose from the dress and stares instead at his own reflection in the dressing-table mirrors. The top of the dressing table is covered in jars of stale make-up, perfume bottles and a set of silver brushes. A pair of panties dropped in a heap against a lacquer jewellery box.

'He drinks because he's bored,' says Webster, trying to bend Conrad's arms into the sleeves of a black nylon nightie. 'He's bored and he's lonely. And he's getting old. It's time he got out of here and found a place to sit in the sun.'

'What's stopping him?' says Frank, watching Webster in the mirror.

'He won't leave the house. He doesn't even walk in the garden. He's been living in the shadows so long the sunlight would probably blind him.'

'Why do you stay with him?' probes Frank. This house feels like a fortress built to contain a madman's dream, its dungeons haunted by the lewd leviathan of a wife.

'I don't know,' sighs Webster. 'We understand each other. We've grown old together . . .'

Frank picks his way downstairs and steals into the jungle hothouse. The moonlight streams through the canopy, bleaching the cobbled path and starching the undergrowth that leads to the ornamental pond. There is silence but for the splash of water and the mutterings of mice. The heat from the steam pipes fogs the ground and rolls in the roots of the trees.

He follows the path as far as a glade where velvet moths with luminous eyes have gathered to feast on waxen flowers. He stands patiently, listening, waiting for Valentine to emerge from the forest. He can sense her watching him from the shadows, catches a trace of her poisonous scent through the soft smells of jasmine and stephanotis.

After a while she steps into the clearing from the gloom of a thicket. Staring. Suspicious. Her long hair loosely tied in a knot.

'Did you put him to bed?'

Frank nods. 'He's sleeping,' he says, to reassure her, but finds himself whispering, nonetheless, knowing they're trespassing in Conrad's secret sanctuary. Who guards this kingdom while he sleeps? Crocodiles with diamond collars. Vampire bats, folded neat as black umbrellas, keeping watch for him in the trees.

'Where's Webster?'

'I think he's gone to roost,' says Frank. A frog as big as a bowler hat crawls from its lair in the shrubbery. Somewhere behind them, maddened by moonlight, cicadas have started their frenzied singing.

'Let's walk.' She slips her hand through his arm and presses herself against him as they venture deeper into the jungle.

'Did you ever trade tales with a caravaneer in the deserts of Afghanistan?' she says, when they've strolled a little way through a corridor of giant ferns.

He screws his face into a frown, serious, thoughtful, pretending to tick through a thousand adventures and voyages, as if he's a seasoned traveller, a veteran of the wilderness, a man who has been to Belize in search of the golden jaguar. 'I've had a honeymoon in Nice, a weekend in Amsterdam and a business trip to Birmingham.'

'You've been to the south of France?' The news is greeted with wild amazement. He might have said that he's sailed around the Rings of Saturn alone in a short-sea schooner.

'Yes.' He pauses, pleased with himself, sucking at the heat of this tropical night.

'Tell me about it!' she says, eager as a child demanding stories of serpents and castles.

So Frank tries to describe the town and how, in the early morning light, he would climb the hills behind the medieval streets to look down upon the Bay of Angels where yachts drifted on a placid sea already shining like molten glass and how, in the glaring afternoon, he lingered in the shade of pavement cafes, feasting on seafood and chilled white wine, to emerge through the pungent twilight to join the strollers on the shingle shore; and how at night the sky seemed as soft as soot, astonishing after London where night never fully penetrates the city's murk, and in this darkness an avenue of floodlit palm trees along the Promenade des Anglais. And he remembers his room at the Hotel Negresco, and Chinese rugs on the floor and the big carved bed with its canopy and rose-pink sheets; and the view from the balcony and the great glass dome of the Salon Royal. And he remembers the hordes of American students, the Parisians on parade and the shuffling old Africans who tried to sell him souvenirs from plastic shopping bags. And Jessica is somewhere down on the beach, laughing and flirting, dark as a gypsy with mocking eyes, but here his memory fails him.

'I want to see it,' says Valentine. 'I want to see the great tombs of Giza and the burning ghats of Benares and the ice flows of Baffin Bay. I want to see San Fernando and Tierra del Fuego. Pukapuka and Tonga. The Tasmin and China Seas.' The land beyond the security fence, beyond the iron hand of the city, is a world of lakes and palaces, cannibals and camelopards, mermaids and monopodes.

'What happened to Afghanistan?' he says as she takes his arm and they're strolling again on the winding cobbles.

'I want it all, Frank. Everything. I have to get away from here. Don't you understand? I'm suffocating in this house . . .' She turns to him, squinting, her face blurred with tears. She tries to swallow back her frustration, snuffles and blinks as the tears spill down. Her throat is flushed. She attempts a breathless, sobbing laugh and wipes her cheeks with the back of a glove.

'But you're free!' he protests. 'You're free to go anywhere in the world.' He can't comprehend how she might regard herself as a captive, suspects her of raising obstacles to prevent her from taking the risk of breaking loose from the family. It's different for him. He's worked all his life at the treadmill, making just enough money to keep himself working, dreaming of having the freedom to pick and choose how to spend the days. The freedom to stay at home. The freedom to travel abroad. Time can be bought and sold but only the rich can afford it.

'I can't even leave the house without an escort,' she says sharply.

'Tell him you want to take a trip,' says Frank. 'He wouldn't want to stop you. Where's the harm in it?'

'You think he'd let me out of his sight?'

'Have you ever tried to face up to him?'

'I once tried to run away,' she confesses.

'What happened?'

'He sent Webster after me.'

'How old were you?'

'Seventeen.'

'If we can find you a ladder perhaps we can get you over the wall. You could make another dash for freedom.' He looks up into the treetops and imagines fireflies swarming, trails of sparks in the canopy.

Valentine sniffles and grins. 'You're lovely,' she says and places a kiss beneath his ear. Her mouth is hot and red as a pomegranate.

'That's what you say to Webster.'

'That's different.'

She stretches forward and grasps the back of his head in her hand, staining his face with kisses, pecking at his eyes and nose, the edges of his mouth.

'Isn't this rather sudden?' he whispers, pulling away, not daring to respond for fear she is leading him into a trap. 'We hardly know each other.'

'I've changed my mind. Shut up and kiss me.' She grinds herself against him. Her hands pull frantically at his shirt.

He hesitates, splits open her mouth with his tongue, sliding quickly between her teeth. She tastes of sorrow and wine. The black dress, fine as cobweb, rumples beneath his hands as he gently works at the buttons. One. Two. Three. The dress falls apart with a shrug of her shoulders, slithering over the tips of her breasts, loiters for a moment around her hips before fainting away at her feet. She is left wearing nothing but a

162

pair of black lace panties and her long satin evening gloves.

'Quickly!' she whispers. 'Follow me!'

Frank squirms from his clothes with the speed of an escapologist as Valentine disappears again. He hurries in pursuit, pushing through a screen of tufted grasses, scrambling on tree roots and trampling orchids. His bare skin prickles with excitement. His cock grows heavy and stiffens, a tusk in the glimmering moonlight.

He finds her waiting for him beyond a tangled curtain of creepers. She is kneeling in a tussock of moss beneath the shade of a sprawling shrub that spills its flowers like confetti. The shrub clings to fragments of a granite column, half-submerged in the vegetation. The knucklebones of a giant sleeping in the warm, black earth.

'Come here,' she whispers and beckons him forward.

He stands over her and hangs his head, watching as she takes his cock in her hand, fingertips fanned along its barrel, and guides the end of it into her mouth. Her fingers are tapping a tune, dainty yet deliberate, as if she were learning to play the flute.

'Lovely,' she murmurs. 'Lovely.'

She closes her eyes and suckles, her black hair flopping around her shoulders, her breasts loose, her buttocks propped against her heels and spread like a swollen valentine heart. He cries out, trembling, and gathers her fallen hair in his hands, twisting it into a rope which he holds away from her face while his cock slithers loose from her bulging mouth.

'Do you know what would happen if he found you doing this to me?' she whispers, tapping the flute against her chin. He remains connected to the cushion of her lower lip by a quivering silver thread.

'He'd kill me.'

'That's right. You remember. I'm glad you were paying attention.'

He stares as she laps at him with her tongue, probing

and pressing, nibbling with her teeth, as if she were teasing herself with some delectable morsel before seizing it again in the melting heat of her mouth.

Flowers, small as sequins, cascade against the curve of her back. A lizard with astonished eyes watches them from a crack in the granite. But tonight no ghosts have gathered to mock him.

He remains hypnotised, drugged by desire, while she makes a slobbering feast of him until, as he feels himself losing control, he tries to pull away. But she stops his retreat, wraps her arms about his thighs, grasps his buttocks and jerks him forward, driving him deeper into her throat. He moans and floods her mouth, grabbing at her arms for support as she gulps at his spurting milk, still holding him fast, murmuring encouragement, sweetly squeezing him with her tongue.

For a time they remain locked together, her arms draped around him, her head pressed warmly against his belly, and he gently combs out her hair with his hand, slow and comforting, as if she were clinging to him in grief.

At last he shivers and sighs, saturated with pleasure, and kneels before her, kissing her face, lifting the weight of her breasts in his hands.

'Let's stay out all night,' he says, nuzzling at the hollows of her neck. He glances down at her breasts, the ripe softness between his fingers, the dark halo of a stiffening nipple.

Valentine laughs and cradles his head. 'Are you hungry? We could steal some food from the kitchen.' The idea of it fills her with delight. Creeping through the sleeping house with her arms loaded with fruits and biscuits.

He lifts his face to kiss her throat and the slope of her shining shoulders. 'We'll never find our clothes again.'

'They can't be far away,' she says, climbing to her feet and sweeping the fallen flowers from her body.

'No. Stay here,' he says, catching her wrist. 'I want you naked in the moonlight.'

She grins, pulls at her panties, slips them down her long, white legs and casts them away with a shimmy and kick of her feet.

He picks up the scrap of lace, crushing it against his face like a nosegay. Valentine stands before him, still wearing the long satin evening gloves, confident and smiling, her skin shining opalescent against the darkness of the jungle.

'You don't look very impressed,' she says, mocking him, grinning at the stump of his wilted cock.

He pulls her down, seeking her laughing mouth with his tongue, sneaking a hand between her legs as a wedge against her thighs. She struggles, pulling his ears, bucking to unsaddle him until, with a quick sleight of hand, he sinks an inquisitive finger into the slippery well of her cunt. Then she moans and stops fighting, arches her back and shuts her thighs around his fist.

Slowly he works open her legs but Valentine screams and flings him away. As he tumbles to earth she springs shut, rolls herself into a ball and hides her face in her hair.

Frank scrambles to his knees, startled, staring around, and there, from a crack in the broken granite, a face is glaring back at him. It's the face of a wild demon, punched through a frame of thorns and leaves. The eyes are shocked and staring, the eyebrows shot into bristling exclamation marks. The crapulent features are twisted and swollen, inflated by some internal rupture of hot and poisonous gases. The mouth is an empty, sagging purse. The veins stand out from the nose like a fantastic growth of coral.

Frank stares, transfixed, as the jaws pull apart and the face erupts with an anguished roar. And then he has turned and is running away through the undergrowth with Valentine beside him. The creepers whip at his throat and wrists, trying to snare him and pull him down. A moth, like an angry homunculus, batters itself against

165

his face. Behind them Conrad comes rushing on long, elastic legs.

They have found their clothes and are scrambling to dress when the hunter erupts through the jungle and stands before them, terrible in his nylon nightie, a pruning knife and a brandy bottle trembling in his fists.

'I know what you're thinking!' shrieks Valentine, fighting with the buttons on her dress.

But Conrad's thoughts are too dark and deep to be fathomed. He turns to Frank and fixes him with a long stare, closing one eye and shaking the brandy bottle at him. 'I've been watching you,' he whispers, flicking his tongue around his teeth. 'I've seen the way you look at my daughter. I've seen the way you've been trying to get your hand up her skirt while your feet were under my dinner table. I trusted you, Frank. I brought you into my home. I made you one of the family.'

'If you trusted him why the hell were you creeping around in the bushes!' shouts Valentine, dancing from foot to foot as she tries to fit her shoes. The dress snags and twists on her hips.

'Silence!' roars Conrad. 'You're disgusting! Go and cover yourself – I won't have you walking around half-naked. It's bad for the servants.' This is fine talk for a man in a nylon nightie that barely covers his pecker. He pulls sulkily on his shoulder straps and takes a quick shot of brandy.

'She's a grown woman!' says Frank, in a sudden rush of exasperation. 'Why can't you leave her alone?' His anger is nothing but shame and guilt and a fear of the pruning knife. He takes a step forward, reaching out with his hand like a man approaching a savage dog.

'Hah! Listen to him!' cackles Conrad. 'He interferes with my little girl, breaks my heart and then tells me to mind my own business.' As he talks his fury plays mischief with his face, pinching his mouth, tweaking his nose, pulling at the hair in his flaring nostrils. His ears

166

seem to soften and swell as if they were made from sealing wax and were ready to melt in fiery splashes against his mottled neck.

'Shut up and go back to bed,' orders Valentine, trying to keep the two men apart. 'You look ridiculous. We'll talk about it in the morning.'

Conrad pulls back his head and considers her for a moment. 'No!' he snorts indignantly. 'I may feel different in the morning. I'm going to kill him here and now, while I'm still as mad as a magpie.'

He turns again to Frank, hobbles towards him, hacking at the air with his knife.

'Jesus! Take it easy!' shouts Frank, jerking away from the whistling blade as it narrowly misses his face. He retreats into the shrubbery but Conrad wades after him, cursing and slashing the moonlight. Rule number four: when you find yourself cornered, never attempt to engage your killer in the art of conversation.

'Stop it!' screams Valentine. 'Stop it! If you hurt him, I swear you'll never see me again! I'll walk out of here for ever.'

Conrad gives pause for thought. He shrinks from the attack and turns to his daughter. 'How can you do this to me?' he gasps, his face wilting with dismay. 'How can you do this to your mother? Didn't we give you everything that money can buy? Didn't we nurse you through the whooping cough and the measles? Didn't we give you a fine education? And now you want to break our poor hearts! Why? Why did I work so hard and make such sacrifices if you're going to squander your chances on the first tuft-hunter who shows you his tongue? Don't you have any respect for yourself? What would your mother say if she knew that he'd been tampering with you?'

'She's dead!' shouts Valentine. 'My mother is dead!' Her eyes glitter with hate. The cords stand out in her neck.

'Don't say that!' says Conrad, very shocked. 'Don't even

think it!' He cringes with pain, his legs bent and his elbows pressed against his belly. 'She's alive in this house. She's alive to me.'

Frank emerges from the sheltering undergrowth. 'I'll leave in the morning,' he announces quietly. 'I'm sorry. I didn't want this to happen.'

'It's too late,' mutters the aggrieved pongo, softly sinking beneath the weight of his misery. 'I want you gone from here tonight.' The strength in his legs seems to wither away beneath the ballooning nightdress. 'Take him!' he says to Valentine, as he makes his slow descent. 'Stuff him into the car, drive him down to the river and drown him. I'll give him twenty-four hours and then I'm coming after him.' He falls to his knees with a grunt, spilling the brandy bottle, and looks around in confusion.

'Let's go,' says Valentine, turning her back on her father.

'Twenty-four hours,' repeats Conrad, searching for Frank through the fog in his eyes. 'And when I catch you . . . I'm going to cut off your balls . . . poach them in their own gravy – make you swallow them . . .' He falls back, driving his heels between his buttocks with such a force that it knocks the blade from his fist. He gropes blindly in search of the knife, sweeping his hands in a circle. But it's finished. He opens his mouth, gulps at the air and bursts into tears, wrapping his head in his nightie.

And Webster steps from the darkness, kneels down beside him and gently covers him with a blanket.

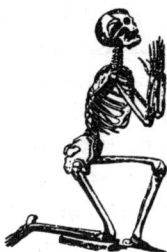

The moon fades in the first grey light of day as the Bentley sweeps through the dirty streets towards the outskirts of Kilburn. The pavements are choked with sacks of rubbish – drunken scarecrows that topple and spill themselves in the gutters. Two women in scuffed leather jackets stand on a corner, staring aimlessly around them, stamping their feet and sipping at cans of export lager. Old men, wrapped in rags and cardboard, are stirring and scratching in stinking doorways. Here and there a few Asian grocers have started unlocking the steel cages protecting their narrow shopfronts. Alarm bells are sounding the cockcrow of dawn.

Frank sits in the front of the car, wiping his eyes and raking his chin, trying to stay awake. He's so tired that his head feels weightless, as if it's floating away from his shoulders. He needs a shave and a clean shirt, a hot bath and a long sleep.

'Are we going to the cemetery?' he says, trying to make conversation to push against the silence that has settled between them. They made their escape like a couple of delinquent children, running from the house while Conrad bellowed threats from his bedroom window. But riding through these ugly streets their excitement has quickly been exhausted.

'Have you got a better idea?' says Valentine and glances nervously into her driving mirror.

'Maybe I should just go home and pretend that none of this ever happened,' he suggests quietly.

'Thanks a lot!' bristles Valentine, banging her fist on the steering wheel. 'I thought I meant something to you.'

'I'm crazy about you,' he says, trying to stifle a yawn. 'But you'll find my passions grow cold when I'm dead.'

She grins at him over the collar of the fur coat she's picked for this cold and frosty morning. 'You can't go home. Your friend Bassett sent the police over there to look for you.'

'A jealous husband with a fake gun?' says Frank doubtfully.

'A crazy man with a loaded shooter. You think he knew it was empty? Tell it to the serious crimes squad,' says Valentine.

'The police went to the house?'

'That's right.'

'How do you know?'

'I checked.'

'How?'

'Simple. I told Webster to send someone out to keep a watch on the street.'

Frank considers this for a time. He's a criminal. The way he threatened Bassett, tortured him with a mock execution, not to mention his fight with the Cocker brothers – that must be worth a charge of assault and even attempted murder, although he doubts the owner of the Golden Goose took the trouble to make a report to the police. He imagines a midnight raid on his house, sledge-hammers punching a hole through the door, torchlight on the stairs, marksmen crouched in the privet. His eyes start to shut and his chin sinks slowly against his chest.

'Webster!' he shouts, jerking awake as Valentine tugs at the wheel to avoid a dog running loose in the street.

'*What* about Webster?'

'He knows about the cemetery. You told me he found it for you. It's going to be one of the first hiding places he checks when he comes after me.'

'Don't worry. I'll buy him a bag of peppermints. Anyway. A few days. It might not happen.'

'And what about you?'

'I'll be fine,' she says, without looking at him.

'I don't believe you.'

'It's time to trust me.'

I can't run away for the rest of my life, he thinks, and then wonders if that's true. For twenty years he's stubbornly tried to build on the swampland of his career and then marriage and now, watching them sink beneath him, he feels nothing but excitement. He thinks of his father's escape, cashing the pension plans, taking a ticket as far as New Brunswick, and begins to understand the need to get out and run, to give death a moving target.

'I should at least go back and try to talk to your father,' he says, as the limousine turns a corner and creeps to the cemetery gates.

'Don't be stupid. The next time he'll kill you. Nobody gets a second chance.'

'It's a mess.'

'Yeah. But it's not your fault, Frank. It's bad timing.'

He steps from the car and walks out to unlock the big iron gates. His breath hangs above his head like a shock of ectoplasm. The sky is filled with thousands of starlings rising from their roosts in the city as they scatter to their feeding grounds in the wastelands and rubbish dumps. The sun casts a low light across the gravestones, sweating the frost from the long grass.

'It's comfortable and the heating works. I think there's a TV somewhere. Try looking under the bed,' Valentine tells him as they open the gatehouse and catch the mouldering, spicy smell of the silent interior. Incense and candles. Flagstones and drains. The smell of solitude. The arched windows scatter spindles of sunlight across the room,

171

revealing the wounds in the battered sofa and the rime of rust on the stove. 'I was going to have it decorated,' she adds wistfully, looking around at the dismal walls. In one corner of the room, pressed behind glass in a bamboo frame, a portrait of Christ in long white robes saluting the world as He floats to Heaven. His hair is straight as a sheaf of corn. His blue eyes are staring vacantly from a face as bright as an apricot. Above His head the sky curdles into thunder clouds. Beneath His feet an impression of smoking mountain peaks.

'How long do we have to play hide-and-seek?' asks Frank, walking as far as the kitchen and searching the shelves. A tin of stale coffee. A packet of salted crackers. A box of brown sugar. An unwrapped block of bitter, black chocolate, cloudy with age, a grey bloom spread like a cataract over its polished surface.

'I don't know. As long as it takes.'

'There's no food.'

'You'll have to starve until I can bring you something.' Her voice is brittle. Her long hair, slumped against her collar, forms a cowl around her face. She looks tired and lost and frightened.

'I can buy my own groceries,' he says, reaching out to catch her waist. He draws her against him, scrambles his fingers under her coat, trying to coax a smile.

'Listen, Frank. You're in big trouble,' she says, slipping her arms around his neck and leaning away from him slightly to watch his face, to be certain that he's paying attention. 'If you're seen on the streets you're a dead man. So be careful. Sit tight and keep quiet.' And she kisses him, long and hard on the mouth, turns abruptly and walks away as if she were leaving for the last time, as if she will never see him again, stepping into the cold bright air and closing the door upon him.

Conrad slowly opens his eyes, twists his head in the pillow and gazes between the voluptuous thighs of his late beloved wife who hangs suspended above him. Painfully pushing against the blankets that still engulf him in odorous heat, he raises one trembling hand to beckon Dawn down. But she's doomed to ignore his agony and remains on the wall, smiling at her own breasts. Lost in a swoon, radiant in her nakedness, mocking him with eternal youth. His fingers stretch out for her, begging to know half-forgotten comforts, before his hand sinks away exhausted, strikes against the bedside table and gropes for the bell to call the maid.

The girl who enters the room is small and thin with bright copper hair that is neatly pinned beneath her cap. She bobs a curtsey at the bed and moves away to open the curtains.

'Who are you?' grumbles Conrad. He groans, shielding his eyes from the sunlight.

'Geraldine, sir.' She turns and smiles, anxious for approval, her freckled face very pale, her green eyes fixed upon him, not daring to stray for a moment from her master's baleful stare.

'Are you new?'

'Yes, sir.'

'Are you willing?'

'Yes, sir.'

'Let me look at your legs.'

'My legs?' She hesitates and stares at her shoes. She picks at the hem of her uniform and draws it gingerly over her knees.

'Show me the length of 'em, dammit!' shouts Conrad, annoyed by her timorous ticklings. 'Are you hiding holes in your stockings?' And to gain a better view for himself he struggles to haul himself upright by wrestling with a bedpost.

The maid grows so pale that the freckles fade on the bridge of her nose. Her mouth starts to quiver as if she might scream. But she somehow finds the courage to gather her skirt in her hands and pull it around her waist to let him peer at her narrow thighs and the ribbons on her black suspender belt. There. It's done. She closes her eyes and attempts to press her thighs shut, afraid that he'll leap from the bed and lick them.

'Ah!' He sighs and sinks back into the pillow, his hands retreating under the sheets to fondle his balls absently.

'Will you take some breakfast?' she begs of him. Standing there, frozen, spindle-shanked, with arms akimbo, she looks like a startled phasma.

'Tell the Turk to make me a glass of cold tomato juice with two raw eggs and plenty of pepper. Can you remember that?'

'Yes, sir,' she says, releasing her skirt and making great work of smoothing her apron.

'Good. Bring it to me. And fetch Webster,' he says and slumps again into stupefaction.

Webster arrives at the bedside bringing with him the smell of strong soap and a gust of spearmint toothpaste. He stands, silent and very solemn, like a man come to pay his respect to a corpse. He's wearing an army field jacket and camouflage trousers tucked into a pair of new canvas boots. A wet toothbrush pokes from his pocket.

'Has he gone?' says Conrad, peering at him with a jaundiced eye.

'He's gone.'

'And Valentine?'

'She asked for breakfast to be sent to her room.'

'That girl deserves a good spanking,' says Conrad. 'He was a married man! My daughter was running with a married man. Did you know that? What does it mean? The world's gone crazy! The people have gone crazy! I don't understand them any more. How can you hope to understand people who walk around the streets in plimsoles, eating Chicken McNuggets and drinking tinned beer? How can you believe in them? It might have been different if Dawn hadn't demised. A daughter needs to talk to a woman although, God knows, I've tried to be a mother to her . . .' He punches at the blankets until he unearths a blue satin dressing gown which he throws around his shoulders.

'Children grow,' sighs Webster. 'You can't protect them forever. A lot of girls her age are married with two or three kids.' He walks to the window, his new canvas boots making little gasping sounds on the carpet of marigolds.

'Bog-trotters, the lot of them!' shouts Conrad. 'Verminous rag-pickers! I was born with nothing – I didn't climb so high to watch my daughter crawl back to the gutter. She's beautiful. She's rich. She has a smatter of education. She's choice enough for royalty.'

'Remember the old days?'

'What old days?'

'I was thinking of the Tufty Club in Frith Street,' says Webster. He turns from the windows, hands pushed deep in his trouser pockets, and walks as far as the dressing table, sits down and reviews himself in the mirrors. 'We used to go down there to look at the girls and watch Freddy Alpino at his private table, drinking champagne and plotting murder. Remember Freddy? They used to call him the Pig. He ran all the rackets in London . . .' He pauses, watching Conrad's reflection in the glass.

'So what?'

'He retired and bought a Greek island.'

'That's right.'

'He lived like a lord in a stone fortress and tried to debauch all the local girls,' Webster reminds him. 'He always loved dark and hairy women,' he adds, tapping his fingers against the bristles of a silver hair brush.

'He died of the pox!' growls Conrad. The wages of sin is death. He crawls from the sheets and swings his legs overboard, making the brocade canopy shiver and leak a trickle of dust.

'But when he retired and left town there were gang wars in the streets. Every kid with a blade in his pocket wanted to cut out a patch of turf,' continues Webster, steering the conversation away from the weaknesses of the flesh. 'Remember Jungle Johnny from Brixton? We had to have him put away when he tried to come north of the river. And Fat Willie gave us trouble when he wanted a share of the restaurant racket.'

'It was a tough time,' says Conrad.

'But we took the protection business and most of the entertainments. We took control of the streets.'

'That's because we had talent,' says Conrad proudly. 'We had discipline.' He shuffles to a rosewood wardrobe and peers at his hoard of ballgowns and frocks.

'We also had to spill a lot of blood,' says Webster, turning from the mirrors to watch the wardrobe.

'An occupational hazard,' says Conrad, scowling at him. 'I never heard you complain. You made a good living.'

'That wasn't the reason I risked my neck,' says Webster. 'We used to be a family.'

'We're still a family,' says Conrad, 'and no one is going to pull us apart.'

176

'No,' says Webster sadly. 'It's finished. The times have changed.'

'Talbot is still out there somewhere,' Conrad reminds him. He removes a cotton dress from the rail and hangs it in the crook of his arm while he scowls at its pattern of yellow lilies. He knows it won't stretch to his bulging gut but he might squeeze into it again if he wears a panty girdle.

'Talbot is a clown,' says Webster. 'Don't waste your time on him.'

'What are you trying to tell me?' Conrad demands impatiently. A gold bracelet for the yellow dress. A coral necklace if he wears the black skirt and cardigan.

'I'm trying to tell you that perhaps it's time we left London and found *ourselves* a place in the sun. You've made enough money to buy Bolivia. It's time you made peace with yourself.'

For a moment Conrad looks flummoxed and then such an expression of incredulity spreads across his face that even Webster feels shocked by the suggestion. 'I can't leave here! I can't desert Dawn's memory!' gasps Conrad, clutching the dress against his throat.

'And you can't waste the few years you've got left to you trying to keep Valentine out of mischief. She's a grown woman. She can pick and choose her own men. She can make her own mistakes.' This is very dangerous talk but Webster knows the risk.

'So that's it!' shouts Conrad. 'Valentine sent you to beg for mercy.' He throws the dress at the bed but it falls against the railings and flutters to the floor in a heap.

'I came here to speak for Frank,' says Webster grimly. 'He saved my life. I owe him something.' He stands up, banging against the dressing table as Conrad storms towards him.

'No!' growls Conrad. 'You owe me *everything*!' His eyes are mad. His breath is sour. Through the miasma of stale perfumes his skin has the smell of horse meat. 'I want you to go out there and find the bastard. I gave

177

them my word. It's a matter of honour. No one is free to play hide-the-sausage with the daughter of Conrad Staggers. I want you to bring me his head on a plate – I'm going to stick it on a pole.'

At that moment the maid appears at the door with a glass of chilled tomato juice set on a black lacquer tray.

'What is it?' roars Conrad.

'A glass of tomato juice, sir, with two raw eggs and lots of pepper,' the maid whimpers, trying to raise her skirt while she keeps control of the tray.

'Drink it and get out!' bellows Conrad.

The maid plucks at the glass and drains it in several, sobbing gulps, turns and scampers back to the kitchen.

'If you go after Frank,' says Webster, 'you'll make Valentine hate you for the rest of your life. She'll never forgive you.'

'She needs a damn good spanking,' grumbles Conrad, stamping towards the bed. 'You didn't see them together. He was touching her private parts. Touching my little girl!' He kicks at the yellow dress on the floor, hooks it with his toes and sends it flying across the room. 'God dammit! I want that bastard brought down!'

'I can't do that for you,' says Webster.

'What?' The old man turns on him again, his face bloated with indignation.

'I can't do it.'

'What's wrong with you?'

'I'm tired,' shrugs Webster. 'I'm tired of the beatings and killings. I'm tired of the tantrums and squabbles. I'm tired of watching you swagger around in dead women's underwear. I want to go fishing.'

Conrad turns in a circle, spinning with fury, and slaps at the rails of the bed. 'What's happening to the world?' he shouts. 'What's happening when my own bodyguard turns against me?'

'I'm not your bodyguard,' says Webster, retrieving the yellow dress from the floor. 'I'm your nurse.'

'Get out!' rages Conrad, snatching the precious garment and pressing it to his chest. 'I'll find another man for the work. Someone who doesn't have your sort of scruples. I'll send for Kadinsky.'

Webster looks startled. His eyes betray a glimmer of fear. He stares at Conrad for a moment, trying to make sense of this announcement. 'Kadinsky died eighteen months ago. He was shot by the Syrians after his argument with the Phalangists.'

'Hah! He flew into Paris last week. He's been working in Tripoli, raising money for good causes.' Conrad looks triumphant, snorting and nodding his head as he tramples about the room.

'How do you know?'

'I've been in touch with him.'

'He's a terrorist, for God's sake!' protests Webster. He builds bombs into airline luggage. Rapes and tortures hostages.

'A freedom fighter,' Conrad corrects him.

'He's a mercenary,' insists Webster. An international bounty hunter. He tracks and kills for money. Men, women and children.

'A professional.'

'He's a psychopath!' He works with an assault rifle, usually a Kalashnikov, but when he wants to make an impression he switches to an Uzi with a folding stock.

'An idealist.'

'You can't let him loose in London to butcher your daughter's boyfriends!' shouts Webster.

Conrad grins. A fat Mikado in a dressing gown. 'I can do anything!'

'You're crazy!'

'Get out,' snaps Conrad. He lunges at Webster again, stamping his foot and shaking the dress in his fists.

'You're making a big mistake,' says Webster as he turns to leave the room.

'Tell it to Kadinsky!' Conrad shouts after him. 'Tell it to Kadinsky!'

Valentine brings Webster to the North West London and Metropolitan All Saints Garden of Rest early in the afternoon.

'There's nowhere else to hide him,' she says anxiously, as Frank appears to help unload the Bentley.

'I've been fired,' says Webster cheerfully.

'We'll try to find somewhere else in a couple of days,' says Valentine, darting a kiss at Frank that misses his mouth and catches him on the side of the nose.

'I can sleep on the floor,' says Webster. 'I don't need to share the bed.' He looks up at the flint cottage and flicks a peppermint into his mouth.

'I'll be glad to have the company,' says Frank, smiling, grasping the hand of the man he thought was coming to kill him.

But Valentine looks sulky and nervous. She stands sentry in the front porch watching the tombstones for signs of malevolent resurrections. The monuments shine against the darkness of yew trees. This love nest in a graveyard no longer appeals to her sense of humour.

'Why the hell did you bring so much luggage?' she complains to Webster as he drags a heavy wooden chest over the threshold.

181

'I brought everything,' he says, grunting beneath the weight. 'If we don't need it – we'll throw it overboard.'

Frank helps him to push the chest against the wall where several large suitcases have already been assembled beneath the portrait of Floating Jesus. He recognises the broken lock and the mouldering leather straps on the chest. Webster has stolen Conrad's collection of love letters.

'What went wrong?' he demands, when they've emptied the car and have finally closed the cottage door. It feels like a doll's house with the three of them squeezed in this tiny room.

Webster sits down on the chest and sets out to explain what's happened to him in the last few hours but it's clear from Frank's face that he's making very little impression. Frank hasn't grasped the full implications of Webster's sudden appearance. His visitors have brought him the spoils of a raid on the Turk's kitchen and he's more concerned with picking at the bones of a cold roast chicken than ruminating on Conrad's plan for revenge.

'Who's Kadinsky?' he asks from the sofa when Webster has finished his story.

Webster shakes his head and looks to Valentine.

'Remember the Barcelona bombings three or four years ago?' she begins patiently. She is sitting on the staircase, still wrapped in her big fur overcoat. Her hands inside the pockets are holding the coat against her knees.

Frank shrugs. Every night he used to sit and watch the TV news and wonder at the violence in the world. Skinny kids with hunting knives killing housewives in supermarkets. Mass graves found under turnip fields in the frozen twilight of Eastern Europe. The heads of fat dictators rolling in the African dust while government troops loot towns and rebels raze villages. Terrorists seizing aircraft in the sweltering heat of distant airports. Earthquakes, famines and rumours of war between the quiz shows and panel games.

'A lot of policemen were killed when their bus exploded

on the way to a football stadium,' explains Valentine. 'That was Kadinsky's work. But everyone blamed the Basques.'

'And then a young Basque leader died in an ambush walking his wife to church. And that was Kadinsky,' says Webster. 'But everyone blamed the police.'

'I don't get it,' says Frank.

'Kadinsky works for Kadinsky,' says Valentine. 'As far as he's concerned, when you finish a job the perfect way to cover your tracks is to murder your employer. You have to be crazy to hire him.'

'And Conrad is crazy,' says Webster.

A silence settles between them. The chest creaks under Webster's weight. Beneath the window, the radiator belches through its fat iron pipes.

'How long before he gets here?' says Frank. The chicken is greasy. He's lost his appetite.

'A few days,' says Webster. 'He's in Paris.' He hangs his head, stares at his new canvas boots and wipes the back of his neck with his hand.

'We've got to be ready for him,' says Valentine. She stands up and clatters downstairs, brushing past Webster to reach the window. 'If we can take him by surprise. There's a chance.' She glances nervously at the sky.

'I'm an old man!' protests Webster, trying to lever himself from the chest. 'I should be collecting my pension and going on a sunshine cruise. I should be sitting on the promenade deck, wrapped in a tartan blanket, watching the girls in the exercise class trying to touch their toes.' He bangs his knees with his fists and scowls. 'I shouldn't be standing in the rain in some dirty London backstreet waiting for a man like Kadinsky to cut my throat with a razor.' He stops trying to raise himself and sinks slowly back again, settling his weight on the creaking timbers. 'There's one way to beat him,' he says after a moment's meditation. 'We can make a run for it.' He brightens and smiles. 'We'll buy ourselves passports and papers and catch the first flight to the sun. If we're lucky we'll have disappeared before he gets into town.'

'You're a fool!' snaps Valentine. 'Kadinsky will follow you everywhere. You know that. He'll hunt you down. He's patient. He may have to wait years but he'll strike you off his hit list.'

'Let him wait!' says Webster stubbornly, waving her doubts away with his hand. 'If I'm lucky I'll have died from sunstroke in Florida or been knocked on the head by a jealous husband.'

'No!' insists Valentine. 'You can't run away from him!' She looks at Webster with a flare of panic in her eyes, her mouth stretched tight, her hands pulled from her pockets to drag the hair from her face.

Webster shakes his head and looks across at Frank for support. 'What do you say about it?'

Frank stares at the palms of his hands as if he could read the lines and creases. He admires Valentine's spirit but he trusts Webster's fighting instincts. There's a time to stand your ground and a time to cut and run. Give death a moving target. 'We can't sit here like the three little pigs waiting for him to blow the house down,' he says at last. 'I vote we take a chance and make a run for it.' All aboard the Trans Siberian Express. Bombay Night Mail. Blue Train to Cape Town. The world is waiting for them.

Valentine sags against the window. Her face hardens with disappointment and she lets a dark strand of hair fall back against her eyes. 'I'm not coming with you, Frank,' she says slowly. 'I'm warning you. If you follow Webster you'll be leaving me here.' And before Frank finds his voice again she has turned to fling back the cottage door and escape.

'Valentine!' Frank shouts and springs from the sofa.

'She's just like her father,' says Webster smugly.

'Give me a few minutes,' says Frank, to leave Webster sitting, sulking, on his pirate's chest.

He runs from the cottage and follows Valentine along a broad drive that leads to a capsized mausoleum clenched by monstrous claws of ivy. The air is cold and smells of earth and wet gravel. The sky is the colour of smoke as the afternoon sinks towards darkness.

'What happened to the caravaneers in the deserts of Afghanistan?' says Frank, walking carefully in her footprints as they pick a path through the long grass. 'What happened to feasting by starlight in the mountains of Turkistan?'

'They were dreams,' says Valentine. 'Nothing but dreams.' She looks exhausted. She hasn't slept since the night before last and her eyes seem bruised by the light. She huddles into the fur coat and presses the collar against her mouth.

'Come with me,' says Frank. 'We'll go anywhere you choose.' Pineapples on the Ivory Coast. Bananas on the hills of the Windward Isles.

'You still don't understand,' she says desperately. She turns to face him in the shade of a granite column supporting an angel with broken wings. 'Listen. Kadinsky isn't some overweight bruiser you can hit with the back of a shovel. He's a terrorist. You can't play cat and mouse with him. If you turn your back on this man he'll kill you.'

Frank looks up at the angel and remembers how Conrad had tried to threaten him with the Cocker brothers, transforming them into bogeymen who would chase him through all eternity unless he stopped to confront them. They didn't look so formidable when he finally caught them trying to cover their bollocks in a cheap room at the Golden Goose. And Hamilton Talbot. The mad dog of the underworld. A sad old man in yellow gloves with a rented schoolgirl on his arm.

'Come with me,' he says again. He's hardly had time to make his declaration of love. He can't believe that he's losing her. How can she go back home when they've

185

risked their necks to set her free from its dungeons and empty corridors?

He reaches out to claim her again by pulling her roughly into his arms but she jumps back from him, twisting her ankle and crying out in surprise.

'I can't do it, Frank! I can't travel half way around the world just to watch you get killed. We'd always live under a death sentence. We'd always be looking over our shoulders. Webster knows that.'

'Damn Webster! I'm asking you to come away with me. We can go anywhere you choose . . .'

'And I'm telling you that it's too late!'

'I'll stay,' declares Frank, trying to act like the warrior. 'We'll help Webster out of the country and I'll stay here and take my chances with you.'

But this offer to be a sacrifice in the interests of keeping her affections fails to have the desired effect.

'You're dead without Webster,' she tells him bluntly. 'You're a civilian, Frank. You wouldn't stand a chance without his skill and experience. He's cunning. He's a survivor. Whatever happens, you must stay with him.' This is no time for flattery. Frank is an easy target. He's an innocent. That's what makes him so attractive. That's why he'll get himself killed. She turns, wanting to get away from him, seeking the sky beyond the reproachful eyes of the mutilated angel above them.

'Are you telling me to leave?' says Frank. 'Is that what you want? Are you telling me to leave you alone?' He's frightened by her determination. He isn't ready for this confrontation. He needs time to think. He wants time to puzzle it out.

'It doesn't make any difference, dammit!'

He snatches her arm to stop her escape but she pulls away, losing her balance and sprawling over the hump of a grave. She hits the ground with a yelp, supported on hands and knees, embracing the burial mound with her coat.

Frank follows her down, straddles the grave, wanting to pull her up again. But she shakes herself like a dog and scrambles through his legs.

'Don't touch me!' she warns him, restored to her feet. Her face is flushed. The heavy coat is streaked with mud.

'Do you want me to stay or go with Webster?' he demands stubbornly and knows that he's already lost the battle to prise her apart from her father.

Valentine takes a breath and throws back her head defiantly. 'I don't care what happens! You can both go to hell!' she shouts, smacking at the ruined coat.

'If you don't come with me. If Webster gets me out of the country. We'll never see each other again.'

'So what?' she spits at him. 'I'll go back home where I belong. Don't worry. I won't be crying myself to sleep over a stupid dumb bastard like you!' She turns blindly and struggles among the graves, searching for the safety of the path.

Frank remains standing, turned to stone. He watches her run to the Bentley and drive away in a spray of loose gravel. And then he walks back along the path and slowly closes the great iron gates.

Kadinsky arrives on a late-morning Air France flight into London. He's travelling on a German passport and comes disguised as a tourist. He's tall and lean and walks through the crowded terminal with the slow, deliberate stride of a prosperous funeral director. His blond hair, retreating from the temples and high forehead, hangs from the back of his head in a short ponytail that has lately been dyed to an unremarkable shade of brown. The mouth is large yet pale and touched with the smile of a man who has just found himself delivered, without delay or misfortune, to the desired destination. The sun-bleached eyes stare out unblinking from a face that is nothing but polished bone.

He wears a dark trench-coat and carries an old leather overnight bag stuffed with the basic armoury of a traveller abroad. The bag contains a small Nikon automatic with three rolls of film, clean shirts and underwear, a waterproof washbag and shaving kit, a Michelin guide, an English phrase book, a street map of the city, a map of the London Underground, a travel clock and a carton of cigarettes.

The good tourist takes a cab from the airport to the city outskirts where he enters a small hotel, bleak as a lazaretto, in which special arrangements have already been made for him. He's received in a gloomy entrance hall by a large Jamaican woman in a nylon duster coat and a pair of Reeboks with green knitted ankle socks. After a few words of introduction she guides him to a room on the second floor where she leaves him alone to inspect his surroundings.

He sets down the overnight bag and paces the worn carpet, rattles the window and draws the miserable rags of curtain against the view of a drab backyard filled by an empty pigeon shed. He examines the furniture, fiddles with the lamp in the ceiling, checks beneath the mattress on the narrow bed. He searches the bathroom, inserts an inquisitive hand behind the pipes of the small wash basin, strokes the carcass of the water heater bolted into the wall.

Satisfied that nothing has been ignored, he removes his trench-coat and jacket and arranges them neatly on the buckled wire hangers he finds in the plywood wardrobe. Then he sits down on a chair and waits for the bedroom door to open and admit the object of his desire.

After a few minutes there is a scuffling in the corridor beyond the room followed by several whispered protests until the door is flung wide to reveal the Jamaican woman returned and leading a girl by the hand.

The girl, a sulking strumpet of seventeen, looks nervously at Kadinsky and glances quickly around the room at the wardrobe, the bed, the curtains that sag on the dirty window. Her dark hair hangs in greasy curls. Her eyes look stung by her caked mascara. Despite all the efforts that might have been made to titivate her sullen features, she's already licked the colour from her pouting mouth. She is wearing a floral cotton smock and old beach sandals that slide beneath her feet. She is short and pale and pregnant.

Kadinsky leans forward in his chair and surveys the girl from head to toe with his bulging assassin's eye. And then he raises one hand in approval and lets it fall like a flag.

The Jamaican housekeeper grins and bids the girl undress, giving her some encouragement with a friendly cuff to the head. The girl flinches and reluctantly sets to work. The smock is raised to reveal a pair of heavy thighs and the rim of a greatly swollen belly pushing against her underpants. The stretched skin marked like a curving silver tracery. Small tufts of hair beneath her arms. A plastic necklace at her throat. The straps of a stout maternity bra cutting into her shoulders. She struggles with her underwear, reaching around and beneath her belly in a clumsy attempt to pull down the pants. But now the older woman takes charge, yanking the pants down the girl's legs and snapping open the bra to release a pair of blue-marbled breasts for the general admiration.

The girl stands naked, hands clasped under her belly as if she were holding a boulder, watching Kadinsky watching her with his mad, unblinking stare. She feels herself hypnotised by those eyes, sinking beneath his influence, until she is rudely shaken awake and ordered to mount the bed with an urgent poke in the ribs from her keeper. She settles herself in the mattress, turned slightly towards the window to relieve the pressure on her spine while guarding her buttocks from assault by tilting them at the sheltering wall.

Then Kadinsky walks to the bed and slowly stoops to look at the girl, lowers his face to her body and trawls his nostrils against her skin. She shivers and covers her breasts with her arms. He takes her hand and nuzzles her shoulder, snuffling in the damp, sour smell of her armpit, sniffing out the faint trace of lavender soap buried in the fold of her elbow, catching his breath at the fresh dab of rose and geranium scent evaporating on her wrist, inhaling the odour of dog and tobacco clinging to her fingertips.

The frightened girl struggles and tries to pull away but her keeper threatens her with violence and kicks the bed until she surrenders herself again to Kadinsky's examination.

This time he takes her foot, sniffs at the rank smell of rubber sandal, pulls open her toes to release their rank and musty odour, shovels along the length of her legs, trailing vague and elusive flavours until he pauses to linger at last in the thick, ripe smell of her thighs. And here, at the roots of her pubic hair, he inhales her secret vinegars, stirring memories of childhood nightmares, death and estuary mud, fear of the dark, rotting fish, glues rendered down from animal bones.

The girl cringes into the mattress, twisting her legs and pulling away from his flaring nostrils. The beads on the plastic necklace bury themselves in the folds of her neck.

Kadinsky blinks and his eyes darken. His fingers flutter over her body. He grows more demanding, snuffling for the scent of milk curdling in her bulbous nipples, the traces of sweated salt in the knobbles along her spine, hunting for the smell of entrails in the socket between her jerking buttocks, dipping his nose into all her cracks and crevices until she can endure it no longer and lets out a long cry of misery, fighting him away and rolling from the bed to hobble weeping from the room, still chased by her angry gaoler.

Kadinsky, thus satisfied, retires to scrub his hands with a plastic nail brush, cleans his teeth with an index finger, combs his hair, retrieves his jacket and coat and, having suitably rewarded the girl with enough money for a christening mug, quietly leaves the house to present himself, without further delay, at Conrad's security gates.

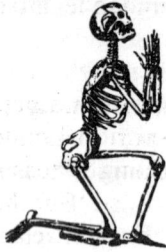

Conrad receives his visitor in a corner of the jungle hot-house. He's dressed for the occasion in a full-length black silk ballgown with a diamond necklace and matching earrings. He's standing beneath an ornamental palm that shoots like a fountain from a mighty Chinese bowl embossed with ceremonial dragons. Kadinsky, the trench-coat folded over his arm, sweats softly and opens an envelope containing the photographs of his targets taken by the security cameras hidden around the house. He leans against the edge of the bowl and studies the eyes of his victims.

'They'll be together,' says Conrad. 'The old one is crafty. He knows enough to look after himself. The young one is a noodle-brain but he's quick on his feet and he's plucky.'

'Are they running or hiding?' asks Kadinsky. His voice is so soft that Conrad must strain his ears to catch it. The words seem to float from his mouth like a whispering through a keyhole.

'They'll have taken cover,' growls Conrad, slapping the wall of the great bowl as if testing for the hollow ring of a priest hole among the roots.

'Do they know they'll be hit?'

'I gave them a friendly warning,' Conrad confesses, 'so they'll probably try to leave the country. Spain. Morocco. Florida. The old one is soft. He's going to chase the sun.'

'Are they clean?'

'No. They'll need passports and papers.'

'It's easy to find a passport in London.'

'That's true,' agrees Conrad, teasing the bunches of ribbons that decorate his waist. 'But they'll want to search out a man called Picasso. He's an artist. His passports are perfect. They won't be making any cheap mistakes. When you've found Picasso you'll find your targets.'

'Where does this man work?'

'Soho. Somewhere. You'll have to make contact with Ronnie the Scrubber. You'll find him at the Peekaboo Club along the back of Berwick Street. Threaten to break his fingers and he'll take you straight to Picasso. He's very obliging in that direction.'

'It shouldn't be difficult,' says Kadinsky. He returns the envelope to Conrad while he searches for a handkerchief to wipe the sweat from the back of his neck. Parakeets mock him from the treetops. Behind them, deep in the undergrowth, a tiger moans in its sleep.

'Make it fast. And make it nasty. I don't want them buried in pine boxes. I want them hosed from the walls and ceiling. What have you brought with you?'

'A camera. A Michelin guide. Three hundred Lucky Strike,' says Kadinsky mildly. He knows how to pack a suitcase bomb. He knows how to pack an overnight bag.

'What do you want?' says Conrad.

'What can you give me?'

'If you want to make a mess I can give you a shotgun. A Remington 870 packed with birdshot. That's enough to mincemeat a horse.'

'You're talking close-range work if you want that sort of penetration,' says Kadinsky, after a moment's reflection.

He doesn't look impressed. He wipes his hands in the handkerchief, polishes his fingernails.

'You want something heavier?' says Conrad, pulling nervously on his nose.

'I'd settle for an HK MP5 with 30-round mags. High impact. Deep saturation.'

'It's a problem finding the ammo,' says Conrad cautiously. This man is talking army-issue 9 mm sub-machine-guns! He's talking burgled military stores. He's talking Irish cabbage fields.

'I'll take a box of grenades if you've got a shotgun that fires them,' Kadinsky bargains with him. 'A Mossberg would be enough.'

'Grenades?'

'I'd prefer mortars.'

Conrad grins and grinds his teeth. Windows melt like sugar. Bricks turn to biscuit. Smoke. Flames. Bones burn. Blood boils like gravy. He'll teach them a lesson. He'll make them regret they abandoned him.

He retrieves his handbag from a clump of lilies and scratches inside for a few moments, spilling several lace handkerchiefs, a Swiss army knife and a large security whistle.

'Take a look in the gun room,' he says, offering Kadinsky a black key on a length of string. 'Whatever you need for the job.'

There is a crackling in the undergrowth and a maid appears with a tray of savoury morsels and glasses of chilled champagne. She approaches Kadinsky, attempts a curtsey, and holds out the tray before him.

He trades the trench-coat for a champagne flute and as the maid struggles to fold the coat on her shoulder he leans forward to sniff her skin, his nostrils flared, his eyes turning cloudy with desire.

'Good health!' barks Conrad, jerking his glass of champagne to his mouth and splashing his fingers and chin.

'You're wearing Dawn's diamonds,' says Kadinsky,

accepting a fancy tidbit. A wafer of toast trimmed with a curl of raw ham as pink and tight as a rosebud. He sniffs it lovingly, inhaling its ripe and naked odour, before slowly inserting it into his mouth.

Conrad looks startled, touches the necklace at his throat and is soon so befuddled with misery that he fails to enquire how Kadinsky should know the name of his wife.

'Twenty years,' he grieves. 'Twenty wretched miserable years. Twenty years of solitude.' He slumps against the Chinese bowl, wagging his head and staring forlornly into the jungle.

'I thought it was thirty,' says Kadinsky, staring at Conrad suspiciously.

'Twenty,' Conrad corrects him. 'She was young and she was beautiful and God Almighty snuffed out her life. She demised in the Caribbean. Stolen away. Swept out to sea with the mermaids and porpoises.'

'I didn't know.'

'It's true,' growls Conrad. 'Swept out to sea with the porpoises.'

'I came to your wedding,' says Kadinsky.

'I don't remember,' frowns Conrad. He stares at Kadinsky, casting back into his crowded memory, licking the edge of his champagne flute.

'It was 1962. I was fresh out of the army and working as a sniper in Algeria. I thought I'd found my vocation. But the shooting stopped in March and I never got paid so I came to London. I wanted to raise enough money to take me to the Sudan. I needed the price of a ticket. They said you could find me work.'

'What happened?'

'You invited me to your wedding.'

Conrad nods in approval making the diamonds flash on the fat truffles of ears. 'It was a huge affair. We had the best of everything. Harry Goldberg did the catering. The Beverley Sisters did a cabaret. They treated us like royalty.'

'I've never forgotten it.'

Conrad beams, puffed out with pleasure, and rinses his mouth with another glass of champagne. 'You'll join us for dinner,' he belches. 'You can meet my daughter. You'll enjoy that. You're going to be killing her boyfriend.'

'Does she know?'

'Yes!' says Conrad in surprise. 'We don't have any secrets in this family!' And he instructs the maid to show the assassin to his room.

But Valentine fails to join them at the dinner table and when Conrad sends someone to search her out he's told that she's retired for the night and has barricaded her door.

'Sulking!' he grumbles. 'They don't like it when you punish them. She's lucky I didn't give her a spanking.'

'Plucky girl,' says Kadinsky, cutting into a ripe cheese and watching it leak across the plate. 'Pugnacious like her mother.' He leans forward and draws up its dank odours of urine and rotting straw.

'Ah!' Conrad sighs and slips back into a reverie. 'Dawn was a glutton for punishment. Did you ever see her spanked in *Bullwhip Beauties*?'

'I believe the pleasure escaped me.'

'It's hell for leather in the old barn when the Grinning Gaucho gives Dawn and Dolores a taste of his tackle!' shouts Conrad, reciting the plot from memory.

'It doesn't ring any bells,' says Kadinsky.

'You must have seen *Bullwhip Beauties*!' says Conrad, hiding his disappointment in another glass of brandy. 'It's a classic. Dawn wears a special corset with stainless-steel wrist and ankle restrainers. Handmade. Natural leather.' He draws an hourglass with an undulating sweep of his hands and then smacks the hands together, locking the fingers, shaking them in the candlelight, describing a pair of invisible handcuffs. His face is flushed. His wattle quivers with excitement.

'Perhaps I was working abroad,' says Kadinsky, hoping

196

to pacify him. He fills his mouth with cheese and sets it melting through his teeth.

'We'll watch it downstairs!' cries Conrad, banging his chest with his shackled fists. 'We'll watch it together. Bring the bottle.' And he guides his guest from the pleasures of the table to the secrets of the basement.

Kadinsky escapes in the small hours of the morning with Conrad asleep and the Grinning Gaucho still flogging Dawn and Dolores with bullwhack and pizzle.

He steals through the silent house in search of his room along unfamiliar corridors. The brandy hurts his head and he finds himself tormented again by the smell of the pregnant halfwit unwrapped for him on his way from the airport. He tries to rekindle the memory of her pungent body, the rancid odours of skin and hair, when a bright breeze of perfume shocks his nose and throws him from the scent. He pauses, turns and locates the source of the intrusion lurking in the shadows of an antique cupboard.

'You're Valentine,' he whispers. The maids smell of nothing but soap and cologne buried in a broth of kitchen odours. Conrad smells like a pickle barrel fashioned from oak staves and iron rings. This must be Valentine or the living ghost of her mother.

A young woman steps into the light. She's wearing crimson silk pyjamas and a pair of brocade slippers. 'So you're the hired help,' she says softly, gazing at him with her beautiful Bedouin eyes. He's older than she imagined him but he's lean and hard and dangerous. She remembers the stories of his killings in Southern

Angola. The torture camps. The burial pits. The murder of women and children. 'How does it feel to do another man's dirty work?' she demands, trying to balance her trembling voice.

'It feels good!' he whispers. And when he smiles she feels her mouth and throat turn dry.

'What are you going to do to them?'

'I don't know what you're talking about.'

'Don't play games with me!'

'I'm here to follow your father's instructions,' he says simply, watching her with his pale eyes.

'He's a sick old man. He lives in a fantasy world.'

'I'm here to make his dreams come true.'

'Why don't you leave us alone? We're nothing to you.'

'I never break a contract.'

'How much is he paying you?'

'He's paying the price,' says Kadinsky and wonders if she's planning to raise a ransom. He doubts it. She'd have to pick her father's pockets and, besides, if she pays him ransom money he'll have to forfeit a good day's sport.

'You won't find them. You're too late,' she says defiantly, flicking her head to throw a gleaming curtain of hair swinging against her neck.

'Is that right?'

'They're heading for Glasgow.'

'It's cold in the north at this time of the year,' whispers Kadinsky.

'So what?'

'The frost gets into an old man's bones. Burns in the blood. I heard they'll be going south.'

'I don't care if they fry or freeze to death!' snaps Valentine, glaring back at him. 'They're nothing to me.' Her heart is pounding. He knows everything! He knows the direction of their escape. He'll track them down like runaway slaves and dig them out of hiding.

'You're not telling the truth,' says Kadinsky. He purses

his lips like a coquetting corpse. 'I think you care about one of them. I heard you were a naughty girl . . .'

'That's none of your business!' Her courage breaks down as she struggles to smother her tears. She curls her fingers into fists. She won't cry. She won't give him the satisfaction.

Kadinsky smiles. 'I heard he gave you a royal shagging.' He likes that. Royal shagging. It makes him laugh. It's something he heard in Amsterdam.

'You're disgusting!'

'Is it true?'

'Go to hell!'

'Is it true?'

'He didn't touch me.'

'Prove it!' He steps forward, breathing through his mouth in shallow spurts to protect himself from the volcanic heat of her many perfumes. If he can get close enough, if he can penetrate the pyjamas, there's a chance he'll catch the scent of her skin, the sweat of fear on her shoulders, the gloss of terror between her thighs, and that will give him the power he requires to gaze down into her soul.

'I don't have to prove anything to you,' she says, backing away from him. He's driving her into a wedge between the cupboard and the wall.

'Would you rather send an innocent man to the gallows?'

'What are you going to do?' She glances into his bleak face and finds something flickering in his eyes, some tiny flame of excitement as he stares up and down her pyjama buttons.

'I'll strike a bargain with you,' he whispers.

Valentine shakes her head, cringing away from his outstretched hand.

'I can smell if you're telling the truth,' he murmurs as he creeps forward, 'and if you're telling the truth we'll say no more about it. But if I can smell him on your skin . . . if I can smell where he fondled you . . .'

Valentine strikes the skirting board with her heels and flattens herself against the wall with her hands protecting her stomach. She wants to shout and scream, strike back at him, kick him where it hurts and run to the Turk for help. But she can only stand and watch in fascination as Kadinsky's hand reaches out to the collar of her pyjamas.

'I won't hurt you . . .' he gasps as his fingertips touch her neck, flutter down to her breasts and pick at the jacket buttons.

She shuts her eyes and whimpers, waiting for him to seize her with his cold and murderous hands. But Kadinsky grunts and recoils in horror, snatching away his fingers as if her skin had scalded him, retreating from the astringent assault of jasmine, tuberose and vanilla; musk, amber and frankincense; hawthorn, honeysuckle and cedar; lavender and sandalwood. Her poisonous brew of bottled scents stings his nostrils, burns through his delicate mucous membranes, scouring his nose and making him sneeze.

'You're disgusting!' Valentine tells him again, quickly pulling her jacket together. She doesn't know what's happening here but she's quick to seize the advantage.

Kadinsky gropes for his handkerchief to shield his mouth and nose from destruction. It's as if he's been caught by a violent fit that all but cripples him. He gasps and chokes and sucks at the air like a man in danger of suffocation.

Valentine ventures forward and to her great astonishment Kadinsky starts to retreat, stumbling along the corridor. 'Do you know what my father would do if he knew you were trying to fuck me?' she hisses triumphantly as she chases him to his bedroom door.

'You're a stupid girl!' growls Kadinsky, turning abruptly and making her stop in her tracks. His eyes are wild. His voice is reduced to the merest whisper. 'Did you think I would shag you like a tart?'

'You'd do anything!'

'You're wrong. I have very particular inclinations. You'll discover them for yourself if you try to interfere with me.'

'I'd rather kill myself!' she spits at him.

He springs forward, grabbing her hair and twisting her savagely to the floor. 'Oh, but that's essential!' he whispers into her face. 'And while you're still warm I'm going to strip you and wash down your corpse . . .'

Silence settles over the house.

Valentine bolts her bedroom door and lies awake in the dark waiting for Kadinsky, shrunk to the size of a woodlouse, to scramble up through a crack in the floor or batter with black crow wings against the shivering glass of the window.

Kadinsky sleeps softly, dreaming of the long, malodorous summers he spent as a boy exploring the town drains and butchers' shops, urinals, kennels and public laundries.

The Turk in the basement dormitory, having locked the house and set the security systems, is left with nothing but to count the maids and, finding none murdered or missing, snaps out the lights and tiptoes to bed, thankfully wrapping himself in the blankets.

Conrad, alone in the cinema, sits and continues to stare at Dawn who looms majestically over him, taunting him with her loose-limbed peformance, mocking him with her youth and beauty. His hands are stretched out in supplication. His eyes are brimming with tears.

Silence settles over the house adrift in the rain-drenched night.

Valentine is woken by a pair of maids wailing at her bedroom door. When she throws back the bolts and demands to know their business they cannot speak but find themselves struck dumb with terror, grasping her by the wrists and running her down the corridor towards the marble staircase. The ribbons fly from their aprons and their legs are flashing like angry scissors. They can't stop running until they reach the family doctor, standing guard at the steps to the basement cinema. And here they promptly abandon her and hurry away, hand in hand, to howl in the freedom of the kitchen pantry.

'What's happened?'

'He's gone,' says the doctor softly, placing a hand on her shoulder, and he lets the monocle fall from his eye as a token of respect for the dead. 'One of the maids found him sitting in front of *Bullwhip Beauties* at five twenty-five this morning. She said he looked so peaceful she thought he was asleep until she noticed that his teeth had fallen out. That's when they called for my services. I'm sorry.'

He dips into his pocket and removes a top set of porcelain teeth wrapped in a large blue handkerchief. Valentine stares at the teeth, the pendulum swing of the monocle, and continues to wait for the floundering physician to give her some word or sign to tell her this is only a dream that will pass in another moment or two and she'll find herself in bed again with the maids waiting to serve her coffee.

'I want to see him,' she says at last.

The doctor takes her hand, folds her fingers into a fist and presses the knuckles against his mouth for the comfort of it. 'His heart stopped,' he murmurs. 'We shall have to take him away. You understand. It's routine. We'll want to examine him before we issue the death certificate.'

'Yes. Whatever you think.'

'I'll write you a prescription. Is there anything in particular? I can give you something to calm you down, something to perk you up, something to keep you awake, something to put you to sleep . . .' he says, staring mournfully into the folds of her dressing gown.

'No. There's nothing.'

'Why don't we go down and say goodbye to him?'

'Yes.' She allows the doctor to fondle her arm as he leads her down the stairs. His clothes smell of mentholate snuff. She notices, for the first time, a crumpled pair of surgeon's gloves hanging from his jacket pocket. The cinema is cold. The lights have been turned down. The curtain is drawn against the screen.

Here rests the Mirrors of Mars, the Darkness at Noon, the Storm in the Eye of Phosphorus.

Here rests the Grand Panjandrum of Paddington, the Hammer of Highgate, Golem of Golders Green, Mayhem of Mayfair, Doomsday Dundreary, Last of the Mohocks, King of Buncombe, clan chief of the Gaberlunzie, Beelzebub the Babbler, Napoleon in Fancy Nylons, Attila the Hen, Jumping Jack-pudding, Baron Bruiser, the Sultan of Sleaze.

Valentine stares at her father and finds him reduced by death to nothing more than a fat old man in soiled knickers and a faded frock.

He sits in his favourite chair, his head bent to his chest

and his arms thrust between his knees. The black silk ballgown sags from his chest, breaking in waves around his splayed legs and spreading across the floor. His skin is dreadfully white. His nose and mouth are turning blue. The air is pickled with urine and brandy.

'He didn't suffer,' says the doctor gently.

'His heart,' says Valentine, venturing as far as the chair and staring at the empty brandy bottle caught in the folds of his skirts. Sad and unlovely old man. She wonders if she's expected to weep. She feels nothing. She is empty. She has been abandoned.

'His heart,' confirms the doctor. 'And his liver and lights. I gave him advice. He never listened. Did he make any arrangements? Do you know if he left instructions?'

'Instructions?' She gathers her courage and removes the necklace at her father's neck, fumbles with the diamonds that dangle still from the blue and bristling ears. A pity to waste them. Is it true that diamonds melt in fire?

'The funeral,' says the doctor. 'The final resting place.'

'I want him cremated,' says Valentine firmly. 'I want his ashes sealed in a bottle.' She slips the earrings into a pocket, wraps the necklace in her fist.

The doctor glances at the bereaved but doesn't care to question the wisdom of her decision. Grief reveals itself in a thousand different disguises. 'Would you like me to remove his frock?' he suggests. 'Perhaps we could find him some pyjamas. It might be more appropriate . . .'

'He's wearing his favourite gown. Don't disturb him.'

'I've already phoned for an ambulance. Do you want me to leave you alone with him?'

'No!' Valentine shakes her head and steps away from the corpse. 'I think I should go and speak to the maids.'

The doctor smiles and screws back his monocle, fussing around the dead emperor like a little haberdasher, pulling at the lines of the gown, arranging the tucks and pleats, letting Valentine make her retreat.

Kadinsky, aroused by the noise of the maids and the

shimmering scent of death, lies in wait at the top of the stairs. A jackal excited by carrion. He's wearing a loose cotton dressing gown and a silver chain at his throat. His bare feet are sheaves of bones, wrapped in strings of green vein.

As Valentine emerges he scoops her violently into his arms, making her yelp as she wriggles loose and presses herself to the wall. The necklace clutched in her fist sparkles like a fire-drake's tail.

'What happened?' he whispers, restless and grinning, nodding towards the cinema stairs.

'It's finished,' she says briskly. 'You can get out.'

'He's dead?' says Kadinsky and whistles.

'My father no longer requires your services.'

'I never abandon my clients,' he says, reaching out with a lazy hand to pull at her sleeve.

'You no longer have a client!' she says fiercely, snatching her sleeve away. 'Don't you understand? You don't have any business here. This is my house and I'm telling you to leave.'

'I never leave unfinished business,' he says, smiling, scratching his jaw with his fingernails.

'What does it take to get rid of you?' she hisses. 'What do you want? Why can't you leave me alone?' Her pleading leaves her strangled and she swallows hard, tasting the salt of tears in her throat.

'Let me look at the necklace,' he says suddenly, snapping his fingers.

Valentine stares at the fire in her fist. 'It's old. Genuine antique,' she says hopefully, surrendering the diamonds.

Kadinsky grunts and stares at the stones. He weighs them, rattles them, holds them to the light, sniffs at them suspiciously. He glares at them through narrowed eyes, holds them to his mouth and breathes on them, allows them to swing from his bony wrist.

'Take it,' Valentine urges him. 'Take the necklace and leave me alone.' Her heart is pounding. She'll give him rubies and amethysts. She'll give him sapphires and strings of opals.

Kadinsky smiles, watching the tears as they start to spill from her dark and glittering eyes. 'It's not enough,' he whispers and throws the necklace to the floor.

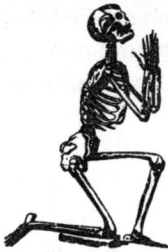

The morning is cold. The sky, washed with rain, gleams like a polished steel bowl. Frank and Webster stand among the tombstones feeding a bonfire with the contents of Conrad's treasure chest.

'It's time she had a Christian burial,' says Webster, tossing letters into the fire and perhaps, by this simple act of cremating the dreams of her thousand tormentors, they are helping to lay Dawn to rest.

The fire eats away at the mildewed declarations of love, promises of unholy wedlock, death threats and sporting photographs of their authors wearing hoods and gauntlets in corners of suburban sitting rooms.

The smoke gathers the pamphleteers into a dark and wobbling column, rolling them together, a tower of corpulent satyrs wielding handcuffs and corkscrew dildoes, pushing them as high as the trees where it gradually dissolves in the sunlight.

'When are we going to leave?' says Frank, as they throw the empty chest to the fire.

'Are you ready?' says Webster, slapping his jacket. His pockets are stuffed with money, fat rolls of banknotes retrieved from the floorboards in the attic. His vest has been lined with travellers' cheques. He's equipped to travel the world.

'There's nothing to keep me here,' says Frank, yet finds himself glancing towards the gates, still hoping that Valentine will appear to join them in their great escape.

'We'll go down to Soho and pick up some passports and then we'll be as free as the birds,' says Webster.

'Is it really that simple?'

'People disappear every day of the week. Hundreds of them. They walk away from their lives and vanish. You know that. You've done it yourself.'

Above their heads the serpent of dreams uncoils in a sparkling flight of chains, shackles, curry-combs and bastinadoes. The fire crackles and spits as it drives out the last of the demons.

'And Kadinsky?'

'Kadinsky won't bother his head. By the time he gets here and starts the hunt the trail will be cold. And we'll be burning our feet on a coral beach on the other side of the world.'

'And Valentine?'

Webster kicks at the scattering embers. 'She's a survivor. She won't come to any great harm. When we've settled ourselves we'll send her a ticket and tell her to come for a visit. We'll buy ourselves a villa and keep a few rooms for guests.' He's still a fugitive and yet he's already planning barbecues and beach parties, sending out invitations to friends.

Frank looks out towards the far wall of the cemetery where the rhododendrons are pushing their way through the ranks of headstones. He won't leave without Valentine. He'll take Webster to the airport and help him catch his flight to the sun. And then he'll come back into town and find a way to reach Valentine without getting caught in Conrad's trap. He's resolved to tell Webster at the boarding gate when there's no time left for arguments. Webster must get away from here. After all the years of fighting Conrad's battles he's earned the right to walk around in a straw hat and beach towel.

He's been awake for most of the night trying to work out a plan for survival. He knows he can escape Kadinsky by finding a suitable foxhole. There are thousands of cheap hotels in this city. He'll rent a room and sit in the dark, waiting for the danger to pass him. The footsteps in the corridor beyond the door. The telephone that rings at midnight. He'll rent a room and fill it with silence. Webster and Conrad are old street fighters. They believe the universe to be in a state of perpetual conflict. Their lives are nothing but trials of strength. Frank has been taught to avoid confrontation. His own life has been an elaborate game of surrender and compromise. He'll survive again by imitating death. He'll win his freedom by enduring a term of imprisonment. Despite all the talk of a blissful old age, he suspects that Webster has resigned himself to meeting a sudden and violent end.

'Did you bring a gun?'

'Shooters?' says Webster with a look of disgust. 'We don't need shooters. We're going to make a fresh start.' And to demonstrate his commitment to their new life he trudges back to the cottage and returns with a pile of his own precious scrapbooks and throws them onto the funeral pyre.

The Peekaboo Club is a basement beneath a bookshop in a passage linking Berwick with Brewer Street in Soho. A neon sign fizzles on a frosted-glass door: Take Your Own Photos of our Lovely Nude Models. The passage is stuffed with key-cutters and tattoo artists, bed shows and massage parlours. The air is heavy with the stink of hotdogs and deep-fried doughnuts. Tourists shuffle through this arcade, silent and staring, heckled by pimps and beckoned by rent boys, checking their street maps for direction as they fondle the clasps on their money belts. At night, when the lights turn the cobbles to rhinestones, the passage becomes a circus freak show filled with whispered promises of dangerous delights.

Frank and Webster arrive in the early evening, pushing through the market in Rupert Street, avoiding the drunks, the dippers and junkies, ignoring the tarts, the touts and the tourists, and find themselves, delivered at last, beside the bookshop window.

'Keep your eyes open and your mouth shut,' says Webster softly as he checks the address.

Frank open his eyes on the bookshop window and peers at the rows of magazines. Beaver Bondage. Gut-bucket Glamour. Prosthetic Parade. Wet-Nurse Wonder.

Frollicking Fatties. Beneath the magazines, shelves of vibrators like curious plastic gherkins. In one corner of the window inflatable rubber women with faces like goldfish are folded into dusty boxes. Behind the boxed women, displays of leather underwear, rubber pants and aprons.

He follows Webster through the frosted-glass door and down a steep staircase where they find themselves in a corridor guarded by a girl in a cardigan and a pair of old trousers. The girl sits in a torn armchair wedged beneath the stairs. A small table beside the chair is covered in cheap cartridge cameras, packs of film, a dirty ashtray and copies of *Hello!* and *Chat*. After the noise of the street above them the silence seems startling.

'It costs twenty quid,' the girl tells them, without moving from the chair. An electric fire glows at her feet. 'We supply the camera, the film and the model of your requirements guaranteed in the nude. That's me.' She looks at Frank and tries a smile as she pulls herself from the chair and draws back a curtain to reveal the little studio.

They are staring into a shabby basement room containing two chairs, a paraffin stove and a black sheet tacked to one wall as a backdrop. A plastic shopping bag on the floor spills a jumble of crumpled underwear.

'I can work in different costumes if you want something special,' the girl tells them as she kicks at the bag with her foot. She picks out a scruffy nylon bra and holds it against her cardigan like a mad woman picking through charity clothes.

'Spare me the sales talk,' says Webster, turning his back on the studio. 'Where's Ronnie the Scrubber?'

'Who wants to know?'

'His mother.'

'Fifteen quid,' says the girl stubbornly, directing herself at Frank. She looks so cold and bored. Her face has the shine of candle wax, a dark rash spreading around her eyes, her long nose peeling raw at the nostrils. 'Twenty-four pictures. Different poses.'

'Ronnie the Scrubber,' says Webster.

'He's not here.' The girl pulls a little wad of Kleenex from her sleeve and dabs at the tip of her nose, unpicking the damp paper ball, turning it inside out, dabbing her nose again.

'Where do we find him?'

'Ten quid,' haggles the girl, still trying to work on Frank. 'Ten quid. Semi-nude. Twenty-four pictures. Different poses. No extras. Guaranteed. You can afford ten quid.'

Frank smiles, tries to imagine her cardigan as part of her bump-and-grind routine. Is she alone in this mousery? Where there's a girl at work there should be a pimp in waiting.

'Give me the price on Ronnie the Scrubber,' says Webster, putting his hand in his pocket.

'You're narks!' snorts the girl in disgust and having reached this dismal conclusion retires again to the comfort of the armchair. 'It's frigging cold!' she adds miserably as she wraps herself in her arms.

'What do you keep down there?' enquires Frank, pointing towards a small door at the end of the corridor.

'I dunno. It's private offices.'

The words Strickly Private have been daubed on the door in thick red paint. Webster leans his weight against it and the door springs open on twisted hinges to reveal a dimly lit storeroom. The girl turns her back, crouched in silent misery as the narks disappear in the twilight.

The brick vault is filled with crates and boxes, bales of books and magazines. Clockwork cocks from Hong Kong. Suction pumps from Korea. A deflated rubber doll hangs from a hook on the wall like the freshly boiled skin of a woman, cooked and boned in hell's own kitchen.

Beyond the crates, a gaunt young black man with a mane of tangled daglocks is stretched on a camp bed flicking through copies of *Gang-Bang* and *Gobble*. He's wearing a Terminator sweatshirt, jeans and fancy ostrich boots. His fingers are covered with heavy gold rings. His head, plugged into a Walkman, trembles with self-inflicted chorea. On the ground beside the bed, within the lazy sweep of his arm, a tin of rolling tobacco, an empty hamburger carton and a bottle of Old Kentucky bourbon. Frank and Webster have reached his bed before he knows they are in the room.

'Hey! Don't you read? It says Pry-Vit! Right? You got shit for brains?' He leaps from the bed, tossing the magazines aside, ripping the Walkman from his ears, crushing his tobacco tin with the heel of an ostrich-leather boot.

'Ronnie the Scrubber!' beams Webster, strolling among the stacks of boxes while Frank sits down on the bed and flicks through the *Gang-Bang Christmas Special*. 'Where's Picasso?'

'I dunno nothing! Right?' shouts Ronnie, retrieving his tobacco tin from the floor. But he looks scared, startled awake by these strange intruders, glancing around for fear there are others beyond the door waiting to smash his skull with hammers.

'You're a cheap little smack-head, Ronnie,' says Webster sadly, breaking into a carton of dildoes. 'I don't have time to play games with you. Tell me where we can find Picasso.'

'I don't know him!'

'You worked for him.'

'I worked a lot of different places. You know what I mean? I done all sorts of work. Right?'

'And you worked for Picasso until he threw you out.'

'What's it worth? Everything worth something. Right?' says Ronnie, satisfied now that they've come to trade and taking courage from the hunting knife that he likes to keep hidden inside his boot. Nobody leans on him. Right? Nobody frightens Ronnie the Scrubber.

'It's worth a lot to me, Ronnie,' declares Webster. 'It's worth the effort of driving this boner up your arse.' He

215

holds the dildo in his fist and smacks it through the air like a cudgel. It's a truncheon of epic proportions, long and curved, as thick as a man's wrist, the glans resplendent above a collar of hard rubber nipples.

Ronnie spits through a chink in his teeth and wipes his chin with the palm of his hand. 'You know the Yardies, man? You get heavy with me. Right? You know what they going to do to you?'

Webster sighs and shakes his head like a man grown tired of a taunting child. 'You want me to hurt you, Ronnie?'

'I dunno nothing, man! I dunno nothing!'

'Poke him!' shouts Webster.

Frank throws down the magazine and pulls himself from the bed in time to catch the weapon as Webster throws it towards him.

'Shit!' growls Ronnie. 'Shit!' He slouches forward, reaching for the blade in his boot, but Webster knocks him down with a neat slap to the side of his head that sends him spinning against the bed.

Ronnie, his face buried in blanket and daglocks, struggles to get away, pumping with his elbows and knees, but Frank and Webster have thrown their full weight behind him.

'Take his knife!' says Webster, as they hold their victim against the bed.

'Leave it alone, man!'

'We need the blade, Ronnie,' says Webster, the sympathetic surgeon. 'We're going to cut through your belt to help you out of your jeans.'

Frank squirms around and catches Ronnie by his legs. Talk, you dumb bastard! How far do they have to take this threat? Ronnie may not be impressed by his fate but it scares the bejabers from Frank. Dear God! Talk, you stupid stubborn bastard! Say something to save yourself from the wrath of the Taiwan Tickler. He finds the handle of a knife protruding from the top of a boot, pulls it from

216

its hiding place and the rush of steel against ankle bone proves enough to break Ronnie's nerve.

'Fantastic Travel!' he splutters through the heat of the blanket. 'Fantastic Travel! That's all I know, man!'

Webster turns him around and pins him down with a hand to his throat. 'Give me the address.'

'It's somewhere along Beak Street. Right? I don't know exact. It's called Fantastic Travel. Right?'

Webster seems satisfied with this snippet of information. He takes the knife from Frank and throws it across the storeroom while Ronnie crawls from the bed, pulls at his sweatshirt, strokes his daglocks.

'Thanks for your help,' says Frank cheerfully, smacking him in the chest with a tattered magazine.

'I dunno nothing,' says Ronnie, watching them retreat before searching for solace in Old Kentucky. 'I dunno nothing.'

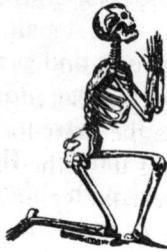

They are walking down Brewer Street when Frank remembers the dildo still clenched like a rolling pin in his fist. There's nowhere to throw it and no pocket big enough to contain it.

'Do you have any peppermints?' asks Webster, slapping his tongue against his teeth. He strides forward, glancing anxiously at his watch, determined to reach Fantastic Travel before the door is locked for the night.

'No,' says Frank, stuffing the dildo under his jacket. 'I never carry them.'

'I need something,' grumbles Webster. 'Scrubber Ronnie always leaves a bad taste in my mouth.' So they pause at a little tobacco shop and while Webster buys a tube of mints, Frank whips open his jacket and plunges the offensive weapon into an ice-cream freezer where it disappears in the frost and snow, lost among the chocolate Cornettos.

Fantastic Travel is wedged behind a barber's shop and an empty grocery store. Between the posters in the window they can see a solitary figure sitting at a long counter, reading and smoking a midget cigar.

'That's our man!' says Webster, pressing his nose against the glass.

Frank is looking at a rumpled old man in a grey suit with a wilting bow tie at his throat.

'I think it's our man,' says Webster, cracking a pepper-mint.

'Let's go and talk to him,' says Frank. It's getting cold and the street is filled with a grey diesel fog. But when he tries to enter the shop he finds the door locked against him.

Frank bangs on the door until the old man is annoyed enough to scowl from the counter and wave them away with a skeleton hand.

'Open the door, you daft bugger!' shouts Webster. He pulls a roll of money from one of his pockets and thumps it against the glass, grinning and nodding his head by way of encouragement. There must be five hundred pounds or more pressed in that dog-eared bundle.

The sight of so much money, waved in happy mummery, has a galvanising effect on the old man, who plugs the cigar in his mouth and hurries forward to unbolt the door.

'We're looking for Picasso,' says Webster as they step quickly into the shop. The place smells of rubber mats, newspaper print and smoke. Fluorescent ceiling panels cast a spluttering light on racks of leaflets, brochures and guides. A poster on the wall above the counter depicts a girl in a swimsuit having the time of her life in Botswana surrounded by dusty, grinning bushmen.

'I'm Picasso,' smiles the old man and cocks his head, squinting at Webster over a pair of bent wire spectacles. 'I know you. I've seen you. What's your name?'

'Webster Boston,' says Webster.

'That's right!' exclaims Picasso, pulling the cigar from his mouth. 'Webster Boston. Who's that?' he demands, nodding at Frank.

'Frank Fisher,' says Frank.

'Frank Fisher!' smiles Picasso. 'I knew I recognised that face. How can I help you, gents?' He glances hopefully at the pocket where Webster has stowed the money.

'We need passports.'

'That's easy enough.'

'We need them tonight.'

Picasso plugs back the cigar and ponders Webster for a long time.

'Late travel plans?' he says at last.

'Something like that.'

'The sudden urge to get away? Clean break? Good for the health? Doctor's orders?'

'You've caught the drift of it,' says Webster.

'Government property, passports,' says Picasso.

'Worth a lot of money in the wrong hands, I should imagine,' says Webster, tapping the buttons on his shirt.

'Bad business if they get stolen. Best to keep them under lock and key,' says Picasso, nodding to a small office at the back of the counter. 'What was your name again?'

'What names have you got?'

Picasso bolts the door to the shop, ushers them around the counter and into the office, where he unlocks a tall cupboard to reveal the entrance to a secret workshop. This room, with its high ceiling and tessellated floor, has been cut from an old-fashioned scullery lost a hundred years before when the building was chopped and divided into a warren of offices. A rusty skylight has been sealed with wet leaves and pigeon droppings. An extractor fan in the wall has been stuffed with rags. A wooden bench, in the centre of the room, is cluttered with bottles of inks and solvents, boxes of rubber stamps, scalpels, spoons and engraving tools; glues, clips and masking tape; the humble paraphernalia of a man who is master of his craft.

'Sit down and make yourselves comfortable,' says Picasso, switching on the lights and waving them into a cracked leather sofa.

'How long does it take?' says Frank.

'A passport? It takes time. Do you want a drink?' Picasso blinks around the room, searching for a bottle of whisky.

'No, we're anxious to get away,' says Frank, unsettled by the old man's ditherings.

'Patience,' says Picasso. He sucks at the butt of his cigar and blows a wobbling ring of smoke at the ceiling.

'If there's something we can do to help . . .' says Webster. He pulls the roll of money from his shirt and tosses it at the bench.

'It's the labour that is so expensive,' says Picasso, brushing a spill of ash from his sleeve, and Webster is obliged to remove a second and third bundle of notes from his person before the old man is sufficiently encouraged to set about his work.

'The old British stiff-back was a beauty,' he says, opening an ancient safe set in the brickwork beside the sofa. He stashes the money and retrieves a heavy, brown envelope. The envelope contains a dozen passports in various stages of construction. 'In the old days, with a bottle of solvent and a blunt die, you could switch a passport in half an hour.' He splits the envelope and scatters the contents over the bench. 'These modern European passports are bitches.'

'They look like coupon books,' says Frank, peering at the assortment of pages that Picasso begins to arrange beneath the light of his lamp.

'Cheap and nasty but intricate,' says Picasso. 'Machine readable. Protected with plastic security shields. There's no trust left in the world. They have to be taken apart every time you recycle them.'

He takes their photographs with a Polaroid passport camera and sets out to match their portraits with suitable new identities from the small selection before him.

'Can you do it?' says Webster anxiously.

'A whisker short of perfect,' chuckles Picasso. 'Two white males of uncertain age. No distinguishing marks.'

The mug shots are lightly glued in position and the finished inside back covers, complete with serial codes and computer check digits, are fed through a lamination machine, taking care to ensure that the plastic coating bleeds a fraction into the gutter for the sake of appearances. There should be a narrow margin of plastic peeping through on the inside front cover. It makes the difference. He's a stickler for detail. An artist.

'Have you made your travel arrangements?' he enquires as he checks the effect beneath his lamp.

'I want to feel the sun on my head,' says Webster, stroking his skull. 'I want to feel the sand in my shoes.'

'I can get you down to Spain on a flight tomorrow morning. It comes as a package. Cancellation. Seven days. Half board. Courtesy bus to the hotel. Welcome drinks. Complimentary tickets for the folk and flamenco dancing . . .'

'We were thinking of something a trifle exotic,' says Webster, looking very disappointed. 'Sumatra. Java. The South China Sea.'

'Tomorrow morning?'

'Yes.'

Picasso shakes his head and smiles. 'Take my advice and fly down to Spain. Why make life so difficult?'

'We'll take it,' says Frank, afraid that Webster is going to start an argument. As the passports take shape he feels overcast with guilt knowing that, whatever passage they pick tonight, he'll abandon their plan tomorrow in favour of finding Valentine.

He watches while the interior pages, printed with elaborate cobwebs the colour of broken veins, are carefully paginated and stitched together again by running them through a sewing machine.

'That's the ticket!' says Picasso. 'You can buy a visa in Spain that will take you to South America. I'll give you the name of a man who can help you to grease a few palms. You'll find him at the Hotel Suncrest in Alicante.'

'South America?' says Webster suspiciously.

'Panama. Ecuador. Peru. This time next week you could be looking at the Pacific with nothing beyond but paradise.

222

Tahiti. Samoa. Fiji. Scattered strings of islands as far as the Coral Sea.'

Webster grins and turns to Frank with his face bright with pleasure. 'What do you think, Frank?'

'It sounds good,' admits Frank and marvels at the way Picasso has turned a week in Spain into a prospect of blue lagoons and distant jungle volcanoes.

The familiar claret covers, gold embossed with their coat of arms, are pasted into position and the finished passports are set to dry.

'Ronald Wister!' hoots Webster, reading aloud from the back of his book when he finally takes possession. He repeats his new name several times, rolling it around his mouth to savour its unfamiliar flavour.

'Denzil Plowman,' says Frank, checking his own identity before slipping the passport into his pocket.

'I'm famished!' says Webster. The business is complete and he's ready to celebrate. 'Let's go down into Chinatown and have a big bowl of noodles.'

'That's a very generous invitation,' says Picasso, pulling the spectacles from his ears and wiping his eyes with his sleeve. 'But my wife is waiting at home and I have to finish your paperwork.'

'Spare ribs with plum sauce,' says Webster, hoping to tempt him away. 'Bean curd soup with chicken threads.'

'You're trying to get me into trouble,' grins Picasso, leading them from the workshop and switching out the lights.

'If you change your mind we'll be at the Nan Cheng,' says Webster, watching the old man rummage beneath the counter.

'Send me a postcard from Alicante,' says Picasso. He presents them with their flight tickets, hotel vouchers, complimentary cards for the Star Lite Beach Club and six free luggage labels, all neatly packed in a red, white and blue Fantastic Travel folder, and the fugitives return to the streets.

'We'll spend the night on the town,' says Webster as they walk through Golden Square towards the lights of Piccadilly. 'We can sleep on the plane tomorrow.'

Frank walks beside him in silence, isolated and withdrawn, already divorced from the ordinary world like a sick man preparing for surgery. He has twelve hours left to make a decision. Twelve hours before the flight leaves for Spain. His sense of doom increases with Webster's exuberance. When they reach the airport tomorrow morning will he watch Webster Boston the bruiser change into Ronald Wister the tourist and take to the skies without him? What's left for him if he stays behind? The idea of reaching Valentine by circumnavigating her father already seems impossible. Returning to the gatehouse unannounced, taking her by surprise, he's half-afraid he'll find her in the arms of another man. Nothing is certain. Nothing can be trusted.

The gardens of Golden Square are deserted but for a solitary shadow stalking through the shrubbery. The shadow calls out to them and reaches out a hand clutching an empty alms-dish in the shape of a waxed paper cup. Webster ignores it. Frank pokes in his pockets and throws a cascade of coins on the ground.

Emerging from Lower James Street they walk briskly through the narrow corridor of Sherwood Street, where a few old drinkers have already settled down for the night pressed against the warmth of the ventilation shafts set in the buttresses of the Regent Palace Hotel; and turning at Dunkin' Donuts, on the corner of Glasshouse Street, they are swept into Piccadilly Circus on a rushing tide of noise and lights.

Here, beneath the neon scaffolds, the pavements are crowded with people, laughing and eating, smoking and spitting, swearing and calling to one another; swilling from every direction, swarming from the steps of the Underground, dashed against railings and floodlit doorways, spilling over the glittering streets and pushed into frightened, trampling herds by the sudden jolting of heavy traffic.

Here are shop girls and filing clerks, secretaries and paper shufflers, surging forward to Leicester Square, already late for the last performance. Here are car thieves and card sharks, Jack the Lad and Jack of Diamonds, trawling the night for the smell of excitement. Here are wives of the senior board, hunchbacked by furs and diamond earrings, come to fork prawns at the Cafe Royal. Here are fat corporation men, seized by satyriasis, dreaming of mixing business with pleasure. Here are crocodiles of salesmen wearing identical travel suits with paper badges pinned to their collars: Fullers' Link Chain & Gate Convention – please return to the London Hilton. Here are the lost and found, the blessed and the damned. Here are hawkers of dogmeat burgers, candyfloss and coloured sherbets, postcards and tinsel souvenirs. Here are tarts touting, dippers drifting, totters picking the waste bins and gutters, and gangs of swaggering hobbledehoys everywhere saluting the night with cans of Carlsberg, smack, crack and poppers.

The multitude swarms and surges, pulling Frank and Webster forward, lifting them from their feet, bearing

225

them aloft and throwing them down again like casks on a storming ocean until, when all direction seems lost, they are slung from the rim of the vortex into Shaftesbury Avenue where they hurry, impatient and angry, to the gates of Chinatown.

The night is scented at last with star anise and coriander. The pavements are piled with baskets of fruit and dried fish, gourds, cabbage and salted eggs. Shop windows are filled with curious trinkets, books in impossible languages, charts of traditional acupuncture. The five elements and their seasons. The officials aligned for cosmic balance. Frank's spirits lift again, bewitched by the sudden shift in surroundings, until they reach the Nan Cheng, set in a gloomy terrace along a cobbled back street.

'It's a modest enough arrangement,' admits Webster, surveying the scuffed red paintwork and panes of dirty glass. A faded menu, mounted in a bamboo frame, hangs from greasy cords in the window. 'They save their energy for the food. It was voted Triad canteen of the year.' Nothing can smother his bright, good humour. He's here to celebrate and nothing is going to stop him.

A young Chinese waiter approaches them as they push through the door and leads them to a table against one wall. The table is laid with red paper napkins, a bottle of soy sauce and a glass egg cup filled with toothpicks. The restaurant is empty. Tonight the Triads must be eating French or Italian. Elaborate silk and lacquer lanterns, hoary with dust, hang from a tongue-and-groove ceiling. Posters on the walls provide a series of sentimental views of mountains and pagodas. A beaded glass curtain conceals a passage that leads to the lavatories and kitchen.

'You want a drink?' the waiter asks them as they settle themselves on the narrow chairs. He's wearing a green shirt with black polyester trousers, cut very low at the hips and polished at the pockets and seams. His broad face holds an expression of vague but universal contempt.

'Two beers,' says Frank.

226

'And tea,' says Webster. 'China tea.'

'Two tea,' says the waiter, snapping open a notebook and scratching an entry with a ballpoint pen.

'China tea,' confirms Webster.

'And two beers,' says Frank.

The waiter presents them with menu cards and disappears through the beaded curtain.

'You've got to stop thinking about Valentine,' says Webster gently, while they meditate on the merits of sweet and sour quick supper special. He glances at Frank across the top of his menu.

'Is it so obvious?'

'Yes. Think about stuffed squid and spicy noodles.'

Frank drops his card and rattles the toothpicks in the egg cup. 'If I hadn't made such a fool of myself we wouldn't be in this mess. Maybe I'll have the bean curd and pickles. Do you want to share some rainbow rolls or shall we have the pork pancakes?'

'Pork pancakes,' says Webster, beaming. 'She's a lovely girl, Frank. Vain. Stubborn. Cantankerous. Selfish. Just the way I like 'em. I'm surprised I'm not in love with her myself.'

'I thought you were.'

'Let's wait until we're a thousand miles from here before we start feeling homesick,' says Webster, pulling open his paper napkin and trying to stuff his collar.

'You ready?' asks the waiter, returning with their drinks.

Frank runs his finger down the menu. 'We'll have seventeen. Twenty-one. Thirty. Thirty-three and a small forty-nine.'

'No thirty-three.'

'Twelve?' suggests Webster.

'No twelve,' says the waiter.

'Twenty-seven?'

The waiter looks puzzled. 'You want twenty-seven *and* twenty-one?'

227

'Yes.'

The waiter pauses, waiting for them to change their minds, and when it's obvious they're too proud to admit their mistake he gathers up the menu cards and strolls away to share the joke with the kitchen.

The food, when it arrives, is hot and delicious. Stir-fried squid and red peppers. Fat slices of omelette stuffed with pork and shrimp. Steamed fish. Deep bowls of spicy noodles.

'I should have been stronger,' says Frank, dipping into a bowl of pickles. 'I should have stopped her from going home. How is she going to handle Conrad?'

'It makes it easier,' says Webster. 'He doesn't care about you and me. He just wants to keep a hold on his daughter.'

'But she can't stay with him in that house. It's monstrous!'

'Give it time,' says Webster. 'Give it a couple of months in the sun while the old devil calms down and comes to his senses. It can't last. Valentine knows how to deal with him.'

'What happens if something goes wrong?' says Frank.

But Webster isn't listening. He's staring at the door to the street, his chopsticks dangling in his fingers, a noodle slithering from his mouth and falling against his sleeve.

An elderly man, supported by two large bodyguards, enters the restaurant and shuffles painfully to their table. He's wearing yellow kid gloves and an overcoat with an astrakhan collar. The men who flank him are built like blacksmiths dressed in voluminous raincoats.

'Most rewarding!' says Talbot, directing himself at Webster. 'I was rather afraid we had missed you!' He allows himself a cadaverous smile and looks around at the empty tables.

Webster leans back in his chair and stares at his aged adversary, considers the size of his bodyguards, measures the room from the ceiling to floor, counts the bowls of food on that table. 'How did you know we were here?' he asks, clacking his chopsticks together.

'Johnny Mango saw you in Brewer Street,' says Talbot. 'A man visits Soho at night to indulge his earthly appetites. You blunt your own carnality by irritating your gastric juices. Foo Yung. Hot Yang Chow. Diabolical mistresses. I checked the Tang Chun and the Nan Hai and here you are in the old Nan Cheng. You're getting careless. I'm disappointed. A few brief years ago you wouldn't have made such a mundane mistake.'

'I see you've found some new bruisers,' says Frank. He turns his head slowly to stare at Talbot, his heart pounding, his hands smoothing the tablecloth, clutching the coarse edge of wood beneath it, ready to overturn the tables and go into battle with a restaurant chair at the slightest indication from Webster.

'Shut your mouth when Mr Talbot is talking!' shouts the right flank, whistling through a broken nose. He's a ponderous brute of a man with his raincoat buttoned as far as his chin.

'And put your hands on the table where we can see to break them,' adds the left flank, scowling, riding up and down on the balls of his feet. He's taller than his companion, with a blue tattoo on his thick white neck and the face of a large bull terrier.

Talbot looks at Frank and shakes his head. 'It's time you went home, my young friend. I've no immediate quarrel with you.'

Frank looks past Talbot, across the restaurant, towards the freedom of the street, where a man has paused to read the menu hung in the window. The man, remote as a shadow, has a green and red sports bag under his arm. He leans forward against the window, shielding his eyes against the reflections in the glass, peering briefly into the restaurant.

'You're wrong, Talbot. I was at the Golden Goose. I helped to put down the Cockers.'

'Don't take any notice of him,' says Webster. 'He wouldn't hit a fly with his handbag.'

'We're in this together,' says Frank fiercely. He's tired of being bullied and taunted. After all the preparations they've made to smuggle themselves from the country, he'll be damned if he'll surrender Webster to this decrepit gangster. Nothing is going to stop them walking out of here. 'If you're picking a fight with him,' he warns Talbot, 'you're picking a fight with me.'

'That casts a darker complexion over the proceedings,' says Talbot, frowning. He ruminates upon the confession as he taps his shrivelled fingers lightly against his chin.

Frank feels the world slowing down around him. Everywhere he casts his eye objects are revealed with a new and astonishing clarity. The grains of rice still glued to the tips of his chopsticks, the blisters in the glaze of the blue and white bowls, the pattern in the weave of the table linen, like rows of chicken claw prints, the sparkling ripples of the beaded curtain as the waiter approaches them.

'You want a drink?' demands the waiter, directing the party to a neighbouring table.

'Shut your mouth when Mr Talbot is talking!' shouts the right flank, taunted beyond endurance. He lashes out with an arm and catches the waiter full in the chest, knocking him to the floor.

'Sodding Chink!' growls the bodyguard, checking his raincoat sleeve. 'He nearly made me lose a button.'

'Kick his bollocks – learn him a lesson,' says the left flank with a lop-sided grin.

'You kick him!' says the right flank indignantly. 'I'm wearing new shoes.'

The waiter springs back to life, cursing, yelling towards the kitchen for help, his face alight like a jack-o'-lantern.

Webster starts to rise from his chair, catching a bowl with his thumb and making it catapult from the table.

Frank grabs the table, tilting it forward, knocking down

230

glasses and bottles, splashing the beer and soy sauce, scattering rice and noodles and toothpicks.

A large Chinese cook pushes through the curtain. He's wearing nothing but canvas shorts and waving a meat axe in his fist. His face and shoulders are glazed with sweat. A blue dragon uncoils from the pit of his stomach and swells against his chest. A fabulous serpent with hooked wings and devils' claws. Its eyes are giant pearls. Flames feather from its open jaws.

'Freeze!' shouts the left flank nervously. He flicks open his raincoat and whips out a steel Colt Combat Commander from a leather horizontal shoulder rig.

Frank and Webster slowly subside into the wreckage of their table. The waiter falls to his knees and presses the palms of his hands to his skull. The cook drops the meat axe and lifts his arms in the air, stretching his loose and bulging stomach. The dragon twists on its flexing wings. The meat axe clatters to the floor.

The right flank unbuttons his raincoat and pulls out a small-frame Chiefs Special snubby, thrusting it hard into Frank's face while the left flank, whistling with excitement, waves the big Colt at Webster's throat.

Talbot smiles and takes a moment to gloat upon his victims' faces, the way they close their eyes against death, the way they gulp at the air as if drowning, terror flooding their arteries and pouring its poison into their hearts. It's a deeply disgusting spectacle.

'Goodnight! Goodbye! Farewell! Adieu! You must excuse me if I step outside but I really can't afford to splash this coat and I've never liked the look of brains.'

He turns and shuffles away from the sight of his vanquished enemies, huddled still at their table, trapped between the wall and their silent executioners. He reaches for the restaurant door and the cold clean air of the street. How he hates the smell of Chinese food! How he loathes the sight of blood!

Frank retreats, shrinking into the shell of his body,

231

pulling into his own darkness, searching for Valentine, wanting the memory of her face as a talisman to protect him. It can't end here, without warning, cut down by a rented firing squad over a supper of pork and shrimp omelette, with no time for counsel or confession, chanting the thousand names of God, pleading for time, begging for mercy, hoping for angels to sweep down and save them, brushing death away with their arms.

The window falls like a sheet of ice and a thunderbolt fills the restaurant with a whirling, incandescent wind that lifts the furniture to the ceiling and makes the lanterns explode into cascading blossoms of light. The tables spin and carelessly throw out their skirts. The chairs roll and tumble, one upon another, as nimble as circus acrobats.

The killers bend like burning trees. Their raincoats spout flames. Their melting shoes take root in the floor as the wind divides into a thousand flying knives.

Frank is thrown back, his face scorched and his ears filled with boiling wax. A splintering table swoops down on him, the long legs striking the wall like spears.

A yellow kid glove, still filled by the weight of its owner's hand, yet separated from its owner's wrist by a distance greater than the span of an arm, slaps the blistering tabletop with an angry gesture of defiance.

Frank is drenched with blood, grains of hot glass and soft plums of viscera. The air burns black as it turns to smoke. And then there is nothing but silence.

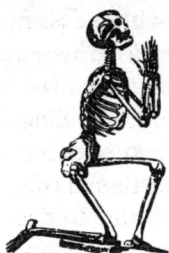

Kadinsky stands in the street and stares through the smoke into the ruins of the Nan Cheng. All around him men are shouting, women are screaming, dogs are barking, alarm bells are ringing, rattled by the shock of the big grenade. Faces appear at shattered windows. A crowd gathers at the top of the street and fingers are pointed in his direction. But Kadinsky stands his ground, smiling and unblinking, staring into the flames of hell, searching for signs of lingering life. A burning windmill of arms. The spillings of a disembowelled waiter. The fire shines on his face and turns his eyes into rubies. The smoke fills his nostrils with the stench of urine and scorched hair, melting plastic and hot blood.

At last he packs the grenade launcher into the green and red sports-bag and tosses it into the flames. The target has been destroyed. No signs of hostile activity. It's time to return to base and sink a few cold beers. He'll push through the gawping crowd, escape this maze of backstreets and reach the shelter of the Underground. He'll go back to the house and claim Valentine as the spoils of war. She's the only one left alive who can link him with these killings. Scrubber Ronnie is buried beneath a box of Tormentor ticklers with his throat slashed from ear to

233

ear. Old Picasso tried to struggle and had to be kicked to death. He'll drown Valentine in the shower, softly and slowly, feeling her sinking under his fingers, washing away her perfume and spices, before he takes his final pleasure. He'll carry her to bed and bury his face long and deep in the marvellous odours of her failing body. Tomorrow he'll have lunch in Paris and take a night flight to Africa.

The crowd grows bolder, shuffling forward to gain a better view of the slaughter. But as Kadinsky turns to retreat, something catches his attention. It's a movement of muscle and bone, a head still connected to a collar, something crawling on its hand and knees from beneath a blazing tabletop. Impossible! The sky fallen and the dead risen. The figure crawls away through the rubble and another corpse stirs into life and gropes towards the back of the restaurant.

Kadinsky curses, plunges into the heat of the fire, pushing towards the darkness of the passage that leads to the lavatories and kitchen. When he reaches the top of the kitchen stairs he pauses, sheltering against the wall, to pull a Glock 23 automatic from the lining of his jacket.

He knows from bitter experience that some men prove difficult to destroy. They survive grenade and rocket attack, buried in mud, cushioned by corpses, and emerge from battle with nothing but bruises. They walk away from shotgun blasts, bend the blades of bayonets and catch pistol bullets with their teeth. Bad luck to fight beside such men. Dangerous to keep their company. They draw death away from themselves and onto the heads of their companions.

He rams a magazine of soft lead hollowpoints into the grip of the Glock and checks his pockets for spare ammunition. Two full magazines. The first packed with Hydra-Shok and the second filled with heavy grain Pro Load. Satisfied with his fire-power he creeps down the narrow flight of stairs and into the restaurant kitchen.

The kitchen covers a large basement with walls of white

ceramic bricks. The floor beneath his boots is puddled with oil and wet scraps of food. The smoke extractor in the ceiling vibrates and thunders, shaking the pots and pans on their shelves and rocking a basket of fish perched on the edge of a torn zinc counter. A rice pan boils on a range of gas burners. The ovens are hot. The door to the cold store is hanging open. There! Mark it. Hit hard and take cover.

Kadinsky sprints across the kitchen, fires loosely into the cold store, destroying a bag of dragon shrimp, several chickens and a bucket of bean curd, twists around to cover his back and comes to rest behind the zinc counter.

He changes position, moving along the length of the counter, sweeping from left to right, firing at random. He knows they are trapped in this kitchen. He can sense their fear in the air around him. He gazes up at the smoke extractor. The fire in the restaurant is starting to buckle the ceiling timbers, bringing down snowflakes of paint and plaster. In another few minutes the building will collapse upon itself and come crashing into the basement. But he won't be cheated of his quarry. He knows they are here. He can smell their terror. He gazes around the floor and there, between the stairs and the ovens, is a thin but glistening trail of blood.

He follows the trail to the wall behind the ovens where a broken grating reveals an earthenware pipe twisting into the darkness. It must be an air shaft or part of some dismantled drain, just large enough for a frightened man to adopt as a makeshift coffin. The wire grating has been wrenched from its screws and torn away from the wall, dragging with it a black veil of cobwebs.

Kadinsky checks the laser sight on the Glock and squeezes into the blood-stained chamber.

Frank and Webster crawl from the pipe and search themselves for damage. Frank's face has been scorched and his
jacket buttons have melted. There are tiny puncture marks
on his neck where a flight of toothpicks caught him with
the force of blowpipe quills. His shoes are torn. His hair
sparkles with broken glass.

Webster's face has been badly scratched and his knuckles are blistered. A hole in his vest is plugged with a
smouldering roll of banknotes. Blood fills his sleeve from
elbow to wrist and spills from his fingertips.

'Bugger it!' he grumbles, trying to peer at the gash in
the arm. 'I think I'll need stitching.'

Frank shakes his head and pokes at his ears. The
explosion has all but deafened him, filling his skull with
the clamour of bells.

They are standing in a brick cellar with walls that are
bulging with moss. Far above them a square moon casts a
feeble light through the prison bars of a gulley-hole in the
street. Before them, through a low arch of dressed stone,
lies a second chamber, dark and dripping with water.

It is Webster who catches the sound of Kadinsky
crawling along the pipe behind them. The soft breath
of death. The ticking heart of a tiger. He gestures for

Frank to be silent, waving him forward into the watery chamber.

'Where?' shouts Frank. 'Where!' He's stunned by the sight of so much blood and his head is still baffled by bells.

Webster pushes him into the gloom, along a crooked corridor, as Kadinsky scrambles into the cellar. The ground tilts beneath them, the air grows cold and their feet splash a stinking silt of fermented mud and leaves. The brickwork is cracked and weeping with rust from iron girdles that help support a vaulted ceiling.

The corridor leads to a sudden spiral of stone stairs that sends them sprawling down through the darkness into a shallow sewer basin. Webster shouts in surprise, plunging and thrashing in freezing water. Frank struggles to pull him ashore, dragging him to the safety of a concrete ledge that runs along the wall of the passage. And here they rest for a moment, exhausted and shivering, while Frank makes a brave attempt to examine Webster's tattered arm.

'I can't feel it,' complains Webster, thumping the shoulder with his fist, trying to startle it into life.

'We've got to get you back to the surface,' says Frank grimly. The elbow is shattered. If they don't soon get to a hospital there's a chance that Webster will bleed to death. He stares into the twilight, watching the steps leading into the basin, waiting to catch the shape of a phantom gliding through the water towards them.

'No!' hisses Webster. 'Down and out. We have to go down and out.' He clambers to his feet and lurches along the ledge, steering himself by dragging his arm against the wall. The sewer glows in the sulphurous light from a series of safety lamps, revealing a wide and curving tunnel that beckons them deeper into the system of subterranean canals.

Frank follows in Webster's wake, running forward in a clumsy crouch with his head tucked into his shoulders. A hundred yards away the tunnel meets a junction where several cankerous pipes spout from the walls and drain to a channel of deeper water. The water is fast and bearded with foam, rushing towards a thundering abyss beyond a concrete weir.

'We're trapped!' shouts Webster. 'It's the devil or the deep blue sea!' He peers into the whirlpool and imagines this underground torrent reaching the freedom of the river through fantastic lakes and waterfalls, the river gathering strength as it slides triumphantly into the sea.

'If we can climb into one of these pipes!' shouts Frank. 'There's a chance. If we can work our way to the surface.' He scrambles among the rusty conduits, peering into their throats in a hopeless hunt for a glimmer of light from the distant streets.

Webster leans against the wall and wearily shakes his head. He's breathing hard. His hands and face are varnished with blood and smoke. 'I don't think I have the strength, Frank. I don't feel so good any more . . .'

'I'll help you!' shouts Frank, to encourage him. 'We've got to keep moving along . . .'

But Webster falls to his knees and makes a clumsy attempt to pull the wadding from his shirt, spilling bank-notes into the air, watching them flutter around him.

'What is it?' yells Frank, confused, watching the old man fight to throw his money away. The notes cascade from his pockets in dozens of exploded bundles, swept into spirals, tumbling around the sewer, until they are blown to the licking water and pulled down into the foam.

'It's slowing me down . . .' mutters Webster. 'I can't seem to breathe for the weight of it . . .'

Kadinsky stands in the shelter of the sewer basin and studies the fugitives as they fight to escape with their lives. Their shadows leap against the walls transforming them into dancing giants. He knows that one of them must be wounded, the way he staggers and slumps to the ground, rubbery as a drunkard, raking at his chest with one hand.

Slowly he raises the automatic, grips the weapon in both pale fists and gently concentrates the laser into a tiny medal of light a fraction above Frank's heart.

Webster succeeds in dragging a bundle of notes from his vest with such determination and vigour that the force of it knocks him sideways, pushing Frank to the wall.

The crack of the Glock bursts the stagnant air, rattling the pipes in their sockets and rolling away through the culverts in a distant rumble of thunder. The first shot hits a brick a few inches from Webster's head. The brick falls apart like cheese, scattering crumbs upon his shoulders. The second and third shots are wild, punching at the concrete somewhere beneath the water.

'Get down!' bellows Webster, pulling Frank to the floor and looking for shelter among the pipes.

Kadinsky creeps forward, closing the distance between them and setting his sight on Webster's chest. This time he wants a one-shot stop. This time he wants a killing.

The shock of the bullet smashing his ribcage catapults Webster across the sewer. He sits waist-deep in water and stares at the hole in his chest, trying to cover it with his hands, afraid that his heart and lungs will come tumbling from the cavity. The blood spurts through his fingers and sprays his eyes and mouth.

Frank lets out a great shout of fury, splashing towards him, trying to pull him back to safety.

'Help me . . . help me into deeper water . . .' gasps Webster. His teeth have started chattering. He's shaking so much that he can't control his arms and legs.

'No!' pleads Frank. 'I'm going to get you out of here!'

'Too late. Too late,' gasps Webster. 'Let me find my way to the sea . . .' He pushes Frank away and attempts to drag himself forward, grunting with pain, floundering in the foam, until Frank can endure it no longer and helps to launch him into the torrent.

Webster plunges and rolls like a grampus. The sewer washes his life away in long trailing ribbons of blood. He turns face-down to confront the weir and sails, with his arms outstretched like wings, towards the rushing embrace of the abyss.

Kadinsky stands on the opposite bank and follows Webster's progress with the barrel of the Glock. He fires at the sight of a shoulder, the twist of an arm, the glimpse of a boot as it flips through the water. He fires at the ghost and the ghost of the ghost of the man who dared to defy him. But Webster has already slipped away, beyond the sewers and the dirty river, into the warmth of a coral sea, chasing the late and lovely Dawn among the mermaids and porpoises.

Frank goes crashing into the water, throwing himself at the far bank and making a lunge at Kadinsky before the assassin has time to turn and train the gun upon him. As Frank leaps forward Kadinsky clubs at him with the Glock, stepping back, retreating along the tunnel, trying to keep the distance between them. But Frank swings his fist and catches the side of Kadinsky's face, making him shout in surprise, scuffing the skin from the cheekbone.

Kadinsky touches a hand to his face and smiles. He waits for Frank to hit him again, taunting him by lifting his chin and turning the other cheek, and then cheating him by jerking away and cracking Frank's skull with the gun. Frank stumbles and falls to the ground. He feels himself surrendering to a long and lazy descent, as if he were softly sinking through mud. The darkness floats up through his buckling legs, filling his body, leaving a dwindling rainbow of light swarming behind his eyes.

Now the killer is kneeling over him, smiling and flaring his nostrils, inhaling the sharp scents of gun smoke and blood as they mingle with the stench that leaks from the black, congested bowels of the city. He pokes the Glock into Frank's neck, searching for the hollow under his jaw. It's the end of tonight's entertainment. He turns his own face away from the blast and quickly pulls the trigger. Nothing happens. He springs to his feet and plucks the empty magazine from the grip, letting it fall to the ground with a clatter. He wasted too many shots in the kitchen, shooting at chickens and dragon shrimps, and squandered the rest of the magazine trying to blow out a dead man's brains.

Frank catches him still fumbling with the clasp of spare ammunition. He grabs him by the ponytail, jerks back his head until the neck cracks and bangs his face against the wall. Kadinsky's nose, that cruel snout, shoveller of human stinks, breaks open like a rotting fig. He coughs and snorts blood, spitting and wiping his mouth on his sleeve. The rocket of pain between the eyes has blinded him for a moment, leaving him dazed and vulnerable. He tries to shake off the next assault but Frank still has hold of a hank of hair and, no matter how he squirms and kicks, Kadinsky's face strikes the bricks again, spreading his mouth and breaking his teeth. He moans and stays pressed to the wall, choking on his own blood. His fingers, paralysed with pain, lose control of the automatic.

Frank leans his weight against him, breathing hard, trying to summon the last of his strength for the final thrust of battle. He knows he has to kill this man. He knows that he must not hesitate. And yet they hold fast to each other, clinging like lovers with all passions spent. Their limbs are trembling with fatigue and the hammering of their hearts. Again Frank pulls Kadinsky from the wall by yanking at the ponytail and driving him forward into the brickwork. Kadinsky gurgles and folds at the knees, still hanging by the roots of his hair. Frank lets him drop to the ground and stares in disgust at the mangled features. The jaws grind a terrible grimace. The eyes flutter wildly in their sockets. He wants to retreat from the horror of that face. He wants to escape and run for the light. But turning away from the threat of this man has already cost Webster his life. Frank's disgust turns into hatred.

He drags his victim to the edge of the canal and sinks him, head and shoulders, into the water. The head begins to hiss in a dark broth of bubbles and when the broth clears, Kadinsky is dead. Frank reluctantly loosens his grip and labours to push the body into the torrent, still half-afraid that Kadinsky will spring back to life again, more terrible than before, transformed by some magic into a grinning vampire, ruthless and indestructible. He crouches on his hands and knees and watches the body roll through the foam, banging against the weir, throwing out an arm in mocking salute, before it is swallowed into the darkness.

It takes Frank several hours to scratch his way to the surface, crawling through pipes and dripping tunnels, knowing the labyrinth watches him, mocking his every attempt at escape.

He has lost all hope of finding his way from the nightmare when he catches a faint draught of warm street air, flavoured with diesel smoke. He changes direction, moving against the current, feeling the air brushing over his face, sensing the shift in its ebb and flow, until he reaches a brilliant shaft of daylight, a pillar of fire in the darkness before him. He stumbles forward into the light, shielding his eyes from its glare, and then, without warning, finds himself released at last into a shallow gulley-hole with a broken grating into the street.

He emerges from the catacombs crawling on his hands and knees over the dappled, sunlit pavement. His skin is scratched and blistered, his bones bruised, his clothes drenched in sewer water and blood. He is standing in Piccadilly Circus. The sun is rising over the rooftops and casting shadows into the silent, empty streets. Pigeons strut among the railings where a mad old woman in a poly-thene shawl throws bread from a tartan shopping bag.

Frank shuffles painfully into the sunlight, shivering and

confused. He sits on the steps of Eros and stares down the length of Piccadilly towards the Royal Academy and the Burlington Arcade. He looks around at the great buildings, beautiful in the lacquering light, their rooftops adorned with stone urns and extravagant swags of carved fruits and flowers. Above the towers and sparkling domes, starlings tumble in a chalk-white sky. And sitting here, in the solitude of dawn, the world seems changed and wonderful. He stares, amazed, at the shimmering herringbone tiles on a distant cupola; gazes at the glass of the street lamps, fashioned in the shape of ostrich eggs supporting gilded crests of flame; surveys the graceful bending buildings with their sooty columns and arches. Everything seems remarkable as if the city has been transformed while he was burrowing beneath it.

The old woman hobbles to the steps of the statue followed by a flurry of birds eager to follow her trail of crumbs. She cocks her head and considers Frank with her mad chicken eyes as she mutters in a language of her own invention. She opens her polythene cape to reach a broken handbag and tosses a few small coins at Frank's feet.

Frank looks at the coins spinning, the birds running, the old woman retreating, and when he turns his head again there is a large green Bentley standing at a set of traffic lights, the car door flung open and Valentine walking towards him with easy strides, her long hair swinging against the collar of her fur coat.

He sits and watches her approach, finding nothing to surprise him in this morning of miracles.

'Where the hell have you been?' she complains, sitting down beside him and arranging the coat around her knees. She's wearing her mother's diamonds and a pair of long black evening gloves. Her perfume saturates the air.

'I just went out to post a letter,' says Frank quietly. 'What happened to you?'

Valentine shrugs and stares back towards the Bentley. She wants to explain how she followed Kadinsky as far as Soho and lost him somewhere in Chinatown and then, when the restaurant exploded, knowing that Frank must have perished inside it, found herself aimlessly driving the streets, without direction or purpose, watching the dawn break over the river. She wants to tell him about her father and ask about the fate of Webster and if Kadinsky is dead or alive but, after everything that's happened, she can't summon the courage for so many questions. It's enough to be with him again. It's enough to have found him sitting here, on the steps of Eros, with the stink of death on his clothes but the warmth of the sun in his eyes.

'Is it finished?' she says at last, not daring to look at his face but reaching instead for his hand and pressing the fingers against her mouth.

'It's finished,' says Frank. He glances up at the sky, already overcast by the threat of rain.

'Let's go home,' says Valentine.